Second Time Around

Only two people watched Stephen Armitage die and both swore that the hit-and-run driver must have seen him between the flashing beacons of a zebra crossing even through the murky drizzle of a winter evening. No-one else witnessed the accident. A European Cup football match on TV had kept people and traffic off the streets, especially in suburbs like Kew. Armitage had left his consulting-room just after seven and arrived at Kew Gardens tube station just before eight. From there, he walked towards his house on Kew Green following his normal route along Cumberland Road to Gloucester Road then the green.

Head-down under his umbrella, he was crossing Mortlake Road when the car emerged from the darkness, hurtling through the district line railway bridge like a projectile; it caught Armitage head-on, felling him under its front wheels. Both the man who was walking his dog and the girl who had been buying sweets at the corner shop heard the crunch of breaking bones then a yell that died in the victim's throat: a scuffling, ripping sound reached the witnesses as the car dragged the bundle of flesh and bones and clothes for fifty yards before tearing itself free and accelerating through the lights at the road junction. Neither the man nor the girl managed to get the car number; they both declared that the vehicle had neither headlights nor rear lights illuminated. They agreed on the make, the girl from photographs and the man because he knew the type. It was a French Renault GT.

Other titles in the Walker British Mystery Series

HUGH
McLEAVE
Second
Time
Around

WALKER AND COMPANY · NEW YORK

First published in the United States of America in 1981 by the
Walker Publishing Company, Inc.

This paperback edition first published in 1984.

ISBN: 0-8027-3095-7

Library of Congress Catalog Card Number: 81-50546

Printed in the United States of America

10   9   8   7   6   5   4   3   2   1

One

Any minute now, Irish Deirdre was going to twist his arm or put a half-nelson on him. Why the candlelit table decked out like the altar of a high mass? Why rush to Coopers to buy a haggis and even conquer her own revulsion for the mixture of offal and meal that he as a good Scotsman liked so much? Why allow him to wash all this down with two full glasses of Burgundy? Dangerous for a reformed drunk. But Deirdre kept him guessing by conjuring up a delicious pyramid of Roquefort cheese and finally tempting him with out-of-season strawberries under an avalanche of Chantilly cream. Only at that point did she announce that Stephen and Barbara Armitage were joining them for coffee. At the thought of several boring hours with that pompous young colleague, he nearly gagged on the strawberries and cream. Aloud, he said, "And it so happens that Dr Armitage has made yet another spectacular bound forward in psycho-analytical technique."

"No," Deirdre replied. "If you want to know, Barbara rang me to say somebody's trying to kill him."

"Why have they waited so long? And why does a sensitive and beautiful girl like Barbara want to stop them, whoever they are?"

"It's a patient."

"One who has recovered his sanity, obviously."

"Greg, be serious for once."

Maclean shrugged. "All right, we all go through the phase of thinking every paranoiac has a knife or a gun aimed at us. He'll get over it."

He helped clear the table and slot the dishes into the dish-washer after which he went and wedged his ample frame into an armchair. Constructing a mound of snuff on the back of his hand and inhaling it deeply, he studied Deirdre, his secretary, helpmeet and wife in everything but marriage-lines. With that red hair flickering and flaming in the candlelight and those sapphire eyes, she looked as Irish as a four-leaved clover; she had a spae-wife's uncanny intuitions, a sort of sixth-sense about people. Often he marvelled at the way she deflected needless trouble from his consulting-room door in the shape of everything from hippies and hopeless psychopaths to footloose and moneyed neurotics. She had also weaned and kept him off the bottle.

"And what do you think?" he said finally.

"I think you should treat it seriously and listen to him."

"Do you think he'll listen to me?" Maclean said. "Anyway, I don't like taking in other people's dirty washing."

Every encounter with Armitage set him speculating how a lovely, intelligent girl like Barbara had quit a good job as a medical secretary to marry him. Transference? Even a thousand hours on his couch wouldn't have turned him into a love-object. Hypnosis? With those slimy eyes peering through port-hole specs and that cracked voice! Pity? Yes, it had to be pity for his appearance. Armitage had a pear-shaped head, bald on top; his chinless jaw took cover behind a black, fan-shaped beard. When they had first met, Maclean stared at all that hair in the wrong places and had a double-take, wondering if they'd stuck his head on upside-down. With that face gazing at him from his bathroom mirror, Armitage must have come into psychiatry for his own peace of mind.

Barbara Armitage had fear in her grey-green eyes and the set of her wide mouth; she crossed to kiss Maclean and murmur a thank-you before groping in her handbag for a cigarette. Armitage embedded himself, comfortably, in the sofa. "Well, how're tricks?" he said, running a fancied connoisseur nose over his coffee like a hound over fox spoor.

"Just the usual," Maclean grunted. "Splinting neuroses, giving cracked egos a face-lift and tired libidos an overhaul and sending them back on the assembly-line." He nodded towards Deirdre. "My secretary hasn't found me a decent psycho or schizo in months."

Armitage let the hint pass over his shiny head. He grinned. "You should come and spend a month at the Royston if you're interested in really classic, text-book types." A few months before, he had become a junior consultant at the Royston Day Clinic for psychiatric treatment, attached to the North-east Surrey hospital group. Maclean had met him while giving a course of lectures on aversion therapy for phobias, alcoholism and certain neuroses. He had encountered two types of psychiatrist: those who took their cue from rats, dogs or chimps and transposed animal and human behaviour freely to interpret their patients' troubles; the others opted for the more abstract analytical techniques. Armitage belonged to the latter school and spouted Freud, Jung and Adler by the pailful; he really believed that characters like Oedipus, Electra and probably Medusa, rewritten by Freud, materialized as patients and paraded through the Wimpole Street consulting-rooms he used twice a week; it would take him a long time to learn that he and every other psychiatrist were as good as their own case-books and what they made of them.

"But you have a very interesting case at the moment, Stephen," Barbara prompted. "An amnesiac, isn't he, darling?"

"Hmm, he's not run-of-the-mill, but he's not all that exciting," Armitage said.

"But didn't you say yourself that he might be a genuine multiple personality ... that he might even make a case-history for the British Journal of Psychiatry?"

Armitage blushed and Maclean docked him a mark for

that. Psychiatrists should control their id like their sphincters, or lie more suavely. Did he think Maclean would steal his amnesiac and scoop him in their trade journal!

"Tell Gregor about it," Barbara urged.

"But he listens to that sort of stuff all day."

"Not if he's a real amnesiac," Maclean said. "They're pretty rare." He realized that Barbara was trying to persuade Armitage to discuss the patient she believed was threatening his life.

"I'm not sure myself if he's genuine," Armitage said, finally. After hesitating for several moments he shrugged, then launched into the case-history which he presented with a portentous voice and a style larded with Freudian terminology. In Maclean's mind, it amounted to this:

Just over four months ago, a man in his early fifties came into the Royston Day Clinic. It was after midnight and only a night nurse and a psychiatric orderly were looking after the three patients who had asked to remain that night instead of going home. Both staff members realized that they must give the stranger a bed; he looked completely disorientated, had no memory of where he had been or who he was; nor did he know his name, age or whether he had a family or friends; he had noticed the hospital in passing, entered on an impulse and the night staff had directed him to the clinic. They saw he had not shaved for several days and seemed to have slept rough. From his manner, his clothes and his cultured voice they took him for a middle-class businessman or even an intellectual. At first they suspected he had been admitted to Warlington Park mental hospital and had escaped; but, there and elsewhere, no-one had heard of him.

"No papers to identify him in his pockets?" Maclean queried and Armitage shook his head.

Armitage had seen him the next day when he had finished his morning clinic. To him, the man appeared in a cataleptic shock, or like someone petrified, afraid to move or even to speak. His examination revealed no sign of head injury or deep brain lesion. Nor did he have the appearance of a hysterical amnesiac. For three days, the stranger remained in this frozen mental and physical state, eating little but drinking copious jugs of water.

"As though he were trying to cleanse himself," Maclean interjected.

"I suppose he might have been subconsciously purging some repressed culpability," Armitage conceded.

On the second night, the orderly heard a noise in the ward. Investigating, he found the stranger leaving by the front door, still in pyjamas, obviously sleep-walking. Afraid to shock him by waking him too abruptly, the orderly followed him down the front drive and out the main gate. Just as he was making up his mind to take the man's hand and lead him back, he turned and retraced his steps into the ward of his own free will.

"So, he wanted help," Maclean said.

"Yes," Armitage agreed. "I interpreted this as a subconscious impulse to recompense past guilt and to co-operate in his own treatment."

On the following night, the man roused a whole hospital wing with a nightmare, screaming and bellowing even after they woke him and tried to convince him it was a dream. He refused to believe them and seemed even more terrified of the real world than the dream one.

For four days he maintained silence then began babbling incoherently and afterwards to respond to some of Armitage's questions. His troubles appeared to have begun with blinding headaches which prostrated him, preventing him from getting out of bed, let alone working.

"Did you ever find out what he did?" Maclean put in, but Armitage shook his head.

After the headaches, he complained of nightmares in which someone resembling himself dressed in military uniform was pursuing him. They scared him, these night-mares, for he always ended by dying a horrible death either by hanging or drowning or frying in some fire or acid bath. Even during the day, his mind would seem to switch off and that nightmare would invade and terrify him. On the fifth morning, Armitage visited the clinic to find that his patient had fled during the night. Waiting until the night nurse and orderly had turned their backs, he had collected his clothes and slipped away.

"And you never even got a smell of his name," Maclean muttered.

"Not only that," Armitage said. "He purloined his medical chart and even stole the case notes from the office."

"So, he needed help, but only on his own terms," Maclean mused. "And that meant he didn't intend to confess what he had to hide."

"I thought Stephen should tell the police," Barbara said.

"But I was certain he wasn't a criminal," Armitage said, tugging on his black beard with both hands.

"We're not so certain now," she retorted.

"So you saw him again," Maclean prompted.

Armitage sipped his coffee. Three weeks ago the man had returned. This time he had come not to the clinic but to the psychiatrist's consulting-room in Wimpole Street. Dishevelled and disorientated, he had flopped on the couch and there he lay for hours talking incessantly in an incoherent and somnambulistic whisper. By now fascinated with this man, Armitage had found him a room in a private clinic that he used in Holland Park; in this way, he had spent several hours cross-examining, dropping hints and trying to solve the mystery surrounding him.

One of his nightmares seemed to recur most often: his younger, uniformed *doppelgänger* was hunting him along a corridor with a thousand doors, every one of them shutting as he wrenched at their handles. Suddenly, he had run out of passageway and stood on the edge of what must have been a volcano; he turned to escape and found his double leering at him, then shoving him over the edge and laughing as he plummeted into the sulphurous fumes shot through with flames.

Everything would come right if only he could trace the family that he had lost all those years ago – the Hartmans. And Jane, his first and only love. She was a friend of Lord and Lady Hartman and their daughter, Penelope, and son, Edwin. But like his youth and his past they seemed to have disappeared for ever.

Maclean rose to pick Who's Who from his bookshelves and flip over the pages. "No Lord or Lady Hartman here," he remarked.

"I looked up Burke's Peerage and Debretts," Armitage said. "Not there, either."

And yet the man had described the Hartman manor in detail, down to some of the furnishings, the pictures and even insignificant objects like ashtrays and their magazines, Horse and Hound and Country Life. Trite sayings or remarks by Lord Hartman tripped off his tongue like recitations and he could even name the flowers on the petit point Lady Hartman was working.

"And yet he's talking about twenty-five years ago," Maclean said. "Did he mention where the Hartmans lived – it could have been an Irish or Scottish peerage."

"He tried, but couldn't remember," Armitage replied. "Like most of his youth it seems to have been blotted out by something."

Just when Armitage seemed to be piercing the man's mental shell and gaining his confidence, he once again gave the night staff the slip and vanished, appropriating what notes he could grab from the office. No-one had seen him since.

"What do you make of it all, Gregor?" Barbara asked.

"It doesn't fit into any of the classic psychiatric states or any case-history I've ever met," Maclean replied. "He looks like an amnesiac, but he's obviously emptied his pockets of anything that might identify him, and no man who has lost his memory does that. He's evidently running away from something but not his past like many amnesiacs. In fact, he thinks his only hope is to pick up those lost pieces." He took a pinch of snuff and blew into his hankie. "I don't like the way his double tries to kill him all the time."

"You mean he might have homicidal ideas."

"Suicidal more likely."

"Difficult psychopathology," Armitage interjected. "At the outset I thought it was hysterical amnesia because of the fugue and his obvious terror, then I changed my diagnosis and plumped for multiple personality."

"You didn't think of doing a brain scan?"

"Looking for a temporal lobe tumour or some lesion of the diencephalon or traumatic injury?" Armitage shook his head. "I was sure that whatever he had was not organic. I think he had a personality disorder, probably of libidinous origin."

"You mean he had suddenly rediscovered sex," Maclean said, drily.

"Yes, perhaps," Armitage said. "When he talked about Jane, his first love, his voice and manner underwent a complete transformation."

"I think Stephen is right," Deirdre suddenly put in. "He's a man living a double life without knowing it." Everyone turned to stare at her and Deirdre blushed. She had listened to the case-history and discussion without uttering; and now, when they pressed her to give reasons for her remarks, she merely said, "I just feel it, that's all." She hestitated, then went on, "Well, there's his dream of dying in fire or water or at the end of a rope. They're the dreams of a man who's betrayed himself or somebody else, or committed some dreadful crime or sin."

Armitage shrugged, but Maclean gazed at Deirdre knowing that she often got the right answer for the wrong reasons, or no reasons at all. Crime or religious guilt had struck him as possible explanations, too. "Anybody could be right," he said. "And unless your weird character surfaces again we're never likely to find out."

"But he has shown face," Barbara said. "Three days ago."

"Poppycock!" Armitage snapped, holding up an admonitory finger.

"If you won't tell them, I will," his wife said, then went on, "Stephen was coming home from his consulting-room the other night and as usual walked to Oxford Street to catch his tube to St James's Park, then Kew. He was on the platform in the middle of the rush hour and waited no more than two minutes for a train. Just as one came through the tunnel and people began to press forward, Stephen felt someone thrust or punch him in the back. He cried out ... didn't you, darling?"

"I shouted that he was a bloody idiot," Armitage said. "If it hadn't been for my brief-case I might have been under the train."

"What happened?" Maclean asked.

"I was halfway over the rails and dropping into the pit with the train ten yards away. As a reflex I threw up my hands and somebody grabbed my briefcase and yanked me back onto the platform. I heard somebody shouting at the bloody idiot who cannoned into me."

"He pushed you, and they were shouting that he was trying to murder you," Barbara said.

"No, darling, let's be objective. They said he could have killed me."

"You didn't get a sight of him?" Maclean said.

"No, I caught a glimpse of his back as he was making for the exit. He was nothing like the man who came to me for help – this man was tall and burly."

"Disguised," Barbara muttered.

"It wasn't him, I tell you," Armitage snapped. "What reason could he have for trying to kill me? I'd see your point if he'd confessed something incriminating, or revealed some dark secret. But he didn't."

"How does he know that he hasn't?" Maclean said.

"Come to that, how do you know he hasn't?"

"I suppose I don't."

"There you are," Barbara cried. "Anyway, people like him who're half out of their minds don't need reasons even for killing."

"No, they always have reasons," Maclean murmured. "But who knows them? They're often so deeply submerged that even they themselves aren't aware of them."

"So, a man like the one Stephen has just described could easily turn on the psychiatrist that he has asked to help him?" Barbara asked.

"Alas, yes!" Maclean replied. "We belong to the only branch of medicine where doctors are at risk from patients. We don't kill them with drugs or the knife like some of our colleagues, but sometimes we have to watch they don't kill us."

"Not this one," said Armitage.

"Maybe not. Yet, we can be dealing with a psycopath and not realize it. And they're like nitro – rub them up the wrong way and they explode."

Armitage was not convinced. He had made his analysis and diagnosis and Freud himself would not have shaken them. At the door, while her husband went to fetch her coat, Barbara whispered, "What do we do? Tell the police?"

Maclean shook his head. "No, they're not interested in potential crime. If he turns up again ring me and I'll fix to see him and perhaps discover what ails him. But not to worry."

As they heard Armitage's car pull away, Deirdre turned to him. "I think Stephen should have handed that man over to the nearest mental hospital," she said. "I'm sure somebody did try to kill him."

Maclean murmured that it was probably an accident and a coincidence. But privately he agreed with her. He hoped that Stephen Armitage and his fugitive patient would not cross each other's track again.

Two

Only two people watched Stephen Armitage die and both swore that the hit-and-run driver must have seen him between the flashing beacons of a zebra crossing even through the murky drizzle of a winter evening. No-one else witnessed the accident. A European Cup football match on TV had kept people and traffic off the streets, especially in suburbs like Kew. Armitage had left his consulting-room just after seven and arrived at Kew Gardens tube station just before eight. From there, he walked towards his house on Kew Green following his normal route along Cumberland Road to Gloucester Road then the green.

Head-down under his umbrella, he was crossing Mortlake Road when the car emerged from the darkness, hurtling through the district line railway bridge like a projectile; it caught Armitage head-on, felling him under its front wheels. Both the man who was walking his dog and the girl who had been buying sweets at the corner shop heard the crunch of breaking bones then a yell that died in the victim's throat; a scuffling, ripping sound reached the witnesses as the car dragged the bundle of flesh and bones and clothes for fifty yards before tearing itself free and accelerating through the lights at the road junction. Neither the man nor the girl managed to get the car number; they both declared that the vehicle had neither headlights nor rear lights illuminated. They agreed on the make, the girl from photographs and the man because he knew the type. It was a French Renault GT.

When they ran to pick up the sodden figure of Stephen Armitage from the road and drag him to the pavement he was already dead.

To the young CID men who drove out from Richmond police-station to take their statements and study the accident scene, it amounted to nothing more than another hit-and-run, probably a drunk who would discover his crime in the next day's paper and hide his car in the garage for a few months until the hunt had quietened. However, they circulated a description of the car and the circumstances, giving this to the press in the hope that a member of the public might help them identify the driver or the vehicle. Nothing hinted at deliberate murder. On police evidence and the testimony of the witnesses, Her Majesty's coroner for Richmond brought in a verdict of manslaughter by persons unknown.

"You should have allowed Barbara to tell them about the tube station attempt to murder Stephen, and the psychopath," Deirdre protested when they were walking away from the coroner's inquest in Kingston magistrates' court.

"No point," he replied. At his insistence, she drove them to Kew Gardens tube station, then to the point where the car had hit Armitage. It seemed clear that somebody who knew the psychiatrist's routine had waited for him to emerge from the station and had aleady timed his passage so that he could drive round the back streets and knock him down as he crossed the road.

Barbara had tea ready for them; she had taken the shock well, only buckling for a few minutes during the funeral at Gunnersbury Cemetery.

"I've been telling Greg that he should have allowed you to give evidence," Deirdre said.

"Barbara knows why I advised against it," Maclean said, draining his teacup. "Have you packed your things?" Barbara pointed to the two suitcases. To answer Deirdre's quizzical look, he said, "She's going away for a bit of a holiday."

"Oh, where?"

"Where nobody can find her."

"What do you mean?" Deirdre whispered before her mouth dropped a notch with comprehension. "I see, she didn't tell them what we knew because you thought they might try to kill her, too. You don't think …"

"We couldn't take chances," he said. "Her evidence wouldn't have made any difference to the inquest verdict but would have warned the murderer that she knew enough about him to be his next victim." He lugged the two suitcases out to the small Fiat and when he returned, whispered to Deirdre, "There was another reason for keeping quiet. We'd have had detectives all over the place. They'd have increased Barbara's risk and made her life a misery. What's more, they'd have sealed off Stephen's consulting-rooms and taken possession of all his medical papers."

"But they might have found the murderer," she came back.

"They might," he conceded. "But I doubt it very much."

"And we're going to let him get away with it," she cried, a flush mounting her high, Irish cheek-bones.

"No, mavournin," he said. "If I know anything about human behaviour, the man we're after will break surface again. Why? Because he's searching desperately for the most elusive and most compulsive mystery of all – his own Self. He needed help once and he'll need it again. And perhaps he'll come to me next time."

"And murder you, too," Deirdre breathed.

"I'll stay off tube station platforms and zebra crossings," he grinned.

Crammed into the small car, they set off for Euston station. Barbara had decided to go as far north as she could to stay with friends on Skye in the Western Highlands. As they pulled away from the kerb, Maclean suddenly whispered instructions for Deirdre to drive twice round the green. In the wing mirror he was watching the car behind them, driven by a man he had spotted at the inquest, then at Kew tube station and now at Barbara's house. "It's all right," he assured the two women. "He's a policeman." On their second circuit the man realized they had detected him and was making for a phone-box. Maclean reasoned that only the police had the organization to pick them up and tail them through London.

When they had seen Barbara off, they returned to Maclean's Harley Street consulting room where he asked Deirdre to ring Armitage's secretary and fix an appointment to visit his consulting-room that afternoon and collect his case-books and other papers.

"She says the police were there last week and have taken a lot of stuff," Deirdre said, cupping a hand over the mouthpiece.

"Tell her we'll be at Wimpole Street in half an hour."

Three quick calls confirmed his suspicions. Since the police were treating it as a manslaughter case, no member of the Richmond or Scotland Yard CID had visited Armitage's rooms. At the Royston Day Clinic and the private nursing-home in Holland Park where the amnesiac stranger had spent several nights, a man claiming to be a detective investigating the death of Dr Armitage had come and collected some of his papers; he had even remarked that the police suspected a former patient of perhaps plotting to kill the psychiatrist. Maclean jotted down their description of the man.

At Wimpole Street, the matronly woman who looked after Armitage and three other doctors in the building, explained how the detective had called. He cut her short, saying, "The detective was as big all-round as I am, only he had muscle instead of fat." She nodded, blushing, then led them upstairs to the second floor.

From the neat rows of files, case-books and tapes, he would never have suspected that anyone had searched the rooms. Fortunately, Armitage kept a clean desk-top and had a place for everything. His large room he had divided into two, keeping a cubicle with only a couch, one chair and a bedside table – nothing that would distract a patient's mind during free-association periods. In the next room, his desk and files, his text-books, instruments and a locked medicine cabinet with an emergency drug supply.

Left alone, Maclean and Deirdre began to sift through the case-books, concentrating on February 14 to 18, the dates of the man's final visit to Armitage. Those records had gone. So had a tape cassette for the first of those days, no doubt registering the random conversation of the strange patient. Presumably, the one marked in the book with no name or an X opposite it. Maclean carried the cassette rack through to the inner cabinet and chose the last of the February 14 recordings and ran this to within quarter of an hour of its finish. Armitage had mentioned that the man arrived towards the end of his afternoon sessions. But the tape yielded nothing. It was Deirdre who spotted the Armitage X mnemonic for the stranger, and the disparity between the start and stop numbers of the first cassette on February 15. On this they heard the voice of the man who, in some curious way, had spelled death for the psychiatrist who eavesdropped on him; Armitage must have seen the man overrun the first tape and switched him over to a second.

A babble of confused sound set Maclean wondering if he were playing the cassette at the right revs, but the pitch seemed fine and in a minute he realized that the man was speaking German so fast that he could hardly interpret it. Someone, he said, was always pursuing him – his shadow ... no they had stolen that ... his *doppelgänger* ... Death. But even when they caught and murdered him his own corpse appeared young and tranquil. Why, he asked, should he have these dreams and nightmares which left him with such blinding headaches and feeling too weak to think even.

He was putting this question to Armitage, though Maclean doubted if the psychiatrist had enough German to understand let alone answer it. Finally, Armitage's voice cut across the repeated question as he prompted softly:

"You were talking about Jane and the rehearsals ..."

"Ah, yes ... Jane and I had no lines in the first act, so we'd slip off and make love in the east wing where they had the dressing-rooms and the lecture theatres ... we'd our own secret love-nest there ... we played out our love not with stage words and gestures like the others ... you know, flesh and blood and the senses have their own language, their own memory ... no words can match them ... I thought we'd burned and branded our love into each other's flesh and blood ... and I was wrong ... (Here, he broke down and sobbed and the tape hissed on for half a minute before he resumed) ... I was wrong ... even our love wasn't strong enough to resist them and their tricks ... they were too clever, too cunning, too powerful ..." (Silence).

"What was Jane's name?" Armitage queried in his best disembodied, consulting-room tone.

"Jane had no other name."

"What was she like?"

"Like no-one else ... her skin has the fragrance of honey and roses and jasmin and honeysuckle ... her eyes have opals and diamonds in them ... her hair has sunset flames in its tresses ... she has a voice like spring water over rocks and a smile like letting up a blind ..."

In the pause before the voice continued, Maclean and Deirdre stared at each other as they listened to this rhapsodizing in a grave voice with no inflection, no intonation which lent it an incongruous and yet rather a tragic ring.

"Tell me a bit more about Jane," Armitage's voice said.
After a few seconds, the reply came:
Ich denke dein, wenn mir den Sonne Schimmer
Vom Meere strahlt;
Ich denke dein, wenn sich des Mondes Flimmer
In Quellen malt.
Ich sehe dich, wenn auf dem fernen Wege

Der Staub sich hebt,
Ich bin bei dir, du seist auch noch so ferne,
Du bist mir nah!
Die Sonne sinkt, bald leuchten mir die Sterne.
O wärst du da!

His voice tailed off and he began to cry, a high, keening note like a seagull. Armitage must have considered it either too traumatic or futile to prolong the session, for the tape went silent then came his introduction to another patient.

"What was all that German about?" Deirdre said.

"It's a well-known poem by Goethe about the presence of the loved one," Maclean replied, then began to translate:

I think of thee when the shimmer of sunlight
Gleams from the sea;
I think of thee when the glimmer of moonlight
Plays on the spring.
I see you when at the end of distant roads
Dust spirals rise ...
I am with you, however far away you seem,
You are near me.
The sun sinks, soon the stars will light my way.
If only you were here!

"He must have loved whoever she was very much," Deirdre said in a confessional whisper. "Don't you think it's sad?"

"Sad for him and Armitage and Barbara," Maclean muttered, pocketing the cassette and collecting several books of case-notes hoping they would yield something.

"If only we had the other tape," Deirdre said.

"If only Armitage had told us everything he knew instead of acting coy," Maclean grumbled.

However, Armitage had paid for his reticence with his life. But why? What had his errant patient revealed on the stolen tape or case-notes that compelled him to murder? Armitage had insisted that sex had triggered his personality crises and his attempted flight from the present into the past. This girl, Jane, evidently obsessed him. Had he also confessed to some sexual crime? Rape? Murder? So many criminals found amnesia a useful alibi or ally. Perhaps he had been trying to use Armitage to cover some crime and had gone too far in his disclosures. They had so little evidence about the man that speculation was futile. Somehow, he had to build an identity from the fragments that he could collect.

At both the Holland Park clinic and the Royston Day hospital he confirmed that the burly, heavy-jowled man had performed his bogus detective act. Nothing remained. Yet, from the night nurse at Royston and the matron at Holland Park, he filled out his description of the vanished patient: fairly tall and slim; blond hair grizzling at the temples, blue eyes, regular handsome features with a slight chin cleft. That and the fact that the man spoke cultured English and good German gave Maclean a start.

Deirdre had raised an eyebrow when he stopped during the inquest to give a journalist an interview about Armitage, the brilliant and original young psychiatrist scythed down so prematurely. Let the press use his name prominently and his rivals think he was advertizing and he'd get himself struck off, Deirdre warned. He laughed, then took the odd step of writing obituary notices on Armitage for The Times, the British Medical Journal and the Lancet. Deirdre would have thrown an Irish tantrum had she suspected that he was offering himself as the next target for their mystery patient. If he read the inquest reports, the interview and obituary notices, he might wonder how much Maclean really knew. And he might even come running to him for help next time.

Weeks passed and no-one rose to the bait. Maclean had almost renounced the thought of solving the crime when Kiki gave him an idea. Kiki looked exactly what she was – one of the queens of Shepherd Market or Jermyn Street or whichever beat she paraded. A tall, well-quilted, blond-wigged creature with a blasé expression, she flopped into Maclean's armchair with a nylon hiss as she opened her mink coat and crossed her long legs. "It's Freddie again, ducks," she said, shrugging and squashing her crimson-tipped cigarette in an ashtray. Freddie, he knew, shared her with a thousand other men when he was not serving time; he also acted as her legitimate husband.

"What has he picked up this time?" he said.

"Six months," she sniffed. "And what he did pick up and they picked him up for really did fall off a lorry." She fingered her mink coat. "Just a few pelts almost as nice as this one."

"What can I do, Kiki?" he asked. Years ago he had treated her young sister for depression following childbirth and now half the prostitutes of Mayfair and St James's had come on his books, which didn't boost his stock with his competitors and their pin-striped suits and Sheraton couches, or with a moralistic Irish catholic like Deirdre.

"Freddie's claustrophobic like you know, doc," Kiki said.

"Then tell him to stay out of prison."

"He'd be all right in one of them nice open prisons with his own room and the telly and the Sporting Life and good nosh three times a day." She shot him a smile as arch as Westminster Bridge. "Now if you bit the ear-'ole of the prison headshrink you're pally with in Pentonville and got him to transfer Freddie out of 'is nasty ol' cell ..."

"You're asking me to perjure myself and sin against my oath," Maclean said, mock horror in his voice.

"Oh, we'll make it up to you," she simpered. "You can have it in cash or kind, or ... well, you know what."

Her suggestive sign brought a grin to his face, then lit his mind with a sudden flash of inspiration. He pressed the buzzer for Deirdre. "Bring in that cassette and tape-machine," he ordered. He clicked the cassette into place, switched on the end of the tape and motioned Kiki to listen.

When the tape stopped, he said, "Have you ever heard that voice before?"

"Run it again." This time she concentrated hard, but when the voice stopped she shook her head.

"It belongs to a tall, blond man in his early fifties, greying at the temples, well-dressed, well-spoken, good-looking and well-heeled," he prompted.

Kiki thought for several moments. "It's a good few months ago and I couldn't swear it's the same one but it sounds like him," she said. "Some swine who did in one of the girls in her flat in Curzon Street."

"Can you remember the date?"

"No, but it's in the papers."

"And you'd recognize him."

"Not me. But two of the girls on that beat got a quick shufti at him. They'd know him again."

"If they spot him, give me a ring," Maclean said as he ushered her to the door. "I'll have a word with the prison psychiatrist about Freddie, but he should keep out of stir altogether."

"Thanks, doc."

He hadn't thought of consulting the newspapers, but now he took a cab to Fleet Street where he knew the chief librarian of the Daily World, Stanley Prince. On the way, he recapitulated mentally all that Armitage and the staff at the two clinics had told him; their man arrived on December 2 so he should run through the files for a week or fortnight before that date. His second appearance occurred on February 14, so he would also have to search the week or so before that date.

Settled with the files of several newspapers for the chosen dates, Maclean leafed slowly through them and dissected the fat packets of cuttings on prostitute murders. Of course he realized that prostitutes had an abnormally high mortality from murder as well as sexual diseases, but he hardly expected to trace no fewer than five prostitute killings in the Greater London area for the week preceding

December 2. He studied their pictures, looking for some resemblance between the five victims; but when he analyzed their features no two of them really looked alike. Three of the murderers had already been tried and sentenced; but Maclean noticed that the murder of Kiki's friend, Evelyn Cattell (trade name Ginny) remained unsolved. It had its odd aspects. Her killer seemed to have picked her up at four o'clock as the streets were growing dark; she had taken him to her flat in Curzon Street whereas she normally used one of several hotels; a bundle of five-pound notes in her handbag ruled out theft as a motive; according to forensic experts she had been strangled within half an hour of being seen enter the flat; no other assault marks appeared on her face or body. No sexual intimacy had taken place just before her death.

For the week preceding February 14, Maclean unearthed four prostitute killings. Again, no two bore great similarity. Yet, one of the women did have some features in common with Ginny Cattell. Instinct whispered that perhaps part of the key to the puzzle lay here. A young callgirl called Audrey Sargent, aged nineteen, had been strangled on February 13. Someone had glimpsed her give a man a lift in her car not far from her flat in Fulham Road. Next morning, an Automobile Association patrolman came across her in a copse on Putney Common. She had been strangled but not sexually violated or even touched.

Comparing both half-tone pictures, Maclean discerned very little that matched; however, when he read the police description one thing stood out. Both had titian hair. That phrase from the tape-recording leapt into his mind – 'her hair had sunset flames in its tresses.' For the man who made that recording, who was desperately trying to recreate the picture of the girl who obsessed him, it needed only one point of resemblance. One small feature could trigger his interest, then his excitement and finally his murderous fury when he realized that the girl was not HIS. That she had betrayed him. For that's what he would feel.

Betrayed. Not by his own faulty recollection, but by the woman who had lured him on and tried to seduce him with false promises.

Nevertheless, it baffled him that the remembered feature of a loved one should provoke such hatred and cold-blooded murder. Like the man's amnesia, it seemed illogical, the wrong way round.

Selecting those cuttings that he considered relevant, and the photographs of the dead girls, he had them photo-copied. While waiting, he used the librarian's phone to call Detective-sergeant John Pearson at Scotland Yard and fix a meeting in a Victoria Street pub near the Yard building. A bus put him down at Westminster Bridge and he strolled through Parliament Square crowds flapping in the March wind. Pearson was draining the froth in his pint of beer and ordering another when he entered the bar. He had known Maclean for years, since his uniform days and the Archer Case when the psychiatrist had given the defence advice which it refused and thereby lost their chance to save Archer from the gallows; as a detective, he had invoked the psychiatrist's experience several times to give him character readings and help solve violent and sexual crimes. For his part, Maclean often twitted the big detective for having too much conscience and compassion ever to make detective-superintendent. A Yard sergeant with only one Sunday suit, black-and-white telly and a Mini with 100,000 miles on the clock! Didn't he have any rich friends? Yet those very qualities of uncompromising honesty attracted the policeman and the doctor to each other.

Knowing Maclean's background, the detective ordered him tonic water; he sat running the ball of his thumb over an old knife scar on his chin while listening to the story of Armitage, carefully edited by Maclean. At the finish, he shrugged.

"Even with good evidence ... a knife or a gun ... these pro murders are hard to bring off because of the way they ply their trade. Sex is a secret thing. And into the bargain this one's a strangler … No dabs as well as no weapon."

"But he'll come back."

"To strangle another one and get away with it," Pearson muttered. With a hooked forefinger he knocked the beer froth off his moustache. "We've more chance with the hit-and-run job. From all the evidence he's dented a wing and broken a headlight and knocked a lot of paint off. He'll have to get those things fixed or put the car up for a year."

"Who'd be handling the prostitute murders?"

"Different CID units – but we'll have a watching brief on the Putney Common case and some of the others. I'll find out." Downing his beer at a gulp, he left the pub to return in quarter of an hour. "No joy on the hit-and-run car," he said. "And nothing on your two pros." He grimaced. "They're being investigated by one of the surliest, kinkiest bastards on the detective force – Superintendent Wormwood."

"Wormwood!"

"His name's Bob Gall – so we call him Wormwood."

"If he gets a lead on any of the unsolved prostitute murders or another one turns up like them could you let me know?" Maclean said as they left the pub.

"You're not thinking of defending this one, are you?" Pearson grinned.

"No, but I'd like to have him to myself for a week or two – just to find out why Armitage died, and probably those two women."

"You'll be the first to hear when he turns up again," Pearson said. "And he will. They always do."

"Jack the Ripper didn't," Maclean countered as they parted company.

Three

Behind the consulting-room couch, on the table a red light blinked. Maclean rose and left his woman patient mentally and verbally free-wheeling in the darkened room to tiptoe into the office. "It's your lady friend from Shepherd Market," Deirdre said, slinging the phone at him to demonstrate her disapproval. Kiki's whisper came over like wet emery paper. "He's here," she said. "The geezer with the same voice who was with Ginny."

"Where?"

"In my flat. I'm phoning from next door. I said I'd run out of fags and had to go to the pub."

"Did he pick you up?"

"No, I picked him up. He came down here half an hour ago asking for Ginny. Either he's kidding or he doesn't honestly know she's dead, poor dear."

"Are you going back into your flat?"

"Why shouldn't I?"

"I thought you might lock him in and wait for me."

"And have him wreck my place! Not on your life."

"He could be dangerous."

"All right, he might be dangerous. But say he's not the man your're after, he'll take it out on me. And if he is he'll bust the door down and scarper."

"Well, if you're going back watch yourself."

"I've handled worse."

"Just don't turn your back on him."

"I'm not that kinky, doc "

"Do you think you can keep him there for twenty minutes?"

"If I can't, I'll hang up my mink coat and try another trade."

Maclean returned to his consulting-room where, oblivious of his absence, Mrs Sherwood was still unloading her woes about having unwittingly married a homosexual; it would take him months to persuade her that the sub-conscious doesn't make such mistakes, that she had chosen him because for her sex seemed impure, indecent; with a homosexual husband she could quietly ignore it and give her own neuroses free rein. Closing her session, he hurried downstairs to join Deirdre who had stopped a cab in Weymouth Street.

Within quarter of an hour they had arrived outside Kiki's block, an oldish building with a cage lift running up the stair-well. Deirdre took up her position near the lift and Kiki's flat while Maclean went to the foyer to watch the entrance. When the man emerged, Deirdre had to give the alarm by banging the lift door shut and walking past him towards one of the other two flats on the landing.

Scarcely had Maclean taken up his stance at the door than the lift gate banged twice and he heard the cage descend. A man got out and passed him. Under the soft-brimmed hat and short trench-coat, he could still identify the tall, slim figure that the nurses had described. One thing none of them had mentioned; the rigid set of those regular features. This man had a zombie look, as though existing in some completely different world; he went out the entrance without so much as a glance at the psychiatrist.

In case the man took a taxi and they had to use her car, Maclean waited for Deirdre. As well he did, for she spotted something that he had missed. A Rolls Royce was measuring its pace with the man's as he walked up Curzon Street towards Hyde Park. Both the psychiatrist and his secretary kept well behind both the man and the car. They could see that the driver wore a chauffeur's cap and uniform; behind him and the glass partition of the Rolls sat a woman wearing a mink coat and matching hat; from her profile, Maclean placed her in her forties. At the corner of Park Lane, the car accelerated, turned and caught up with the man who climbed into the back with the woman. They must have watched him enter Kiki's, then tailed him but obviously wanted to stage their meeting well away from the flat and make it seem like a chance affair. Maclean and Deirdre were retracing their way to Curzon Street when the psychiatrist steered her into Shepherd Market. "I'll treat you to a cup of tea," he said.

"You have a patient at four o'clock."

"Behind us," he whispered. "A man in a grey raincoat with a hat and dark glasses." Pushing her into a café, he picked a seat at the rear facing the window; from there, both could see the man enter the self-service chemist's shop opposite and wander round.

"There's a back way out," Deirdre said, but Maclean shook his head. Whoever was following them would catch up or be relayed; anyway, he wanted them to realize he was making progress. They sipped their tea and they waited until Deirdre had rung to cancel his appointment before returning to Kiki's flat to thank her. She had donned working clothes, a floral silk peignoir trimmed with ermine which flapped open to expose a black bra and panties; Deirdre gaped at that, then at the expensive Chesterfield and matching chairs, the Oriental rugs, thick brocade curtains and the accessories like the cocktail bar, colour TV and the original paintings and figurines around the room. Kiki screwed the brush back into her nail-varnish bottle. "Did you find him?" she said in a cloud of cigarette smoke.

Maclean nodded. "Thanks for risking your neck, Kiki," he said.

"With him! I could take on a couple of dozen of his kind before dinner." She sniffed. "Only thing he gave me was cash. I've handled some cold meat in my day, but him, he's really deep-freeze."

"He wasn't impotent?" Maclean queried.

Kiki's blond curls spun as she shook her head. "No, but it didn't seem to belong to him – know what I mean?"

Maclean stifled his amusement as he glanced at Deirdre who was blushing to match her russet hair as she listened to this clinical dissection of a sacred taboo like sex. For all the notes and tapes she transcribed, for all the perversion cases like sadism, flagellation, fetishism, bestiality, transvestism she had to describe, she could never conquer her own inhibitions.

"No sign of violence?" Maclean asked.

"No sign of anything." Kiki lit another cigarette. "We have a Madrid pro in this parish who sees it all like bullfighting and gives them two ears and a tail for a good performance. Me? I wouldn't even raise one small Olé for that joker."

When they emerged from the flats darkness had fallen. As Deirdre drove towards Berkeley Square, Maclean did not notice the figure in the mackintosh hail a cab which dropped into their tracks. His mind was turning over what Kiki had told them: even a woman of her vast experience of male behaviour might mistake that cold-fish type for someone harmless; yet he knew that behind that frozen mask and emotionally bleached and dessicated behaviour there might hide the worst type of psychopath, the man who needed only some small quirk or physical feature to trigger his killer instinct.

John Pearson rang to say he had traced the registration number of the Rolls; it belonged to a company with offices in Holborn called Tekpress Ltd, who published scientific and technical journals and made educational, documentary and instructional and publicity films for science-based industries.

"John, you wouldn't like to check if the firm has a Renault GT saloon."

"Already done," Pearson said. "They've got two, both

registered on the company. What beats me is why they didn't dump the car after the accident and report it as stolen."

"Because somebody like you might have gone nosing around the firm and asking other more awkward questions," Maclean said. "They've got too much to hide."

"You may be right," Pearson said. "Buzz me if you need any help."

As he put down the phone, Maclean wondered if he should hand the whole inquiry over to the police. Two things stopped him and kept Pearson out of the inquiry officially. Armitage's murder would be treated as manslaughter and a clever lawyer would prove that the psychiatrist had stepped blindly in front of the car on a murky, wet night; his client would, therefore get away with a small fine and temporary loss of licence. Maclean felt certain that Armitage's death was linked with those prostitute murders and they, in turn, had some connection with the amnesiac patient and his search for his own identity. That aspect of the case fascinated him. No policeman, especially Inspector Wormwood, would bother to find out why a man had committed murder, merely contenting themselves that he had.

Had he followed Deirdre's advice he would have handed over the whole case to Scotland Yard; she considered his idea of investigating the case himself as mad and dangerous. Then, he always had this tussle with her; she sometimes felt inclined to view psychiatry as a painless exercise in straightening out mental kinks with homely advice and would have filled his working hours with nice, harmless neurotics, from compulsive handwashers and cake-eaters to cat-and-bird phobias; Deirdre had another criterion, sizing up if these patients could pay enough to keep them in high-rent Harley Street; he, on the other hand, would have become involved with schizophrenics and paranoiacs, the acute depressive cases and hopeless alcoholics, seeing some bit of himself in all of them; most of them would touch him for money rather than expect to pay for his help. So, over the years, he and Deirdre had established a sort of symbiosis; she allowed him a percentage of problem people with the sort of mental disorders that had brought him into psychiatry in the first place, while he treated her affluent neurotics.

"Macushla, just look at him as a patient," he pleaded.

"But he's a police case," she countered. "If you suspect he's killed once or possibly more than once, you have a duty to tell the police."

"And they'll do what? – lock him up and drive him really insane. He needs help."

"Stephen tried to help him and look what happened to him."

"He didn't know what he was dealing with."

"And we do?"

"I can tell you this much – the man we saw today didn't kill Armitage," he said. "That man will kill on an impulse and only when he thinks something or someone is threatening his own safety. He wouldn't go in for premeditated murder like a hit-and-run accident."

"No, he's worse," she said. "It's like handling a booby-trap."

"That's right, mavournin," he grinned.

"Well, I hope he blows up in your face," she snapped, but she couldn't camouflage her worried look or the fact that she didn't mean a word of it.

With the information Pearson had given him, he made a second trip to the Daily World library. Soon he was sifting through stacks of cuttings about Tekpress Ltd. Suddenly, the picture of the man who had emerged from Kiki's flat pulled him up short.

It was Laurence Hallam Fisher, founder and head of the Tekpress magazine group.

Fisher's name struck a chord, mainly for the ironic reason that he shunned publicity. Not like many of his kind, in order to back more dramatically into the beam of TV cameras, but because of his shy nature. For a wealthy baron of the technical press, he had earned precious few column inches in any newspaper and Maclean had little trouble reading through his cuttings.

Just over twenty years before, Fisher had started his small empire of technical journals with two popular magazines, Science and You and Medicine and You. After this, he launched a whole series of magazines, fifteen in all, dealing with progress and discovery in science and technology. Maclean scrutinized the list which included Electronic Era, Aviation Monthly, Chemical News, Nuclear Technology, Medical Electronics, Bulletin of Biochemistry, Journal of Physical Sciences and several more of that ilk. No wonder he looked so grim!

Fisher possessed a town flat in Mayfair and a country manor near Sutton. He had a wife, Ruth, and a son and daughter in their early twenties. A recent picture showed the son and his fiancée on their engagement day.

Now in his mid-fifties, Fisher came originally from High Wycombe, Buckinghamshire, where his father had worked as a cabinet-maker in one of the numerous furniture factories; he died when Laurence had just turned nine leaving his widow to rear her boy almost on the poverty line. Still, she managed to keep him at the local grammar school until he was seventeen when he found a job with the county newspaper, Bucks Free Press. Within two years he had quit this paper to join the magazine, Aeroplane, in London. His mother came to the capital with him and they rented a two-bedroom flat in Pimlico. For eight years he wrote about aeronautics, rockets and space research, covering technical meetings in Britain and many of the international conferences on the Continent.

One crumbling, yellowing cutting showed a young Laurence Fisher leaving the train at Liverpool Street station behind a coffin on a railway trolley; he was bringing back his mother's body for burial beside his father at High Wycombe. They had travelled to the Continent by car,

Fisher to report a three-day conference on aerodynamics in Hamburg after which he was taking his mother for a short holiday in Berlin and the surrounding country. On June 17, 1953, on the road to Berlin just beyond the small town of Nauen their car and a lorry had collided; his mother had died instantly and Fisher did nearly two months in a hospital with several broken ribs, a compound fracture of the fibula and a badly cracked forearm. In all of Fisher's story, that car crash and his mother's death seemed the most dramatic and traumatic incidents. So often in Maclean's experience when someone released or slackened his hold on his own identity, it could be traced to some crisis — what Armitage would have called a Precipitating Event. If Fisher had gone off the rails, perhaps this accident had some bearing. And yet he appeared to have put it behind him, for two years afterwards he had founded his first magazines and met and married Ruth Gordon Taylor, a Canadian citizen wealthy in her own right. Maclean noted one other ordeal; the Fishers had lost a second son, aged twelve, drowned in the sea at Brighton.

Maclean photocopied a dozen cuttings and pictures. As he walked into Fleet Street he asked himself again and again whether a man like Laurence Hallam Fisher could suddenly erupt after a blameless life, strangle two prostitutes and possibly engineer the death of Armitage. If so, why? His mind full of misgivings, he turned up Chancery Lane then bore right to the headquarters of Tekpress, a modern eight-storey building. Inside, he ran an eye over the publications list while noting that the lift had no attendant. Up he went four floors before reversing the vehicle and descending into the basement parking area. A couple of dozen cars, presumably belonging to executives, sat behind the firm's delivery vans. But only one Renault, a 20 TS. A close inspection of both front wings and headlights only revealed that if someone had touched them up he was a real professional. Where was the other Renault that Pearson had traced through the licensing department?

Probably in the garage of Fisher's Mayfair flat. Maclean studied the small plaque punched by the concessionaires on the rear panel of the Renault. Sanders Auto Service of Cromwell Road. They had a garage so they'd obviously service and repair the cars they sold Fisher's firm. From a street callbox, he rang the flat in Grosvenor Square. A plummy-mouthed character answered, probably a butler. Maclean put on his best plebeian accent and asked the man if they had a Renault with a registration number that he gave; he worked for Sanders's garage and had been ordered to come and collect the car that afternoon for maintenance and the repair of a broken headlight and some coachwork damage.

"I don't quite follow," the butler said. "Mr Fisher certainly possesses a Renault automobile of that registration number, but he makes no personal use of it. He invariably prefers to travel in one of his Rolls Royce limousines."

"Then where would this Renault be?"

"I have not the faintest conception. Try his office."

"He has a country house."

"Yes, it could be there."

Maclean left the box and hailed a cab to take him to Harley Street. Deirdre had two patients waiting for him and while he listened to the droning recital of their emotional problems he was trying to untangle the knots in his own mind. Somehow, he had to link that car with Laurence Hallam Fisher. There seemed only one way to do that.

"Deirdre, I won't be home tomorrow night," he said when the session finished.

"Oh, and where might I ask will you be going?"

"I have a house to burgle," he said with a straight face. "And if you don't mind I'll borrow your car."

"You'll do nothing of the kind," she cried. "The police will trace it back to me."

"I've thought of that. You'll have an alibi."

"And when they start questioning you," she scoffed.

"Yes, I hadn't banked on that," he muttered. Long ago, he had learned that, like most women, Deirdre had a mission to play the guardian angel; no appeal to her maternal or protective instincts ever failed and he knew that rather than watch him fumble and stumble his way into prison with all the guilt and ignominy this would pile on to her Catholic conscience and bourgeois mentality, she would drive him there and hand him the jemmy or whatever else he needed to commit the crime. All he had to do was act a bit weak-minded. Psychiatry came in handy to solve these domestic problems, he reflected as he thanked her.

Deirdre shook her head in sorrow. Most of her time she spent keeping him out of mischief. But then he'd always been a problem ever since that day they'd carted him into the aversion clinic, an alcoholic fifty times lapsed, given up even by Alcoholics Anonymous, and handed him to her. She had redeemed him then by feeding him whisky and pumping him full of apomorphine to show him how foul the liquor could taste, how it made him so sick that he had to vomit it out of his system. And through her he also forgot the reason he had become a drunk – the fact that he was driving with too much liquor in him the night his wife died in their crashed car. Gradually, he recovered his taste for life and his work. Yet even now she had to watch him, for his sympathies often went to people who were suffering his kind of hell. People like this Fisher. She looked at him, wondering why such a brilliant psychiatric mind had such weak points and flaws in it.

"Wherever you're going and whatever you're doing, I'd better come along and see that you keep out of trouble," she said, primly.

"Thank you, mavournin," he said humbly. "It's the last time, I promise."

Peter Hamlin mounted the two flights of stairs to the office in King Street beside Covent Garden at a run; he pushed open the door with its embossed plaque reading SCIENCE NEWS AND FEATURES AGENCY and nodded to the two men working at their desks and the girl on the tele-printer before knocking at the door of the boss's office. "He's on the phone," Laxton grunted. "The private one." Hamlin lit a cigarette, sat down and watched the smoke curl towards the low ceiling spanned by two dingy fluorescent lamps which lit the office.

Laxton and Boulder were sieving through technical magazines and tapping two-fingered summaries of their more interesting articles; piles of technical journals and newspapers and rows of box files neatly labelled filled the shelves; a Xerox copier stood in a corner beside the telex machine on which Sadie was punching the day's reports and stories which would come up on the machines of their subscribers in Fleet Street and in the provinces. Some thirty newspapers and journals paid for their service, among them Tekpress. But Science News and Features Agency acted as a sophisticated, elegant and intricate cover for their real work – supplying Fisher with information.

As soon as the light button on the small switchboard stopped glowing, Hamlin ground out his cigarette. Knocking, he entered the small cubicle where his chief, Max Anderson, sat behind a parapet of bulky dossiers and In and Out trays as though under siege. Every time Hamlin entered this superheated, sound-proof box he fancied he was gazing at a grizzled reincarnation of Lenin. Those same Eurasian features, the skin stretched so tightly over the cheek-bones that he could map the whole skull; those same fiery eyes with their Tartar slant; that same brilliant mind that sponged up reams of words and figures in the way he sluiced tea down his throat. Talk had it that his blood cholesterol, his blood sugar, his blood pressure, just his blood, had all passed the lethal limits, that two coronary seizures had shortened his stride and his shadow. Hamlin hadn't noticed it. Max Anderson still stepped out the three miles from his Kensington home winter and summer; and, bad heart or no, he could still blow his top in eloquent, four-letter Anglo-Saxon as well as Hamlin had ever heard.

Anderson waved him to a seat, drew off another mug of tea from the electric urn by his side, sloshed milk into it, then said, "Well, Peter, how's the lady-love doing?" His cracked lips retracted over stained teeth in a grin. "Wish I were twenty years younger and in the field."

"Leave her out of it," Hamlin said curtly. His boss always needled him about Anne Fisher, whom he had instructed him to seduce. "I told you," he said, "she knows nothing about her father's real operation."

"She's still his favourite child and our closest link with him," Anderson retorted. "Anyway, even if it weren't a job I gave you, I'd still know where to rout you out of bed in the small hours. Lucky man." He sighed profoundly. "It must be like drawing on a kid glove half a dozen sizes too small ..." His tongue ran, red and moist, over his lips in a way that clamped Hamlin's teeth together.

"Max, when are you going to stop talking like a man who can only talk about sex?" he asked.

Anderson laughed. "When it stops being the biggest drawing-card in this or any other business," he grunted. His index-fingernail rattled along the box files above his head. "Pillow-talk has filled more of these with hard-tack information than all their bugging and spy-in-the-sky sputniks and technical tricks."

"Anne Fisher knows nothing," Hamlin said. "So, don't try to involve her."

"Just keep playing your part and we won't get hurt," Anderson snapped. "Learn the noble art of dissimulation and remember her old man's a spy whose future depends on us."

"Why don't you assign somebody else to the girl and I'll step out of the picture," Hamlin said between his teeth.

"When she's got so fond of you!" Anderson sucked in a

deep draught of tea and scowled at his subordinate.
"What's wrong – you going soft on her, too?" He banged
his mug down. "That's another thing you've got to learn –
emotion and reason don't mix. Sex clears the mind, but love
clouds the judgement. That's your thought for the day."
His grin made Hamlin feel like twisting his buzzard neck.

"I think we should point everything we have at this man,
Maclean," he said.

"Ah, yes, the trick-cyclist. Where've we got to with
him?"

Hamlin threw two type-written sheets on the desk.
"That's a rundown of his movements from the moment we
picked him up at the funeral and the inquest on Armitage
who was a mate of his."

Anderson picked up the report and scanned it with his
eye and index-finger, stopping several times to backtrack
and lift a bushy eyebrow. "He's doing well," he conceded.

"Too well."

"Because he's been lucky so far."

"You mean he found that pro who hustled Fisher into
her bed, then followed and identified him through the car."
Hamlin lit a cigarette and inhaled deeply as he recalled the
scene. "I sweated blood wondering if he'd go to his pal at
the Yard and tip him off."

"But he hasn't, thank God."

"That's not to say he won't."

Anderson took two saccharin tablets from a tiny box,
rattled them like dice in his hand before plopping them into
his tea and watching them froth. "That could be
awkward," he muttered. "But let's assume he did, we'd
have to rig the thing through our contacts – anyway, they'd
have a job at the Yard connecting Fisher with a strangled
tart and a callgirl."

"Not if Maclean found the car that hit Armitage,"
Hamlin said. He went on to describe the steps the psychiatrist had taken that day to trace the Renault. "It'd be a pity
to lose a man like Fisher who's worth twenty agents

because of a stupid hit-and-run killing and some quack who decides to play the amateur detective."

"He's more than an amateur, this Dr Alexander Gregor Maclean," Anderson muttered. "What do we know about him?"

"He's well-known in Harley Street and academic medicine and he's a consultant to several hospitals, including that big one in the East End. He's written several text-books on psychiatry and they say in the trade that when head-shrinks get the heebies his is the couch they go and lie down on. He lives in Bayswater with his medical secretary. She was a nurse and brought him through a drink crisis. She's bog-Irish and more papist than the pope. They're devoted to each other, it seems." Hamlin thought for a few moments, then said, "Oh, I should have mentioned he was involved in the Neil Archer Case."

"The uppercrust psychopath who was hanged for murdering the socialite whore."

Hamlin nodded. "Maclean thought he should have got off on insanity grounds but everybody including the defence lawyer didn't see it that way."

"So, he knows something about murder and he doesn't much like the law and won't go running to the police, is that what you think?" Hamlin nodded. Anderson listened and jotted down notes as his subordinate finished outlining Maclean's career; he quizzed him about the relationship between the psychiatrist and his secretary and about Armitage's friendship with him. "I wonder why he's so interested in Fisher," he mused. "And how long before he runs to the police." He drew himself off another mug of tea and bombed it with two sweetening tablets. "A psychiatrist," he muttered. "He might be just the one to make the right guesses."

"He's made quite a few up to now."

"All right, if he gets too close to the truth we may have to find ways and means of silencing him."

"Should we get some sort of warning to Fisher?"

"No," Anderson barked as though he had already considered and dismissed that notion. "It might frighten him into making even more stupid moves and landing us all in it." Stuffing the typed report and his notes into a dossier he locked it in a desk drawer. "We'll have to keep an eye on this quack day and night and hope he's not clever enough to trace that car."

Four

Deirdre foretold disaster if they carried out Maclean's plan to burgle Fisher's house by themselves. "We're mad," she exclaimed. "We can both get penal servitude for life as burglars." And she quoted reams of legal jargon, obviously culled from her citizen's guide. Maclean tried to reassure her saying that they were not burgling with intent to commit a felony. "So, we only risk ten years without hard labour," he said, tongue-in-cheek. "Anyway, it's academic since we're not going to be caught." A couple of days before he had done a reconnaissance that convinced him they had nothing to fear. A rope ladder would take them over the wall and trees would camouflage them to within twenty yards of the garages; all they had to do then was force the garage lock, have a quick look, and they'd have done the job in half an hour.

Practical Deirdre went to their files and returned with a fistful of case-histories of old lags and sweats from four London prisons; they had all done time for petty crime and Maclean had treated them at some period. "Choose a couple of them to do it," she suggested.

"But that's immoral," he gasped.

"And your burglary isn't, I suppose."

"They wouldn't know what to look for."

At that point she threatened to ring Pearson and confess his scheme and he had to choose between the Yard and the underworld. He chose the latter, selecting two men from her list and briefing them when they had volunteered to help. But he insisted on finishing the job.

At midnight the next night, they drove through South London to Sutton. Two men were waiting for them in the alley alongside the grounds of Fisher's house. Jack (Mug) Hennessey, a punch-drunk boxer whom Maclean had treated for depression, and the burglar that had also offered assistance, Charlie (Chick) Evans. "Chick's been over, Dr Mac. He's picked the locks and all you got to do's have a dekko."

"You gotta watch the dogs, Mister Mac," Evans whispered. "They got two big 'uns."

"And the locks?"

"All fixed, guv. They're self-locking. Just shut them after you and nobody'll know."

"You needn't come," Maclean said to Deirdre, knowing her dread of dogs.

"You're not getting rid of me when I've come this far," she said.

Hennessey whispered they would wait and help them back over the wall. Slinging a rope-ladder over the wall, he held it while Maclean climbed up and slithered to the ground on the other side. He caught Deirdre as she dropped behind him. As they crawled through the bushes, he hissed in her ear that he would go first, identify the garage then signal her.

Inching forward on his stomach, panting even in that cold night with the effort of pushing fifteen stone with his knees and elbows, Maclean reached the shadow of the garages. Earlier that day he had studied them through field glasses and now he made for the bigger of the two, flattening himself against the door. It yielded easily and he slipped inside. Within minutes, Deirdre had joined him. In a corner sat the Rolls they had seen several days before; beside it was a Jaguar and two Minis and at the end lay a Renault. "That must be it," Deirdre said, but he shook his head when he shone his torch on the number-plate. It was the car he had seen the other day in the Tekpress basement.

"It's in the next garage maybe," she said.

They slipped outside and hugged the wall to the smaller garage where Evans had again made it easy for them to enter. "There it is," Maclean said when his torch picked out the Renault GT in a corner beside an Austin. Crossing quickly, he ran the light over the front wings and head-lights; someone had replaced the offside headlamp but even with the torch he could see that the wing all round it and part of the grill and bumper had suffered damage and had been crudely repaired. With a knife he scraped some of the old and new cellulose off the wing and placed this in two envelopes. He was just thrusting these into his pocket when a voice echoed in the garage. "I'll take those," it said.

Deirdre and Maclean whirled round to see two men silhouetted in the doorway where they had obviously been watching all their actions. One of the men pointed a double-barrelled shotgun, a finger on its trigger; the other was restraining two Alsatians and beaming a torch into the garage, blinding the psychiatrist and Deirdre. Either the dogs had got wind of their scent or they had triggered a burglar alarm, Maclean thought. Advancing on him and turning his shotgun at Deirdre's quaking breast, the man held out his hand and Maclean gave him the two envelopes. "But you'll have to get rid of the car," he said quietly.

"And you with it," the man growled.

"That means you're taking on Scotland Yard, doesn't it?"

"You're no copper. You're a quack from Harley Street ... a friend of the other."

"I also have friends in the Metropolitan police who're not only interested in this car, but in the two women your boss was with before they were found strangled."

"Belt up," the man with the shotgun shouted, swinging the barrel of his shotgun round and catching Maclean on the shoulder. Evidently he did not want the dog-handler to hear either about the car or Fisher's escapades.

"I've left my detective friends quite a dossier about you and your master in case I bumped into you," Maclean continued. "Among other things a copy of this tape – one you didn't steal from Dr Armitage's consulting-room." Maclean held up a copy of the cassette he had brought with him and the man snatched and pocketed it. Maclean had little doubt that this was the person who had driven the car that killed Armitage and who had committed those thefts of case-books and tapes; he also realized that he and Deirdre had come within a few phrases of joining Armitage. But now the man seemed hesitant, nonplussed. After a few moments he moved behind them, digging both barrels into Maclean's back. "Lead the way to the house," he ordered the dog-handler and they started in procession for the main building. At the side of the turreted structure, the man with the shotgun opened a heavy oak door which led through the kitchen to what Maclean took for the servants' quarters.

As the man picked up the kitchen phone and spoke to someone in the house, Maclean sized him up. He answered every description from the clinics and hospital: dark, beetling brows, jowly face, squashed nose and chin slightly askew. No wonder he had recognized that tape cassette. From what he said, Maclean assumed he was ringing Fisher although his tone suggested anything but the servile chauffeur. When he hooked the instrument back, he pointed them up a flight of stairs and through a door leading into the vast foyer of the manor-house.

Fisher lived in some style. Marble floors and massive, curved staircase its base surrounded by marble statuary. A mixture of modern and classical painting adorned the panels between fluted and corniced wall pillars; three great chandeliers in Waterford crystal swung from three corniced motifs on the ceiling. Skirting the staircase, the two men prodded Maclean and Deirdre into a library sheathed on three sides with books, its other wall broken by two French windows giving on to the garden and stables. Pushed into two of the button-backed armchairs, Deirdre and Maclean sat with the chauffeur's shotgun a yard away.

A loud buzz came from the entrance hall and the chauffeur handed his gun to the other servant and went to answer it; Maclean heard him apologize and declare that the alarm must have triggered spontaneously. When he returned to resume his surveillance, Maclean grinned and said, "Well why didn't you open the main gates and let the police patrol in?"

"Shut up," the chauffeur said.

Everyone sat silent until the door opened and two people entered, both in dressing-gowns and both in their fifties. Maclean had no difficulty identifying Fisher and his wife from photographs he had seen in the newspaper files. He scrutinized the man closely, registering his first impressions. In Maclean's view, these raw impressions of anyone gave the most vital evidence of character if the mind managed to snap and retain them. For as soon as someone spoke, or smiled, or gestured, the voice timbre, the tenor of what was said, the attitudes struck – all this fudged and falsified what the face and body reflexes revealed.

Fisher's face might have been sculpted from the same marble as the busts and figurines in his foyer. It appeared frozen. And those eyes. Like cones made from gunmetal shading lighter on the rim of the iris then coming to a black pinpoint that penetrated people without seeming to perceive them. Eyes like that Maclean had noted in only one person: Neil Archer, the psychopath and murderer that he had analyzed for his defence counsel. Fisher had those same hooded lids, intensifying his frigid expression; he had also the same deliberate robot gestures.

"So this is the burglar," Fisher murmured in a flat but resonant tone.

"Not a burglar," Maclean corrected. "Your garage

doesn't form part of the house, so it's breaking and entering."

"What's the difference?"

"Twenty years," Maclean replied. "But none so far as you're concerned since you're not going to tell the police."

"Oh! Why not?"

"You know why. You've a car in your garage that killed a prominent medical man."

Fisher turned those curious eyes on the chauffeur and stared at him for fully a minute before he asked in that monotonous utterance, "Is this true?"

"I meant to tell you, Mr Fisher, but your wife thought we should wait until you felt better."

"My state of health has no relevance. How did this thing happen?"

"It was an accident. A man stepped out into the middle of the road without warning. It was dark and wet and I hit him before I knew."

"It was no accident," Maclean put in, then looked at Fisher. "The doctor was a psychiatrist and his name was Stephen Armitage and that should mean something to you."

Fisher seemed bewildered, glancing quizzically at the chauffeur, then at his wife. "Do we know a Dr Stephen Armitage?" he asked and they both shook their heads.

"You consulted him on two occasions," Maclean insisted. "Once at the Royston Day hospital and the second time at his consulting-room in Wimpole Street. If you want proof, let your chauffeur tell you what he did with the medical records and tape-recordings he stole from the psychiatrist's files."

"I've no idea what this man's talking about," the chauffeur said.

"You have the cassette I gave you."

"What cassette?"

"It's all right," Maclean shrugged. "I made a copy."

"What exactly are you after, Mr ..." Fisher interjected.

"My name's Maclean – Alexander Gregor Maclean. I'm

a psychiatrist and a colleague of Dr Armitage. He mentioned your problem to me just before he was killed."

"My problem?"

"On both the occasions that you arrived at his hospital and consulting-room you showed signs of a form of amnesia, he thought."

"Did I?" Fisher appeared to weigh up the statement and be searching desperately through his memory. "Curious, I don't remember ever meeting or consulting your late friend, Dr Armitage," he murmured. He turned his gaze on Deirdre who flinched visibly under those pinpoint eyes. "Who is this young lady?" he asked. Maclean explained that she was his secretary. Fisher rose abruptly, going to a Sheraton table and, pouring himself a glass of water from a jug, he gulped it down, refilled the glass and came back to sit down. While everyone watched and waited, he sipped the water very slowly for several minutes, absolutely silent. Maclean noticed that his hands betrayed as little as his face. No sign of trembling. Yet he could almost feel stress radiating from this man, like a charge building up in a thunderstorm. Was that emotionally bleached look real or faked?

"What did you think, Dr Maclean? About my problem, I mean?"

"Unless you consulted me, I couldn't begin to give an opinion," Maclean replied.

"Know what I think – your friend, Armitage, invented some tale about me, or genuinely mixed up someone with me, or was fooled by someone posing as me."

"You can always check that."

"How?"

"By asking your wife whether you were absent around December 2 or February 14."

"Not that he has any need to check anything, doctor, but I can tell you now," Ruth Fisher said. Her voice had a slight transatlantic twang and he remembered she was Candian by birth. "Apart from trips to Manchester and

Glasgow in November and January, my husband has not been away from home at all.''

"All right," Maclean said. "Then get your chauffeur to give you the tapes he stole from Armitage's consulting-room and the one I gave him tonight. Your voice should tell you if you're the man my colleague was talking about.''

"I don't have to prove alibis or play such games," Fisher said. "I have never had anything to do with your psychiatrist friend.''

"Maybe not – but your chauffeur still admits to killing him.''

"Accidentally," Fisher said.

"A fine legal point."

"Very well, we'll let a judge decide." Fisher turned to the chauffeur. "Wade, you will report to the police investigating this accident tomorrow and tell them precisely what happened. I'm sure they'll understand that your only crime was failing to report the accident or stop when you hit the man.''

"I didn't know I'd hit anything, sir, until next day when I spotted the damage.''

At this statement, Deirdre could not contain herself. "He's lying," she shouted. "He tried to kill Dr Armitage once before by pushing him under a tube. It was deliberate murder.''

"And I suppose you can prove all this," Fisher murmured.

"Of course they can't. Their whole story's absurd." It was Ruth Fisher who uttered the comment; she had sat watching the duel between Maclean and her husband and now felt that she had to call a halt; she got to her feet, took Fisher's hand and motioned him to rise. He stopped her. "First, we have to decide what to do with these two criminals," he said.

"Easy," Maclean said with a smile. "Hand us over to the police.''

"Don't listen to him, Laurence," Ruth Fisher said.

Maclean felt her scrutinize him, her eyes shift slowly over his face then his amorphous figure. In turn, he gazed at her; her filmy dressing-gown blurred the outline of her slender figure just as her blond curls softened her brittle good looks and the rougher contours of her neck. He wondered how much she really knew and had concealed.

"Well, I suppose I should inform the police," Fisher said. "But you'd welcome that, wouldn't you? It would give you both the chance to air your little fantasies about me as well as my chauffeur." He rose, put the glass on the mantelpiece, then said to Maclean, "I'm a quiet man and like to keep my private life to myself. So consider yourselves lucky." He rounded on Wade. "Show them off the property immediately, Wade," he said.

As they left by the front door, Maclean glanced over his shoulder. Halfway up the marble staircase, his hand on the wrought-iron balustrade, Fisher was watching them depart; his face remained a mask except perhaps for the white compression of his lips and the troubled frown over his eyes.

"Get out and stay out or I'll do you in next time," Wade growled as he banged the main gate shut behind them. Deirdre walked or wobbled for several yards before her legs gave and she had to hang on to Maclean for support.

"Know something? – I think you meant us to get caught," she said bitterly.

"What makes you say that, macushla?"

"Never mind." Her voice was trembling. "I thought our last hour had come when that thug pointed his gun at us."

"Oh, he'd have killed us if he could have covered it up."

"We're not going to let him get away with murdering Stephen," she said.

"Nobody can prove it's murder," he replied. "And there's nothing more we can do except ensure he gives himself up and takes what sentence the court decides." As they regained their car they saw that their two accomplices had taken the hint and vanished.

During the return drive he had time to play back the

events of that evening. Wade, the chauffeur, didn't really interest him. Only Fisher. He puzzled Maclean. He looked like a man who had mislaid himself both in time and space, a misfit. But then he was probably doing what most of us spent our lives doing – searching for ourselves. What made him so interesting was that he appeared to have found so little of his real Self. Those doubts about his amnesiac flights and meetings with Armitage looked genuine. Who knew? They might be. That static face came into Maclean's mind. Fisher looked nothing like a man who would have run to any psychiatrist for help; indeed, he seemed in full possession of himself. Nothing like a man pursued by his *doppelgänger*. Nothing like a man seeking some lost love that he called Jane.

"You forgot to get your tape back," Deirdre said, cutting across his reflections.

"No, I meant him to keep that. Whether or not he remembers lying on Armitage's couch, he'll get a shock when he plays it back. He's given away more than he intended."

"He gave me the creeps," she said. "Do you really believe he strangled those two women?"

"I'm not sure," Maclean said. "And I wonder if he's sure himself of what he's done."

Ruth Fisher did not accompany her husband upstairs straight away. As she left the library, her daughter, Anne, was standing by the entrance and stopped her. "I heard the row and thought daddy was having another one of his nightmares and came down. What was it all about?"

"Nothing much, darling."

"Wade with a shotgun and two people who'd been breaking into the garage! And you call it nothing much."

"I meant nothing to worry about."

"But I heard most of it and it sounded serious to me. After all, Wade did knock down and kill this psychiatrist …"

"Wade's a fool not to have confessed to us."

"He has too much influence here, that's the trouble."

"Your father owes him a lot and he's completely loyal," her mother snapped. "Wade probably wanted to spare your father any more worry." And with an injunction to her daughter to go back to bed she crossed the entrance hall and mounted the stairs.

Anne watched her. Sometimes she wondered why her mother and Charles Wade seemed almost conspiratorially close and so protective, both of them, about her father. What had gone wrong in this household in the past five months? It had started when her father began to have those nightmares which wakened the whole house; she had even discovered him wandering around the grounds in pyjamas one freezing night when she had returned late from the hospital dance. Yet he rejected her mother's advice and hers to consult their doctor. He'd merely been overworking and would get over his bad spell, he had said.

And why did her mother lie to him and to the psychiatrist about the two occasions when he had disappeared for nearly a week at a time? It had stopped them all in their tracks, thinking he was dead or had been kidnapped. Everyone had hunted for him in those few places that he frequented. She had urged her mother to seek police help only to meet point-blank refusal. Her father did not like fuss. Fuss! When most of his friends had given him up for dead. Then he had strolled into the house for all the world as if he had just popped out to buy a box of matches or an evening paper.

When she reflected about her father's strange behaviour something else occurred to her; it seemed somehow connected with the fact that Roger, her brother, had brought home the latest cover-girl, Elaine Dancy, and announced that he was going to marry her. At first her father had welcomed the engagement, then for no reason that any of them could fathom he had thrown a tantrum and ordered Roger and his girlfriend out of the house. Anne admitted that her brother was footloose and headstrong and had hardly endeared himself to his father by choosing to become a newspaper and magazine photographer instead of joining him at Tekpress; however, it seemed ridiculous to take it out on him and his girl who was a cut above the average model; now they were living in two rooms in Battersea trying to imagine what had hit them. Like everybody else.

Anne worked as an almoner for hospitals in the Surrey region. She had heard of Gregor Maclean, the psychiatrist. Now, she went into the deserted library to take down Who's Who and the London telephone book; in the first directory she discovered a good six inches about the psychiatrist; in the second she noted his Harley Street and home addresses. They might come in handy one day.

Laurence Fisher had not returned to his bedroom, but had gone straight to his private study on the first floor, over-looking the main drive. He waved Ruth out of the room when she tried to persuade him to come back to bed. Once alone he unlocked a drawer and pulled out his personal diary to consult those weeks that the psychiatrist had mentioned – ending December 2 and February 14. Four blank days around the first date and five around the second. Usually meticulous, he even entered trivia in his diary if nothing important had happened. Why hadn't he recorded anything for those dates?

He vaguely remembered his return in February and tried to recall where he had been on those missing days; but he fared no better now than he had then. Only scattered fragments of that blank period had clung to his mind, splintered pictures and shards of remembrance like the hypnagogic images that tricked the mind between waking and sleeping, or echoes of sounds long dead. He had a hazy recollection of surfacing mentally in a hospital ward, of finding his way home (although he might have dreamt this). Everything else had erased itself like one of those plastic notepads. Some faces and places he sensed he had encountered before. So vividly. Yet his mind had dark areas that he feared he would never explore. This house, for instance, he felt he had seen before the actual fact. On first sighting it, a matching picture formed in his mind like a print in a developing tank; this study and other rooms reminded him of rooms he could never have imagined. When they had made enough money to buy a large mansion and he and Ruth were house-hunting he had summarily discarded scores of period houses. For he could envisage exactly what he wanted. And when he had first clapped eyes on this eighteenth-century Adam building something clicked and he bought it without even visiting more than a couple of the twenty-odd rooms. He had not confided to Ruth that some time, some place, though so long ago that his memory had fudged the events, he knew this house. She had marvelled at the decision and authority with which he chose the furniture and other trappings – Chesterfield sofas and Hepplewhite table and dining-chairs, down to the pattern and type of Axminster rugs and the handles of the Sheraton desk at which he now sat, puzzling at the autonomic reflexes that had dictated his choice.

He knew it had something to do with the months – or years? – of intensive training they had given him. But what he did not know was HOW they had indoctrinated him so impeccably to operate for years like some well-oiled computer. That they had obviously erased. But in the past months he had begun to gain some small insight into their mehods. He realized they had used dozens of Pavlovian techniques to which he had submitted willingly, allowing them to stifle his own reflexes and afterwards to fill him full of new ones from the soles of his feet to the crown of his head. Only at certain times did this realization break through; for most of the time he remained unaware of how and why he acted as he did. Yet he felt pleased that some small recess of his brain had escaped their brain-washing and reprogramming. His masters had given him this training to protect him, so they said. Spies who lived and worked in strange company, strange society, often made stupid mistakes; spies who fell in love became too vulnerable to self-betrayal, to betrayal of their masters or betrayal of their lovers; spies who stepped up in the world might succumb to easy living and the rotten doctrines of the bourgeois society and sell their souls. So he had volunteered for their conditioning, had become a Faust in reverse and made a pact to renounce everything for his ideals.

For more than twenty years he had fooled them all; in Tekpress he had built up a foolproof system of collecting and collating information and military and industrial intelligence which he passed on to his contacts through his associate, Norman Blount; he had his own circle of informants who worked in government departments and procured secret papers for their masters; he had become a prominent member of the community, risen above suspicion and the whisper even ran that he might appear in the next honours list with a knighthood.

He was fireproof. Norman Blount might fall, his other informants might be trapped. But never once had he stepped inside the embassy in Belgrave Square; nor had he ever met this or that attaché, planted by the security services to spy. If anyone cared to inquire into his private or business life, every bit of information arrived on his desk legitimately – although much of it he could not use because it was secret and covered by government D-notices precluding publication.

How then had things begun to go wrong? First he had quarrelled with Roger, his son, over that scheming whore who was obviously after his money. On his part, it seemed more than a quarrel, a sort of brainstorm. He had, however, felt in his heart – how, he could not guess – that his son's girlfriend spelled danger for him and his whole family. Perhaps he had been too hasty and too harsh throwing them both out. That episode had shaken him; it had also forced him to try to recall his own youth and there he had butted against the barrier that someone had erected in his mind against just such behaviour and self-analysis. That way lay all the taboos they had constructed and, at the end, madness. He sensed all this and strove to forget his boyhood, youth and everything they had signified. They had made forgetfulness easy, too.

Before accompanying the psychiatrist and his secretary to the gate, Wade had handed him a cassette. He gazed at its label bearing Maclean's name and Harley Street address; for several minutes he sat weighing his decision before crossing to the cabinet injecting the plastic box into the tape-recorder and switching on.

Armitage's voice had a familiar echo, yet he could put neither face nor name to it; even the timbre and inflections of his own voice when replying to questions and talking about Jane sounded like some stranger's in his ears. Was he really uttering Goethe's Nähe des Geliebten? Where had he learned it? Probably at school. But why recite it in German? And why break down after a few halting lines and cry?

Yet, he could not deny that it was himself on that tape, perhaps a part of his secret and genuine Self infiltrating his mind. For he felt a lump rise from his chest and emerge through his throat as a sob. Tears wet his eyes. He wiped them away then grabbed two handfuls of his blond hair and tugged fiercely as though trying to expunge the thought or emotion that had animated the tears. Whatever had moved him he had to cease to think about; for even that mental effort made his head throb and pulse, alerting him to danger, raising spectres. To his right, something stirred and he started, his skin prickling with the fear that it might be his younger double come to taunt him again.

"I thought you might like some tea, daddy," a voice murmured in his ear. A hand reached out to close the diary and replace it in the drawer. He turned his gaze on Anne who had slipped into the room and was pointing to a tray with a teapot and two cups and a plate of biscuits on the gueridon by the fireplace. Taking his hand, she drew him to a chair, sat him down and poured him a cup of tea.

"You know, he's quite famous," she remarked.

"Who?"

"The psychiatrist who broke into the garage."

"I don't like psychiatrists. They're like priests, parasiting and preying on people's weakness, fear and ignorance."

"But they say he's different – even his fellow-psychiatrists consult him when things go wrong with a patient, or themselves. Like Armitage, the man you're supposed to have seen."

"I saw nobody of that name and don't try to convince me I did," her father snapped.

"But, whether you did or not, Dr Maclean might be able to help you," she suggested.

"By breaking into my home," he growled. "I don't need his help, or anybody else's."

Anne grasped his hand and said softly, "Daddy, somebody's going to have to tell you that you've changed – you're not yourself."

"Not myself!" Those words went in like a poison dart. He glared at her. "What do you know about me ... what I am and what I feel?"

"That may be our trouble," Anne said calmly. "We've never really got to know each other in this house."

"Well, if you don't like the way I act or my house, you can follow your brother." Wrenching his hand out of hers, he strode across the room and banged the door behind him. Anne gazed after him, baffled by his reaction and wondering what made him fear doctors so much. Especially psychiatrists. He obviously felt that Maclean was breaking into his private world as well as his home. Strangely, she guessed that the psychiatrist had intended him to feel that way.

Five

Deirdre shivered. Although as a nurse she had witnessed some harrowing cases, morgues still gave her the creeps with their cloying tang of iodoform and chlorine overlying the smell of death, with their dank, cold atmosphere. However, she braced herself and followed Maclean, John Pearson and the morgue attendant to Locker 12. Steel runners hissed and they were gazing at the latest strangulation victim. Pearson flipped open his notebook and read them the details: Shirley Mainwaring, aged twenty-three, from Nottingham by way of Tite Street, Chelsea. Full-time pro and part-time call-girl who picked up men in her car and used hotels rather than her flat. Found strangled with her silk stocking in a third-rate Victoria hotel. Maclean studied her. Her russet hair still flamed against the green formica of the slab on which she lay. That interested him. For three weeks now, he had visited London morgues whenever Pearson alerted him that a prostitute with red, russet, chestnut or auburn hair had been found dead, preferably strangled.

"I wondered if she'd fit your picture," Pearson said. "She'd been raped."

Immediately, Maclean shook his head. "No, my man doesn't rape. In fact, something always seems to stop him from having any sex play with his victims."

"Jack the Ripper didn't either."

"I know, but this man doesn't rip anybody, and he doesn't hate them. That's what's so funny."

"He lets go too quickly, then."

"No," Maclean said, thinking of Kiki's sexual experience with Fisher.

Maclean had confessed some of his suspicions about Fisher to the detective-sergeant but had sworn him to keep silent as far as the official investigation went. Pearson promised to do nothing – at least until Inspector Gall or some other Yard man pointed the finger Fisher's way. Although he did not think Shirley Mainwaring had any connection with Fisher, he nevertheless dictated her description to Deirdre, trying to imagine what those bleached features must have looked like before someone throttled her life away. "Her eyes, John?" he asked.

"Blue," Pearson said.

In this way, Maclean built up a sort of photoportrait of the red-haired prostitutes who had been strangled, but neither mutilated not sexually violated. So far he had collected four and, from their common features and those of the women he had already traced in newspaper files, he had constructed a composite face. "Funny," he said to Deirdre. "It's not unlike you. Maybe you're his type." She did not share the joke. He was hoping they might pick up the same sort of victim around the date that someone reported an amnesiac like Fisher who had wandered into a hospital looking for help. It was a slender probability but it kept his and Pearson's interest alive. Not Deirdre's. She urged him to give up the quest, fearing that the stranger might pick him as the next victim and arguing that Wade had confessed and was serving his sentence.

Charles Wade had indeed gone to jail. He had pleaded guilty, thus avoiding having to give evidence and reducing the hearing to a few minutes; his lawyer had made the most of the murky night and emphasized the discrepancies in the accounts of the two witnesses. Wade had escaped with a sentence of three months' jail and, since he had already served three weeks on remand, would be released in just over a month. Wade had acted as bodyguard as well as chauffeur rarely letting Fisher out of his sight even at Tekpress; Maclean wondered if the unguarded Fisher might not seize the chance to cut loose once again. If they had solved Armitage's murder they had certainly not avenged the psychiatrist, let alone pierced the mystery of why he had died. Fisher might not have ordered his death in so many words, but Wade had evidently killed to protect his master. So, did Fisher who had instigated the crime get away with it?

Deirdre listened to these arguments, realizing only too well that he did not give a rap for Armitage or Wade. Fisher fascinated him and his Harley Street practice and everything else could volatize while that problem filled his mind. So she bowed because neither of them would enjoy any peace of mind until he had resolved that case. Also because she loved him.

Pearson nudged them, thanked the morgue attendant and whispered that he had a date with Wormwood later that morning. If they wanted to see the other stiff at Kingston, they'd have to move quickly. He drove them on a mad slalom through the London traffic, his siren scattering buses and lorries like a bow wave. When they got there, the coroner's officer, a plain-clothes policeman, led them round the back through a rose-garden to the morgue, a low, brick building. At the door, Deirdre turned saying she'd had enough of morgues for the day and was going to treat herself to coffee and biscuits in the hospital canteen. Maclean and Pearson walked to the table on which the office had laid out the body. Maclean gave one glance and shook his head; she had violent, reddish-orange hair – out of a henna bottle – but her skin had the tawny sheen of a half-caste, probably from somewhere in the Caribbean. "You get back to Inspector Wormwood," he said to Pearson. "I'll pick up Deirdre and take a bus to Richmond and the tube from there."

On entering the canteen Deirdre's expression told him something had happened. "I've just met Fisher's daughter," she whispered.

"What's she doing here?"

"She's an almoner and spends one day a week here. She wants to see you about her father."

"How did she know you?"

"She saw us that night at the house."

Maclean went and bought himself coffee and returned to their table. "Nobody saw you talking to her?" he asked. She shook her head, saying that the two other men in the cafeteria wore hospital uniforms. Maclean thought for a moment. To have someone in the Fisher household might prove invaluable; but not if the people who were following him learned that the daughter had made contact. Even here, after that wild drive, he would not swear that they had shaken off their tail. Who were they? That was another mystery. Pearson had checked everyone and everywhere in the metropolitan police force and nobody had ordered surveillance of the psychiatrist. They had assumed that it must have been one or two people on Fisher's staff. Even here, he could take no chance. "Go and pick up Fisher's daughter," he whispered. "Bring her to lunch in an hour and a half to that little restaurant just off Camden Hill. And make sure you're not followed."

"How do I do that?"

Patiently, he explained that she must take the tube from quiet tube stations, letting several trains go through to make sure no-one was following them; she should get out at Holland Park, another quiet station, and walk to the restaurant. "And Miss Fisher must not suspect that anybody might be following you both." Deirdre raised her eyes to heaven, shrugged and made for the door.

Maclean took a roundabout way to the small basement restaurant behind Notting Hill Gate. He had almost given them up for lost when they both entered. He had expected Anne Fisher to look something like her mother with brittle good looks tricked out with lipstick, eye-pencil and other artefacts; but she had strong features and a golden skin without even a trace of powder; she had frank cornflower-blue eyes, the colour of Fisher's own; she had his straw-yellow hair which she swept back straight, accentuating her facial bones, and tied in a chignon at the nape of the neck; she had the innocent beauty of a gazelle. Yet, she was Fisher with light in her eyes and mobility in her mouth. Maclean seated them, ordering three grilled Dover soles before turning to Anne.

"So, you saw the scene the other week," he said and she nodded. "Tell me, what did your father really think of it all?"

"Frankly, I believe he was baffled." She sipped her glass of white wine, then said, "He needs help. Badly."

"Was I right? Did he disappear on the two occasions I mentioned?"

She nodded. "I checked his diary to confirm it. But he refuses to admit it – even to himself. And I honestly don't think he knew anything about your psychiatrist friend, or what Wade did."

"When did all his problems start?"

Anne reflected for a moment, her blue eyes losing their gaze in her cigarette smoke. "I think it must have started about five months ago when Roger, my brother, came home with Elaine."

"His girlfriend?"

She nodded. "Oh, Roger had a whole regiment of girls before Elaine and my father hadn't even raised an eyebrow. Perhaps it was because Roger was serious about Elaine."

"Maybe your father disliked her."

"No, they got on very well at first. In fact I thought … well I thought they might share some secret."

"You mean they might be lovers."

"I suppose so. Then something happened. They quarrelled."

"Do you know what about?"

"Nobody did. Not even Elaine."

"It couldn't have been a lovers' quarrel?"

"I don't think so." Anne shook her head and sadness

misted her eyes and tightened her mouth. "My father wouldn't have started such a row. He's not a demonstrative man. I've never even heard him say he loved my mother."

"Does he?"

"It's stupid, but I don't really know."

"Does your mother love him?"

"That I do know. She adores him." They had met, she explained, eighteen months after her father returned from the Continent with his mother's body; her mother was then working in London for a publishing house specializing in scientific and technical books; she fell in love with her father at first sight and put up a lot of the money to start his first publication; her family had come from Canada and made its fortune out of department stores in the Midlands and north of England.

"Where did your father learn such good German?"

Anne shrugged her shoulders. "I didn't even realize he could speak it."

Maclean and Deirdre looked across at each other. "But we have a tape of him speaking perfect German," he said.

"I know. I heard it the night you were at the house, just at the end of the cassette he was playing. But that wasn't what stopped me in my tracks. He was crying as he listened."

"Was that so unusual?"

"I'd never seen him shed tears before. None of us had. You probably don't know I had a younger brother, Paul, who was drowned bathing off the pier at Brighton. My father had to go and fetch the body and bring it back to our hotel. Not even that made him cry. He just didn't seem to feel anything." She stopped and gazed at them both. "It was those tears that convinced me my father needed help."

"But is he convinced he needs help?" Maclean asked.

Anne shook her head. "He hates doctors of any sort. He won't even consult our local family doctor about his headaches."

"It's called iatrophobia – doctor-fright," Maclean said

with a grin. "No known cure."

"Can I do anything to get him to seek advice?" she asked.

Maclean shrugged. "He'd be better to come of his own accord," he said. "When he's really scared he'll do what he did before – wind up in a casualty ward where they'll refer him to a psychiatrist."

"I wish you'd take the case."

"Maybe he'll pick me next time," Maclean said. "In the meantime keep an eye on him and if he disappears let me know." As the two girls rose to leave the restaurant, he whispered to Anne Fisher, "By the way, tell Roger to keep away from the house for the time being."

"I don't think there's any fear that he'll crawl back, knowing Roger," Anne said. "But why?"

"I don't think it would do your father's peace of mind any good to see him and his girlfriend at this stage." How could he confess that Elaine might have triggered Fisher's mental or emotional crisis, that she might have the looks or the voice or the gestures of one of these women that he had sought out and who now headed Scotland Yard's list of unsolved murders?

Six

For several minutes, Ruth Fisher stood studying her husband, who lay back in the chair his eyes closed, feet and arms splayed. Even in that state of exhausted repose his face looked a taut, tortured mask. On coming home from the office he had flopped into the study armchair and slept. She hated to waken him, but the lantern clock on the mantelpiece told her their guests would arrive in just over half an hour. As she watched, his face twitched and he mumbled something too low and too incoherent for her to grasp. She shook him gently. "Laurence, it's after seven – you'd better hurry." His mind visibly groped for his bearings as his eyes opened, then his face relaxed very slightly.

"Hurry! Why? Oh yes, I remember, we've invited Lord Curton and that industrialist bore, Markham, and their wives." And as he hoisted himself up, he grumbled that they'd have done better to watch the box in front of a log fire.

"You've forgotten Norman Blount," she said.

No, he hadn't forgotten Blount since he had invited him for a specific discussion. Blount had conveniently left London to meet their circulation representatives in the provinces the day that Wade had been charged and committed for trial. Fisher cursed the man.

Ruth Fisher looked out his dinner-jacket and ruffed shirt while he splashed water on his face in the bathroom; as she knotted his black bow-tie, she felt his blue eyes on her face, troubled. To conceal her own anxiety she smiled, though dying to ask him what had gone wrong recently, to probe for the mental or emotional lesion and excise it with her love. But Laurence Fisher wasn't the kind of man that even a loving wife could question about himself, that would respond to her or anyone else. Never once, even during their courtship, had he ever confessed that he loved her. At first she had attributed this to shyness, then to something in his past that had forced him to construct a biological shield round his personality in case someone would intrude too deeply. He was also grieving for his mother. In time, her own love had become mute, too, although it had grown no less profound for that. Laurence must have loved her a little even if he seemed incapable of showing it. She had borne his three children. And he did need her and rely on her. That he had conceded many times. For her it amounted to a form of love.

Yet something had happened to crack his shell. For twenty-five years his life had followed un unruffled pattern; she could have written in advance his working and social diary for every hour of every day. Then without warning he seemed to have transformed his whole character. He had not disappeared twice as the psychiatrist and others thought, but on a dozen occasions and for one or two nights at a time. Wade, whom she bribed uncompunctiously to keep an eye on him, had finally admitted that he appeared to be looking for some woman he had known along various prostitute beats in the West End. After the initial shock, Ruth supposed that perhaps this sort of upheaval occurred in men like Laurence who had repressed their emotions for most of their lives. For months after she had met him he had blamed himself for his mother's death. That guilt and self-reproach might have something to do with his unstable behaviour. She wished that he would go and consult some doctor, even away from London or England.

"Darling, maybe I shouldn't mention it, but you had another nightmare and were talking in your sleep again last night," she said, straightening the tie.

"Oh! Interesting?"

"I don't know. I was too scared to listen much. You were screaming then you started babbling something in English and what sounded like German."

"German! I hardly know any."

"I may be wrong. As I said, I didn't listen all that hard."

"A model wife. One who knows the second law of matrimony: Never listen when a husband talks in his sleep."

"Oh! What's the first law?"

"That's for husbands and it makes the second law redundant. Never talk in your sleep. Now let's forget it." Fisher uttered these remarks in his flat humourless voice.

"But, darling, there was one thing I couldn't help hearing," Ruth insisted. "You were shouting a name ... a girl's name."

"A girl's name. What was that?"

"Jane."

"Jane? I don't know anybody called Jane." He stopped brushing the hair on his temples, stared at his face in the mirror and pronounced the name several times as though scanning it with his memory. Then, shrugging, he said, "It doesn't click, it's probably some trick of the sub-conscious."

"Don't worry about it, darling," Ruth said.

They walked downstairs and into the library where their servants had disposed a tray of bottles and glasses for Fisher to serve his guests. Even Moore, his trusted valet, left them alone when he was receiving important guests. Mixing his wife a gin and vermouth, Fisher poured himself plain tonic water and sipped this. Only at meals did he allow himself two glasses of white or red wine; for the rest of the time he remained teetotal.

As they sat down, he observed his wife. She had changed little since their marriage nearly quarter of a century before. Still the same lissom figure which bearing three children had not altered; her blonde hair no more required dye or bleach than her figure demanded strutting with wire and elastic; her only concession to age seemed the make-up and greenish-blue shadow with which she softened the cross-hatching and harder lines of her face. She never needed to tell him that she loved him; but he sometimes wondered if her love would resist the disclosure that spying for her country's enemies was his real purpose in life. Maybe she would accept it as she had everything he had done – not even reproaching him with ordering their son, Roger, out of the house. While he was turning all this over in his mind, Anne made her appearance; she was dining with them that evening because it was her day off. She crossed to kiss her mother, then peck him on the cheek, though she took and squeezed his hand for a moment. With her fair good looks and fine bones, she took after Ruth whereas Roger had inherited his squarer features, broad chest, narrow hips and long arms. Anne helped herself to a whisky and water.

Norman Blount arrived quarter of an hour early as instructed. He had known Fisher for twenty-five years since he had disembarked from Canada and thrown in his lot with Tekpress when they started their first magazines. Now he acted as managing editor of the magazine group. In ill-cut dinner-jacket and baggy trousers, he looked anything but a top editorial executive; but then his appearance did not betray his real function, acting as go-between for Fisher and his spymasters. He kissed the hands of Ruth and Anne before approaching Fisher to hand him a wad of paper that he pulled from an inside pocket. "I missed you when I came back from Manchester – but that's the circulation report for the northern circuit."

Fisher cast a cold eye over it, then said to the two women, "You'll have to excuse us. I've got some rather dull business to discuss with Norman. It won't take long." Pointing to the library annexe, he took Blount's arm and led him there and shut the door.

"I've been waiting to talk to you for more than three weeks."

"About Wade?"

"Yes, about Wade. It was you who ordered him to stage that accident with the psychiatrist – a bloody foolish thing if ever I knew one."

"What was I to do? Wait until that doctor found out who you really were and started putting two and two together."

"His Harley Street friend has."

"Maclean? He won't get far with what we've left him."

"Won't he? Wade's now serving time because of him."

"That's because he was stupid to follow you to that whorehouse in Mayfair. And you were crazy to go there."

"That's my affair."

Blount shook his head, his puffy jowls flapping; he took off his pebble-lens specs, pushed the frames half into his mouth to breathe on them, then wiped them with a grubby polkadot hankie. "Nothing's just your affair and you know it. If you go we all go, and that's why we have to keep an eye on what you do and where you go and who you meet."

"Nobody on your side has any complaints about me, have they?"

Blount kept polishing his glasses, then replaced them on his snub nose. "Not out loud, but they would have if we'd left that girl where you did."

"What girl?"

"The one who picked you up in Chelsea and took you to her flat." He paused, his voice dropping into a sinister, low pitch. "The one you strangled."

"You're mad. I didn't strangle anybody."

"All right, you didn't strangle anybody. But, just in case, Wade and I had to dump the body in Putney Common and clean up the flat behind you."

Fisher stared at him. Was Blount making it up to scare him and wriggle out of his own difficulty; or had he murdered some unfortunate prostitute? He had not even the glimmer of a recollection of such an act. However, Blount did not joke about their job, or about anything. For the first time that he could remember, Fisher felt fear crawl from the crown of his head down his spine and even into the back of his legs. Not only the dread of being caught and convicted of murder, but a deeper more nameless terror of having no awareness of what he had done. Or why he had done it. He caught Blount's eyes, floating and wavering behind his thick lenses, scrutinizing him. "What are you staring at, Norman?"

"Nothing," Blount shrugged.

"You see something, don't you?" Fisher gripped the other man's arm until he winced. "I've changed, is that it?"

"If you want the truth – yes."

"You don't think I've changed sides, do you?"

"No, I don't think so …"

"That means others do."

Blount shrugged. From an inside pocket he extracted a

crumpled packet of cigarettes; he lit one and inhaled deeply
while Fisher watched with a set face. "They whisper – it's
no more than a whisper – that the quality of your
information has dropped off. Some of them say that Fisher
has gone too high to be of much use with hard-tack
scientific and technical information. Others say that if he's
not one of the other side in spirit he's one of them in
fact …"

"They put me here," Fisher snapped.

"Yes, but so long ago that most of them have forgotten or
disappeared and been replaced by younger men," Blount
murmured.

"They forget easily – and remember easily," Fisher said
cryptically. Blount noticed that the hand holding the tonic
water trembled slightly as his boss raised the glass to his
mouth to moisten dry lips. "And you, Blount, you've
worked with me all these years, what do you think – truly?"

"I think you could do with a rest," Blount murmured
with a smile that did not fool Fisher. Anyway, what did
Blount know of his real story? He had gathered no more
than that as a young man they had recruited him while he
was working for British technical journals, had given him
an intensive training course on the Continent before
sending him back to Britain. Of course Blount realized that
they had helped him establish his chain of technical
publications with finance and by giving him distribution
rights in Eastern Bloc countries; also by making
agreements to exchange published information through
technical Press agencies. It made the collection and
transmission of military and industrial intelligence that
much easier and less hazardous.

Blount was scanning Fisher's face as though searching
for some clue to his behaviour. As he knew well, there came
a time when a man's ideals began to erode under
conditioning by the society in which he operated; even the
best had to renew their ideals and buttress their courage
through contact with their spymasters and the fatherland;

otherwise loyalties yielded and broke with insidious pressure from friends in enemy country and the fiction that an agent had to live day after day became reality in his mind and menaced his safety. Tonight, for instance, Fisher had a Tory peer and a capitalist millionaire to dinner, and most of his friends appeared to be drawn from such circles. In Blount's view, his boss had surrendered too much to this hostile society; he had gone too soft.

"Why don't you go away for a holiday?" he said finally. "Take a Mediterranean cruise with Ruth. Have a look at Turkey and the Black Sea ports." Blount was thinking of Varna and Constanta, those ports in Bulgaria and Rumania where Fisher could meet some of the top people of their organization without arousing suspicion and return with his batteries recharged, his faith renewed.

"I'll think about it," Fisher muttered, leading the way back into the library.

Ruth and Anne were talking to the industrialist and his wife who had just arrived. Vincent Markham was managing director of a chemical group producing everything from plastic explosives to drugs and synthetic materials; he advertized heavily in Tekpress and had known Fisher for fifteen years. His wife had a wrinkled, quilted face, its small blood vessels exploded around her flushed cheeks; that, and the horror with which she repulsed even a thimbleful of sherry made Fisher suspect her of having bottles hidden all over her bedroom.

They had been chatting for quarter of an hour when the Curtons made their entrance. Lord Curton, friend and confidant of Tory ministers, a powerful voice in the House of Lords, had the tranquil and dignified face of an Anglican bishop. His wife, now approaching sixty, had the pink skin and lithe movements of a woman twenty years younger. They apologized for their late arrival. Fisher gave Lady Curton his arm and led the others into the dining-room. He placed Lord Curton at one end of the Chippendale table and his wife in the middle between Blount and Markham.

Ruth sat at the other end and he put himself between Anne and Mrs Markham. From there he could observe the Curtons and even listen to both as they conversed with their neighbours.

Curton he had known for ten years; he had almost persuaded him to join the Tekpress board. Curton had other directorships in Canadian paper-mills and printing works; but Fisher wanted him for his reputation among city financiers more than anything else. What he most envied in the Curtons was their pedigree stretching back to before the Norman Conquest of 1066; their aristocracy was bred in the bone. In the fluid light from the two clusters of candles, they looked more authentic than all his period pieces, the Chippendale table and chairs, the Georgian candelabra, the silver salver and silver plate from which they were eating their hors d'oeuvre; in comparison, he felt what he was, a prefabricated character with a gloss of good manners; even in the way the Curtons plied their fish knives and forks and sipped their Sauterne they had such polish; he did not understand why, but to him they looked like aristocrats playing stage parts; they gossiped effortlessly in that modulated drawl, the sort of solfeggio speech that Oxford or Roedean grafted on to centuries of good breeding. It said nothing. No smoke-screen obscured the subject as well as English small-talk. But it stamped them like a superior caste-mark. He had never comprehended why such people had left their imprint on half the world, why their language had become a *lingua franca* and their commercial practice an ideal for everyone. Why, when they themselves seemed untouched and unaltered by contact with foreigners? Even a highly-conditioned and deeply indoctrinated creature like himself found it harder every month to prevent them from submerging him or absorbing him into their society. Blount was probably right. He was already deeply contaminated.

"How was your week-end?" Ruth asked Lady Curton.

"So splendidly feudal I couldn't really credit it," Lady

Curton replied. "I didn't think people lived in that style after the Thirties. We had a whole wing of the house to ourselves with half a dozen servants to look after us."

"Even a golf caddy – a walking one – to carry my clubs," Curton put it. "You know Bateman has a nine-hole course in his grounds and a rough shoot in another part of the estate, the blighter."

"And a herd of bison, don't forget, darling."

"Yes – all done out of vitamins and health foods," Curton grinned. "Thank God no tablets and tonic wines on his table. Very best of French cuisine cooked by a Parisian chef."

"What's the house like?" Anne asked politely.

"Looks like the records office at Somerset House with a few chunks of British Rail Gothic welded on at the corners," Curton said.

"He gave us a fistful of those postcards, darling," Lady Curton murmured, fishing under the table for her handbag and producing half a dozen coloured postcards which she circulated.

Fisher glanced at his and suddenly experienced an eerie sense of having seen it before. A curious amalgam of English and renaissance architecture, the original central building had square, eighteenth-century proportions but a six-pillared Italian portico in the middle; two new wings had sprouted on either side with square, crenellated turrets; a horseshoe stairway climbed to the front door. That house set something clicking in his mind, but like some bagatelle ball ricocheting vainly off the pins and never finding the right slot. Where had he seen a house like Viscount Bateman's – so vividly that he could describe some of the features inside? It would have a curved iron staircase with wrought-iron banister and a wooden hand-rail; it would have a dining-table not unlike this Chippendale one they were sitting round; and a library full of leatherbound, gilt-titled books.

Everyone had gone silent and he caught the others

staring at him. Lord Curton said with a smile: "When are you coming back from wherever you've gone to, Fisher?"

His head spun. "Sorry," he stammered, "I was thinking about a remark you'd made."

"I was saying are you still thinking of going public with Tekpress?"

"Yes, I'd go to the market for capital providing I could keep a controlling interest and was sure of the right financial backing," Fisher replied. "Now if you came in ..."

"Why? You only want my name." Curton paused as though weighing his next statement. "And soon you won't need that."

"What do you mean?"

Curton glanced round the table as if wondering whether to divulge his secret; for a dubious moment, his eye rested on Blount, then on Mrs Markham. "Of course all this is off the record and I'm not sure whether I'm within my rights mentioning it – in fact, I'm damned sure I'm not – but I'm going to." He turned to Fisher. "I've had a sight of the next list and you've been put up for the club."

"The club?"

"Best in London. They pay you handsomely whenever you care to drop in. Excellent smoking-room. Real leather armchairs. Always get a four for bridge. Top-hole service. Cheapest menu in town. Bang in the centre of everything. Lots of friends to bail you out if you drop in it. And you can park your Rolls for a month without a ticket."

"I don't follow ..." Fisher said haltingly and the Curtons and Markhams laughed.

"He means the Lords," Markham grinned.

"The Lords!"

"Why not," Curton said. "You deserve it more than most of them there."

"But ... well, I don't know what to say."

"Say Yes when they ask you and you needn't open your mouth after your maiden speech. Most of them don't."

"It would be a great honour," Fisher muttered.

"Glad to hear you say so. Some folk still think it's the real power house with a lot more influence than the other place." Curton smiled. "I take it you have a blameless past."

"I'd never thought ... I suppose so."

"No *lèse majesté*, consorting with Her Majesty's enemies, no library fines or being had up for feeding parking meters, that sort of thing?"

"No," Fisher said with a forced laugh. "Why?"

"They have to check up before they ask if you'll accept the title. But don't worry. Half the present lot wouldn't be there if they'd told the truth about themselves."

"I've nothing to hide," Fisher said. At that moment his eye crossed Blount's gaze which flickered strangely behind those pebble lenses in the watery candlelight. Blount might think he was playing the part TOO WELL. But hadn't THEY intended just that when they trained him? Wasn't it a vindication of their methods, the supreme honour? Their fiction had become real. Somewhere in that dimly-lit corner of his brain where he had recalled the Bateman house and the trappings, he remembered a gathering not unlike his present company. And he heard his own voice and another, both disembodied, faraway echoes, antiphonal dialogue:

HE: I wonder if I shall miss you, Jane, when we finish our school.

SHE: I know I shall miss you. Just think, in another eight weeks we shan't exist for each other. Old Hartman and his wife will go back to the Schauspielhaus and you'll probably be sent to England.

HE: It's the country I've studied most, so they'll probably post me to Indonesia.

SHE: I'd love to go to England. They say Ah've got a fine north-coontry accent. If tha do owt for nowt, do it for tha sen. I'll often wonder what's happened to you.

HE: I won't be running a left-wing bookshop in Charing

Cross Road with a cypher book and a shortwave
radio hidden under the floor-boards and a microdot
kit.

SHE: No, you'll do something splendid, something very
remarkable. You know, I used to fancy that all
those notions they planted in our heads were real –
that I was really your fiancée and your wife and we
had a country house like Hartman Manor with an
English garden and a couple of kids and two cars.
And we were happy and in love. Is that stupid?

HE: No, it's not stupid. Only impossible. They've seen
to that."

All this dialogue Fisher heard clearly in his own voice
and another that he could not identify. Was it Jane's?
Curious that he who reasoned so much in visual imagery
like a strip-cartoon, who could once have felt and smelled
and almost touched his past, was now hearing voices
without any concrete association. Like some schizophrenic. Why did he remember those words only as
abstractions? Had they lost all their significance? Were
they lines from some half-forgotten conversation? Or his
own youthful, unfulfilled wishes?

Anne nudged him out of his reverie and he realized that
Lady Curton was asking him a question and all the others
were regarding him quizzically. Blount's muddy eyes had
stopped quivering.

"I was saying, Laurence, do you have any idea of the title
you'll take," Lady Curton repeated.

It flummoxed him. In his embarrassment and confusion,
he blurted out the name before he could censor himself.
"Lord Hartman, I think."

"Hartman, Hartman! Not a very English name, that,"
Lord Curton exclaimed. "Where d'you get it?"

"A family name ... on my grandmother's side," Fisher
said. Sweat stung the skin under his collar and he only
breathed again when Ruth signalled the maid to bring the

cheese-trolley and the valet, Moore, to fetch more wine and fill the glasses. With some subtle cueing by Blount and Anne, she steered the talk into safer subjects; like the others, she could perceive that her husband was suffering; he whispered to Moore who brought him codeine for a headache and he had gone silent.

Fisher felt that curious aura that often preceded his migraines; his head throbbed with pressure and he felt as though garish marbles were colliding in his brain. Somehow, he survived the rest of the dinner and the small-talk over coffee and brandy in the drawing-room. Fortunately his guests took the hint and departed early. When he had seen them off at the front entrance, he went to his study, doused the light and lay down on the chaise longue. Ruth and Anne brought pillows and blankets, made him comfortable and left him there. They looked at each other wondering if Curton's disclosure, or something mysterious, had brought on his attack.

Another person felt equally perplexed. Blount had his own theory to account for these strange lapses. Fisher had only shown signs of fright and panic when they had talked about investigating his past. Did he have anything on the police files? Next morning he made a phone call to one of his friends in the Records Office at metropolitan police headquarters. When he met the sergeant in a crowded Pimlico pub during his lunch break and told him what he wanted, the man screwed up his face in surprise.

"But he's your boss, isn't he?" He guffawed. "You're not thinking of using whatever I tell you to blackmail him, are you?"

"No, but somebody else might," Blount lied. He went to the bar and bought a packet of cigarettes and switched it for another packet that he had stuffed with five-pound notes. This he handed to the sergeant. "I just wanted to make sure there was nothing on the file that my boss had forgotten or overlooked, that's all."

That evening he had the information. Laurence Hallam

Fisher had only one misdemeanour: a ten-pound fine for careless driving twenty-seven years before. So long ago that Records had expunged it and it had taken the sergeant four hours to unearth the crime sheet.

That could never have provoked panic in a cool character like Fisher. So what had shaken him? That unsolved mystery worried Blount more than ever.

Seven

To reach the studio on the top floor of the old building in Battersea Bridge Road they had to mount four flights of dingy stairs redolent of damp and dry-rot; Deirdre's nostrils wrinkled at the odour of stale fat and boiled cabbage as they groped upwards. On the final landing, Roger Fisher was waiting for them with the door open; his sister had arranged the meeting and briefed him about their reasons for coming. They followed him into the large room which he and Elaine used for living, working, eating and sleeping. In a corner, a tiny kitchen with a small gas-stove and several cupboards and opposite this a bathroom. "Elaine's gone to the local supermarket to do our shopping," Roger explained.

As they sipped the coffee he offered them, Maclean sized up the large room; a huge fresco of coloured and black-and-white photographs patterned every wall – pictures of nudes from all angles, fashion shots, landscapes and city scenes alternating with press pictures and cuttings. Above the rolled-up leather mattress on which they slept, makeshift shelves sagged under the weight of magazines, printing and developing gear and photographic paper. Roger explained that he used the small bathroom as a dark-room.

He had Fisher's good looks and fair hair. But there the resemblance ended. His face, hands, gestures, his stride as he crossed the room had more purpose, more life. He answered Maclean's questions frankly. His old man's reactions to Elaine completely baffled him; it almost looked as though he'd gone round the twist. "But Elaine will tell you the unabridged tale when she comes in," he said.

"You didn't notice him behaving strangely before you introduced him to Elaine?"

"No. And even after he met her he was all right at first. It was later he started acting edgy – even breaking his own rules."

"What rules?"

"So many you couldn't count them. My old man's as regular as a quartz clock – no smoking, no drinking, never a minute late, never a second wasted." Roget lit a cigarette, poured himself more coffee and stirred sugar and dried milk into it. "Then one evening about five months ago I walk into his study and find him halfway through a bottle of champagne and actually smiling – well, it might have been a touch of wind from the fizz. Anyway, I ask what he's celebrating and he says he's drinking to absent friends."

"Did he mention which ones?"

Roger shook his head. "But one of them must have been called Miller. I say that because he'd written that name all over his desk blotter in every size, type and colour – almost as if having remembered it, he wasn't going to risk forgetting it again."

"You've no idea who Miller is or where he met him?"

"At school I'd guess from the little thumbnail drawings he made to go with the name."

"Did the sketches give you any idea of how this Miller looked?"

"A bit like me in my prep-school days," Roger grinned. At that moment, the street doorbell rang and he excused himself to bound downstairs and help Elaine with the shopping packages she was carrying. Maclean took the chance to slip over to the small dressing-table by the big window and look at the lipsticks and perfume bottles. Returning, he whispered in Deirdre's ear: "Sensuous Strawberry and Wayward Red, Mitsouko and Bandit."

"What in heaven's name are you talking about?"

"Her lipsticks and scent. Remember the names and buy some."

"I have my own preference."

"It's not for you," he whispered. "It's my guess that Elaine unwittingly aroused Fisher in some way, maybe with her scent or lipstick. It could be something like this that Fisher associated with this girl he's searching for." A clatter of feet sounded on the bare boards of the last two flights of stairs. "Mavournin, show an interest in his photography," he whispered.

"You mean that rubbish," Deirdre said, pointing at the nudes in various erotic or suggestive postures, her lips pursing.

"I want some samples," Maclean murmured.

Roger brought Elaine into the room and introduced her when they had stowed away their packages. Maclean hid his perplexity, his disappointment. Not with Elaine's looks. She had the willowy, shapely body of a professional model. Only, her face seemed to bear little likeness to the two pictures of dead prostitutes he had discovered in the newspaper archives; or any of those he had noted in the morgues. She did, however, have a russet sheen to her golden hair. As she helped herself to coffee and lit a cigarette he observed her closely. After all, he was comparing her – a live model – with static pictures and dead faces! Her features and figure might mean nothing. It could be the way she tossed her head or brushed the hair strands out of her eyes; or that mannerism of moistening her upper lip with her tongue tip; or the dimpling cheeks when she smiled, showing perfect teeth. She had a long face, accentuated by high cheek-bones and a strong jaw. She pitched her musical voice a tone or two lower than most women.

What had this girl represented to Fisher? Something more than the living model of Jane, the girl he had loved. Probably a whole world of things. Maclean mused on the strange quirks of human behaviour. So often, father and son chose the same type of woman. Either through some atavistic instinct or hereditary trait, or because of the mother's strong influence on the son. So, it might, he reasoned, be something more than coincidence that Roger had brought home a fiancée who looked and acted like his father's first love.

"So you're the Dr Maclean that Anne's been raving about," Elaine said.

"If she has, I'm flattered."

"She thinks you're the one man who can straighten out her father."

"I might be able to help him – if he really wants help and if people like you help me."

Elaine saw no objection; she recounted simply what had happened from the moment Roger had taken her to meet his parents and stay at Sutton. At first they had accepted her as a person and a future daughter-in-law. She had liked them both, especially Roger's mother; his father she considered rather colourless and interested only in his work. Then suddenly he had started inventing excuses to get her alone, in the study, in the garden, in the grounds.

"I was so stupid, I thought he was trying to flirt with me," Elaine said.

"You led him on," Roger said with mock indignation. "You teased him."

"But nothing happened," Maclean suggested.

"If you mean sex ..." Elaine shook her head. "No, he started by asking me all sorts of questions. Where was I born. What was my mother's maiden name. Where was she born. Where did my maternal grandparents come from.

The whole family tree." Elaine tossed her head back and laughed. "Know what I thought? – he's quizzing me to see if my pedigree's good enough for his son, or I'm just a model girl on the make who's after his money."

"But he was serious."

"Yes, he was," Elaine replied. "Dead serious." Her eyes following the spiralling cigarette smoke as though her thoughts too were gyrating. "And I didn't realize it. I'd begun to believe that he was trying to make me. You know the old line – you remind me of someone I knew long ago. He came out with that."

"Did he say where and when he knew this person?"

"I asked him. He couldn't even remember her name or her face."

"At least he was honest," Maclean said.

"And stupid," Roger interjected. "How could Elaine remind him of this lost love when he didn't even know how she looked?"

"Exactly what I said to him," Elaine exclaimed. "Know what his answer was? – he felt it instinctively because of the emotion I aroused in him." Her face dimpled in a grin as she looked at Maclean and Deirdre. "No, it wasn't just a line with hooks in it. He got quite poetic about her and me – much more poetic than his son." She paused as though wondering whether to continue, then said, "I remember he was talking about beauty, saying that it was never something static. The sea was most beautiful when the sun and wind played on it and a face was at its most beautiful when love played over it."

"Your face, I suppose he meant," Roger said.

"Yes, my face."

"I just don't believe it," Roger said with a laugh. "He sees poetry only in things like climbing circulation graphs of his magazines and profit and loss accounts."

"You don't know your father very well, darling," Elaine said. "Anybody who can quote reams of poetry like him must be a romantic."

"What sort of poetry?" Maclean queried.

"The Romantics – Byron, Shelley, Keats, the Lake Poets."

"No German poetry – Goethe or Schiller?"

Elaine shook her head, declaring that she would never have understood German poetry; then she stopped, her long face pensive. "Come to think, he did babble something strange just before ..."

"Just before he picked a quarrel with you," Maclean prompted.

"I still don't know what it was all about," Elaine muttered. "Or what really started it."

"You probably never will," Maclean said. "But can you link what happened with anything – even a word or a gesture?"

Yes, every incident had branded itself into her mind. During their walks, Fisher had spoken at length about literature and drama; he gave her the impression of having done quite a bit of amateur theatricals in his youth and having wanted to go on the stage. Oh, she knew Roger laughed at this idea, dismissing her father as a Philistine in art and literature; but to her he revealed deep feeling for books and plays and a good deal of knowledge.

"Noel Coward, Frederick Lonsdale, Terrence Rattigan and J.B. Priestley and Somerset Maugham – that bunch," Roger sneered.

"He liked the classics, too," Elaine retorted as though defending Fisher. "Look at his collection of books and plays in the library."

"Window-dressing like everything he does," Roger countered.

To bring them back to the point, Maclean murmured, "Funny that he liked Priestley. Isn't he the odd man out of those modern playwrights?"

Elaine gazed at him, as if suddenly aware of his intelligence. She nodded. Fisher had a collected edition of Priestley's plays so well-thumbed that he must have read it several times, even inserting slips of paper to remind him of certain passages.

"The Time plays?" Maclean hinted, and she nodded.

Fisher could recite long passages from plays like Dangerous Corner, I Have Been Here Before, Johnson over Jordan and An Inspector Calls. It fascinated him, the idea that time did not always flow forward in a straight line but might kink or bend round on itself and play tricks with human beings and their conventional notions, so that people could step forwards and backwards as if riding some time-machine. That and the idea we might come round for a second time.

"Did he fancy that he had — I mean, come round a second time?" Maclean asked, thinking of what Fisher had confessed to Armitage about having seen and done so much before. Armitage had merely assumed this to be the déjà-vu sensation often experienced by mental patients, but Maclean no longer felt convinced that Fisher was suffering from amnesia or schizoid illness.

"I don't know … I don't think so," Elaine said. They had talked a lot about Priestley for another reason; she had belonged to an amateur dramatic society which put on one of his plays, An Inspector Calls. She had played the rich industrialist's daughter who, like the rest of the family, had callously and indifferently done her bit to destroy a girl's life.

"And that's really what led to our row," she said.

"How?"

One evening, half an hour before dinner, she had entered the library to find a book. Fisher was sitting there, alone, with only one light burning. On his lap lay a book which he could not have been reading because of the poor light. Yet he was reciting from it. And she remembered the lines from her amateur dramatic society. It was An Inspector Calls, the scene where the daughter and her new fiancé quarrel over their part in the girl's downfall.

"I thought he was playing a game and I'd be clever and

join in. So I tiptoed over and began to respond to the lines he was quoting. He went quite rigid.''

"Rigid!"

"As if hit with a hammer. I went on uttering dialogue but he didn't turn his head. He sat there like a zombie. And like a fool I imagined he was trying to beat me at my own little game.''

So, Elaine went on mouthing both his dialogue and hers. Suddenly, still without turning his head, Fisher shouted, "Stop it! For God's sake, stop it!" And he clapped both hands over his ears to shut out the sound. Of course, she ceased reciting the lines, wondering just what game he was playing. For a full minute she stood there, in the half-light, watching him with his hands over his ears, his mouth contorted. He must have waited until certain that the dialogue had ceased or he was not hearing voices in his own mind before swivelling his head slowly to stare at her and using his right hand as a shade to see her better. "You!" he said in a croaking voice.

"Wait a minute," Maclean interrupted. "Do you think he recognized you or mistook you for somebody else."

"I've wondered about that," Elaine said. "He looked as though I were the ghost of someone he knew. He seemed really terrified.''

Fisher had risen to his feet and advanced towards her with a funny, still walk; but she saw that he had a wild light in his eyes and for a moment she fancied he was going to attack her; he was clenching and unclenching his fists. Now scared herself, Elaine thought she had better do something. She screamed, "Mr Fisher, it's me – Elaine.''

For a moment he hesitated, then bawled, "It's you, you whore. Get out. Get out of my house and stay out." And he flung the book he was still holding at her; then, as she turned to run, something else flew past her and hit the wall with a bang. She did not stop until she had reached her bedroom and locked the door. When Roger returned twenty minutes later, she described the scene and he went down to have things out with his father.

"He ordered me out, too," Roger said. "Oh, we never got on that well at the best of times, but I wasn't going to stand by and hear him call Elaine a scheming bitch, a gold-digger, a whore who had even tried to seduce him, a tart who wanted nothing but his money. I told him if he never wanted to see Elaine again, that went for me, too. We parted on those terms."

"And your mother?" Maclean asked.

"She's all right. She apologized to Elaine." Roger shrugged. "But she'll always take his part. Even if he committed murder she'd stand by him."

Roger's remark, full of unconscious irony, seemed to round off the interview. Maclean wondered just how far Ruth Fisher's loyalty would go. Draining his coffee-cup, he hoisted himself to his feet and crossed the room to scrutinize the photographs on the walls. When he had finished studying them, he complimented Roger on his talent. "I'd like to buy one or two of these," he said, pointing to some of the nudes and street scenes.

"Buy!" Roger grinned. "Help yourself. You'll find duplicates in those folders." Maclean went to the table and flipped through the fat packets of photographs picking a couple of dozen and hoping Roger did not notice that a good half were shots of his girlfriend, Elaine — full-face, profile, half-profile, clothed and unclothed. He threw the others in for camouflage.

At the foot of the stairs, Deirdre asked, "Did you think Fisher and that girl were lovers?"

"No. And I wonder if anything happened between him and this woman, Jane, that he once loved."

"What do you mean?"

"It may be all in the mind." And to himself he reflected that it was so often the women who lingered in the imagination, the ones that hadn't been slept with, who caused the worst withdrawal symptoms. Was Jane one of those? Untouched? Like the strangled prostitutes?

In the car as they drove back to their flat, he scribbled the outline of Elaine's story meaning to write up the notes more fully at home. Fisher she had caught at a moment when he was holding some dialogue with his subconscious; for him she had created the illusion that she was someone else, a person whose presence frightened him enough to attack Elaine. His lost love, Jane, perhaps. But why attack the woman he loved? Something about Elaine, either her voice or appearance in that penumbral library light, recalled a part of Fisher's past that he was trying to reconstruct. Yet, paradoxically, those who unknowingly helped him rediscover his past ran the risk of being murdered. Elaine Dancy did not realise how closely she had come to being strangled that evening five months ago.

Peter Hamlin was sitting with Boulder in a café in Battersea High Street when Maclean and Deirdre reappeared. "Go and phone Max and tell him he's got quarter of an hour at the most to finish the job," he whispered. Buttoning up his mackintosh he walked quickly through the drizzle to the car he had parked round the corner and took off, keeping one car between him and the small Fiat; in any case, the rain would make it difficult for the psychiatrist to spot him. Across Battersea Bridge they crawled at Deirdre's pace and up King's Road a couple of hundred yards before parking in a side-street. Hamlin observed them enter first a bookshop where he saw the bulky psychiatrist dictate something to one of the assistants; then they both went into a chemist's across the road and began to look at cosmetic tubes and bottles.

Hamlin wandered into the bookshop. "Excuse me," he said to the assistant. "Dr Maclean has just given you an order for some books. He wondered if he'd forgotten one. Can I check his list?" Innocently, she handed him her notes. Maclean had ordered the collected plays of Maugham, Priestley, Lonsdale, Coward, Rattigan, to be sent to his Bayswater address. Hamlin memorized the list, then smiled at the girl, commenting that Dr Maclean had omitted nothing. He made a note to phone the chemist and find out what the psychiatrist and his secretary had bought.

What could this headshrinker want with these plays? He failed to see the connection between this handful of West End dramatists and Fisher. He'd have guessed that Becket or Pinter and their theatre of the absurd had more in common with their kinky contact. But then he hadn't reckoned on this Harley Street mind-bender sticking to his investigation of his friend's murder, finding that tape and a dozen other clues. Hamlin pondered all this as he returned to sit in his car and watch the pharmacy. Maclean bothered him. If he'd been Max, he'd have staged another accident the moment this doctor had located the Renault, quizzed Fisher and had his driver jailed. What if this character with his cherubic looks and Sumo-wrestler body finally linked their man with those prostitute killings and took his evidence to Inspector Gall at Scotland Yard? Their chips would be well and truly pissed on then.

They had warned Fisher to lie low until things grew calmer; three of their men were watching him, inside and outside his home. Yet, if he gave them the slip and went on the rampage again! ... Next time they might not succeed in throwing the police off the track. And they'd lose one of the best operators they'd ever had. If Fisher went, Max would tumble with him. Then the whole set-up, for they were all roped together.

Hamlin wondered about Max. Whether he was playing the game the right way. Those two heart attacks and forty years in this racket had perhaps blunted his skill, taken the edge off his intuition. He hoped Boulder would have tipped him off that this trick-cyclist and his girl were on the way back.

Boulder had, in fact, warned Max and had reached the flat where the team was just finishing. Laxton was photographing the final dossiers they had discovered in the psychiatrist's flat while Max was running several tapes through his high-speed machine to play them back at normal tempo later and see if Fisher had revealed anything vital.

Max paraded a final look round the flat which had two bedrooms, a large living-room and a small study and overlooked Kensington Park. An hour before they had entered with keys that Laxton had palmed from the girl's handbag while she was lunching in her favourite Wigmore Street restaurant; he checked that they had disturbed nothing in their search for clues about Maclean's inquiries. They had found and copied the dossier that the psychiatrist had compiled with the inquest evidence, his interviews, his cuttings from newspaper libraries. Something they did not know: he had given Hamlin, Boulder and Laxton the slip, met Fisher's daughter somewhere and interrogated her. Clever, this mental quack!

Anderson laid another bismuth tablet on his tongue and sucked it; his stomach felt as though someone were attacking it with a blowlamp and paint-stripper at the same time; he could have used a mug of strong, sweet tea. But he went methodically through the bedrooms, thinking that Maclean and his secretary didn't share a bed. He ran his eye over the bathroom then the study where they had unearthed most of the material. He seemed a method man, this Maclean. Everything in its pigeonhole. He'd rumble them if one of those hideous pictures of Highland cattle was an inch askew or a magazine had been moved from the rack. Anderson was satisfied that they had creamed off most of the information, much more than they'd got the whole of last Sunday when they took the psychiatrist's consulting-room apart and finished with a mountain of tapes and documents that had left them no wiser.

When he had done the rounds, he and Laxton donned their gas-board overcoats and caps, a useful disguise for a couple of house-breakers. Anderson flicked open the cover of the fisheye lens and peered through it. "All clear," he said and they slipped on to the landing and downstairs.

Boulder was waiting for them on the corner near Queensway tube station. He would stay and relieve Hamlin when he arrived behind the doctor and the girl. By the time Anderson and Laxton returned to the office, Hamlin was there. Anderson studied the list of plays the psychiatrist had ordered. They had to contain some clue about Fisher, something that no-one had told even them; but what it might be he had no idea. Curious though, Fisher had always reminded him of a character from that bygone time in the Twenties and Thirties when he used to go to the theatre himself. That era obliterated for ever by the war.

Eight

Fisher watched the girl enter with the letter-book and deposit it on his desk for him to sign his day's dictation. "You're new, aren't you?" he queried and she bobbed her blonde head up and down. His personal secretary had gone sick with flu and the typing pool had sent her as a replacement. As she turned to make her way to the door, he paused in the act of opening the leaves of blotting-paper and signing his first letter. Something about the way she retreated struck a chord. Was it the low-heeled shoes? Or the slender, nylon-clad legs? Or the concertina action of the pleated skirt with its diamond pattern sussurating over her calves? Or the sinuous sway of the hips and thighs underneath? Signing the two dozen letters feverishly, he again pressed the buzzer. This time he scanned her face as she returned to pick up the book. Blue eyes, blonde fringe, wide mouth. Something indefinable about her set a pulse thumping in his neck. "What's your name?" he asked.

"Baker, sir ... Dorothy Baker."

"How old are you?"

"Just turned twenty, sir."

"Thank you." Her voice did have a nostalgic ring, a haunting quality of some street song he'd forgotten. And again her retreating figure intrigued and puzzled him. He had the wild desire to summon her, to request her to dine with him tonight, to quiz her about her origins. He discarded the notion. Too risky. It would cause talk in the building. Yet she had disturbed him. Rising, he paced the seventh-floor office, his mind as agitated as the April wind shivering against the expanse of window, or the clouds fleeing across the sky behind the cupola of St Paul's on his horizon.

For thirty years, Jane's ghost had lain buried in some locked mental recess. Then his son of all people has to bring a girl home who might have been her daughter! Well, she could be her daughter. No-one knew where Jane had gone. Maybe she was living here, in this town, and had integrated like himself to the extent of eradicating even the idea and any remnants of her past.

His intercom buzzed and he depressed the switch. "Your car's at the front entrance, sir," the porter said. Fisher looked at his watch. Five-thirty. He'd be home by seven, dine at seven-thirty, watch the BBC news on TV, read a bit and bed early. That was his routine; but tonight he felt he could not face adding to the infinity of days and nights of doing the same thing. Pressing another toggle he spoke to Miss Baker. "Ring my personal number and tell my wife I shan't be home for dinner tonight. I have a late appointment in town and I might spend the night in the flat."

He walked through the circulation department, then the editorial headquarters with its anniversary numbers of his magazines and the present week's covers of several of them pinned to its walls, with layout pages on swivel desks; half a hundred people were toiling on a dozen editions, but those who lifted their heads to nod to him as he made his way to the lift got no response. At the main door, Jenkins, the gardener who was standing in for Wade as chaffeur, opened the Rolls door and edged them into the traffic stream, turning along the Embankment and making for Westminster Bridge then south. A few yards from the bridge, Fisher rapped on the window. "Drop me here and go on home, Jenkins," he said. "And if you try to phone Mr Blount I will sack you. Have you got that?" Jenkins touched his cap and when Fisher had dismounted accelerated the car over the bridge.

For several minutes Fisher stood glancing round him before stepping out across Parliament Square and through the back streets parallel with the park. Head down against the swirling wind, he observed the few people behind him, mostly Whitehall civil servants and office staff going home after a hard week at their desks. However, he could not take chances, loitering from time to time before ducking into St James's station; there, he delayed boarding a tube train to the last minute and again on leaving it at South Kensington. From that point, he walked slowly along to Knightsbridge. He had to admit he enjoyed playing the part of the quarry.

As he strolled, he peered at the cold, wind-blown faces of women and girls in the tide of people on the pavements. Once or twice, his mind lit with the remembrance of a feature and he turned to overtake some astonished woman to study her more closely; he had plenty of material, for girls were spilling out of the big stores just after closing-time; but nowhere did he encounter the face or figure that matched his memory exactly. In a Knightsbridge café he chose a window-seat and drank black coffee while he observed faces, the curve of an ankle or calf, the gait, the whole expression of both features and body. Those who met his gaze noticed a handsome, middle-aged man with a grey mask of a face in which only cold eyes moved. For half an hour he sat there until the street lamps began to glow reddish-orange in the gathering dusk, like the Bengal matches of his boyhood; finally, he rose, paid his bill and left. He caught a bus, changed at Hyde Park Corner in case somebody had spotted him, and dismounted from the second bus opposite the Ritz.

Between Piccadilly Circus and the Ritz and along Jermyn Street few girls were patrolling the pavements at that early hour; so he pushed into a pub and through the bar crowd to order and sip a whisky and soda while casting an indifferent eye on the dart-players and knots of drinkers at the tables. When he left, he wandered along Bond Street and around the hotels in St James's and Mayfair. Now the girls were thickening on the pavements. Not one of them stirred him. For some time he lingered at the south end of Berkeley Square eyeing the cars that circled several times round the garden; on the second or third time round, the driver invariably stopped by him to offer her services. More than a dozen cars drew alongside; faces simpered at him and lips pouted the same questions; but as soon as the women behind the wheel spotted his stony glare they wound up the window and departed.

Disconsolate, he turned away and was marching towards Hyde Park when a car scuffed the kerb beside him and a voice, soft as a flageolet, called, "Can I give you a lift, darling?" Something in the accent or intonation compelled him to look. In the raw lamplight the face seemed spectral. With its fringe of reddish hair, the salient cheek-bones and dimpling smile, she resembled Jane so much that he halted with a start. "What do you want?" he muttered.

"To give you a lift, darling," she said with a laugh; her voice had pitched suggestively upwards at the word Lift. "Hop in, *chéri*," she pleaded, flicking open the door.

Before he had time to settle in the seat beside her, she had slammed shut the door and gunned the car down the street, presumably to avoid inquisitive policemen. Bending left at Park Lane, she circled the roundabout and drove into

Hyde Park following the circuit until they came to the edge
of the Serpentine. There, she pulled the car into a track
beneath the trees. "Where would you like to go, honey?"
she said, taking his hand and caressing it with the points of
her scarlet nails. He tensed, then recoiled from her touch.
"What's wrong, *chéri* – are you shy with women?" she
murmured.

"No," he got out, sensing those nails pricking the back of
his hand like so many red-hot needles and sending their
current up his arm.

"Then where shall we go?" she insisted.

"I don't know ... anywhere you like."

"I know a nice hotel, the other side of the park. It's quiet
and they're friends of mine."

"No. Not a hotel. I might be seen."

She understood. Most of her clients were married men on
the lam from their wives for the night, or provincials in the
capital on business. In both cases they wanted private
treatment.

"Where then?" she whispered.

"Your flat," he suggested.

"That'll cost you, darling," she murmured.

Without answering, he thrust a hand into his inside
pocket and pulled out a wallet which he handed her; even
in the half-light from the park lamps, she noticed that it
swelled with ten-pound notes; feeling them, she reckoned it
contained at least five hundred pounds. What had he done
– robbed a bank? He could have her for the rest of the week
for that! She leaned over to fondle him and kiss his cheek
and sensed him shiver. A droll character. But then in this
trade every other customer had quaint ideas; she met every
type from coy characters like this one to sadists who wanted
to see her suffer, from sexual acrobats who wanted to try
out the Kama Sutra on her to fetishists who had to have her
in a mink coat or as a transvestite in boy's clothing. She
handed him back his wallet from which he nervously
extracted a fistful of notes and thrust them into her hand.

"The rest in your flat," he whispered hoarsely. Starting the car, she steered over the Serpentine bridge and out of the park. Within a few minutes they had stopped outside a modern block of flats behind Kensington High Street; she lived on the third floor, she whispered, as she let them both inside with her front-door key and led the way to the lift.

Her flat had three rooms – two bedrooms and a living-room. Once inside, she helped Fisher out of his coat and threw her own mink over a chair in the hall. As she went to the drink cabinet and poured liquor into two glasses, he appraised her. In her early thirties, he judged. A good age. Slim but well-cushioned figure. Perhaps she could have done with a little more fire in her reddish-blonde hair, but her face pleased him with its classical structure, its amalgam of fine bones and fine flesh; she had intelligent blue eyes and an arch mouth.

She crossed the room with their drinks, raising her eye-brows at her first real sight of him. She ran a hand through his blond hair and petted his face. "What've you got to worry about? You're not a bad-looking fellow." She handed him a large whisky and a bottle of soda.

"What's your name?" he said when they had trinked glasses.

"Hamilton," she said. "Sandy Hamilton."

"What makes you do this for a living?" he asked in that toneless voice that made her wonder if the question really interested him.

She shrugged. "I enjoy it and if it makes men like you forget what their wives do to them or won't let them do with them ..." Again, she clinked glasses and they drank; she had given him an outsize whisky thinking he needed it to take that frozen look off his face and relax him. He gulped his in one mouthful and she fetched the bottle, giggling as she poured him another which he once more swallowed at a go.

She ran practised fingers along the inside of his thigh and sensed him stiffen; she snuggled closer to him, pressing her breasts against him and murmuring about the sexual tricks they would perform together in terms that she had known to set even the most frigid and impotent on fire. She sloshed a third whisky into his glass and watched him toss that over his throat. "Let yourself go, honey," she whispered. As he seemed to unwind a little, she unbuttoned his jacket, slipped it off his shoulders, then undid his tie and shirt; she noticed small globules of sweat forming on his brow, coalescing and dribbling into his eyes. He made no effort to wipe them away. "It's going to be a hard night with this character," she thought, but the memory of that fat wallet encouraged her; she stooped to untie his shoes and pull them off with his socks. Flipping open the top button of his trousers, she unzipped them and eased them off.

At that moment, she caught a whiff of a peculiar odour, not even masked by her own musky perfume. An ammoniac tang. Like stale bleach. It seemed to exude from him. But she thought no more about it. Never before had she smelled fear in any person and if anyone had told her that human fear had such a strong odour she wouldn't have believed it. When she had finished undressing him, she drew him into the bedroom. "Now, you have to do a little work, *chéri*," she whispered, pointing to the back buttons of her dress.

"The light," he said in a thick voice.

"Ah, yes." She had forgotten he was a shy one and went to switch off the overhead and bedside lights. Through the voile curtains filtered jaundiced light from the street lamps, broken now and again by the dazzling flash from some nearby neon sign. Fisher had the uncanny sensation that his own mind was switching on and off like the pink, fluorescent light. Everything around him seemed to float, adrift in this eerie glow – double bed, dressing-table, wardrobe, sofa and chairs.

Sandy felt his fingers groping awkwardly, nervously, for the buttons and she lent a hand, slipping her arms out of the dress, letting it slide then stepping out of it. She peeled off her stockings, let her petticoat slide to the floor and stood in black bra and panties. She snapped open the bra clasp, wriggled out of the halter then took off her panties. She turned to face him. Against the vague light from the window she saw only his naked silhouette; she tugged him gently towards her then drew him down on the bed.

Fisher responded to her invitation. But the moment his flesh made contact with the points of her breasts he felt as though they were searing through him. His blood pulsed thickly in his neck and head. And again, as on several previous occasions, he felt that fear. It invaded and permeated his whole body, a nameless, irrational panic that he desperately tried to control or stifle. He wondered whether to turn and run, or stay and try to make love to this woman. At first sight she had troubled, then excited him. Now she confused him, left him disorientated. On one hand, he wanted her more than he could remember wanting anything for years; everything about her appealed to him – the russet gleam in her hair, the arch curve to her mouth, even the perfume in which she moved. Yet on the other hand she repelled him, filled him with a mixture of rage and revulsion; he even seemed physically ambivalent, shivering and feeling feverish at the same time.

Sandy tried to make up his mind for him. Her lips fastened on his and her tongue darted in and out of his mouth while her hands sought to rouse him sexually. He wrenched his mouth away. "No, no," he groaned.

"Come on, *chéri*," she coaxed, dragging him on to her.

At that instant, he felt a surge of nausea in his chest and throat, choking him. Almost as a defensive reflex, his hands reached for her neck and wrapped themselves round it, his thumbs gouging at her windpipe. Now he realized the truth; it had become a duel to the death between him and this creature who threatened his existence. One thought filled him: Kill or be killed. His hands squeezed hard and he heard a long scream that decayed in her mouth; her legs began to flail and kick desperately beneath him; her hands beat violently at his face, then she dug her nails into his right shoulder while her other hand seized his hair and pulled. He felt nothing of this. Only the tightening vice of his hands round her throat and a click like some small bone cracking. Then her convulsions growing weaker and ceasing, her body going slack and finally lying inert beneath him. Yet, he continued to gouge with his thumbs and even hoist the body up by the neck and shake it as though determined to quench every spark of life.

When he threw her back on the bed and gazed with hatred at the livid face, tongue lolling, framed in that reddish-blonde hair, he suddenly felt weak. A retching sickness came over him and he staggered into the bathroom, leaned over the bath and vomited and kept on vomiting until he had voided all the filth he imagined had infiltrated his system from contact with that woman. He was making his way back into the bedroom when his legs began to wobble, his head spin and his vision go dark until even the dim light from the street lamps went out.

He came to, his head hammering with pain. Where was he? How had he got there. His watch read five minutes to midnight. But what day? He levered himself off the floor. A swathe of light from the bathroom fell across the bed and he noticed the figure of a naked woman on the bed, a grotesque twist to her shape. She was dead. Had he killed her? When? Why? Impulse shouted at him to run and keep running. Stumbling back into the bathroom, he sluiced his face with water, gulped some, then cleaned up the vomit in the bath. He switched off the light, crossed the bedroom into the living-room, gathered his clothes together and began to dress. Remembering his training, he searched for his wallet and found it in a writing-desk; he did not look at the whisky-bottle and two glasses on the coffee-table by the sofa. Before he left the flat he watched for ten minutes from the window to ensure no-one was keeping surveillance from the street below.

At the corner of Earls Court Road and Kensington High

Street, he halted for several minutes, wondering where he was. And who he was. Nothing in his wallet identified him and he could not recollect where he had been earlier that day, or on previous days. His mind seemed even to be erasing the traces of that room with its loathsome corpse. He felt frightened, his head still throbbed and his legs trembled when he took a few steps. However, he had to make a decision which way to travel. A side-street opposite the Odeon cinema seemed familiar and this led him round a crescent and along a tree-lined road beside a park. Halfway along he had to rest on the low wall of a house and wait for his head to stop spinning. Had it been a summer evening, he would have climbed the park railing and slept under the trees. But a chill April wind penetrating his heavy coat forced him to consider searching for a hotel in which to spend the night. Reaching the main road, he wandered up and down hoping to light on a small hotel. No luck. Then, in a street just off Holland Park Road, a large mansion house pulled him up abruptly; it had a double entrance, a drive-way and at least a dozen rooms. Where had he seen that building before? His spent brain kept putting that question but failed to provide the answer. Mentally and physically he felt too drained to march another step. Dragging one foot after another to the door, he pushed the bell and leaned on the portico pillar while waiting for someone to respond. Before the door opened, the resolve that had kept him going finally gave way and he collapsed, unconscious, on the step.

Nine

It took Maclean several seconds to surface from sleep and recognize the voice on the other end of the line as belonging to the Yorkshire night nurse in the Holland Park clinic that Armitage had patronized. "Remember the man you inquired about, Dr Maclean? Well, he's here." Maclean now had both feet on the floor and was calling for Deirdre while he listened to the nurse's explanation of how the man had arrived, half-dead, on the doorstep and was now sleeping as though he had swallowed a handful of barbiturate tablets.

"Keep him there until I arrive," he ordered. "But have his clothes and everything ready."

Should he call out an ambulance from his own hospital? No. Ambulances attracted police and other nosey people. Moreover, if they were still keeping tabs on him it would make their job easier. Telling Deirdre to remake his bed, he rang for an all-night minicab which was waiting for him round the corner when he had dressed and descended. Within five minutes he was climbing the stairs behind the night nurse and following her into the private room where they had put the stranger. He instantly identified Fisher. With little ceremony, he humped him in a dressing-gown to the cab and took the plastic holdall containing his clothing from the nurse. "If anybody ... anybody at all ... family, police, anybody asks any questions about this patient, ring me before you answer. Understood?" She nodded.

Dismissing the cab fifty yards from his flat, Maclean

carried Fisher in his arms to the mansion and up the two flights of stairs to his flat. "You're giving him your bed!" Deirdre gasped as he rolled the limp figure between the sheets.

"We can keep an eye on him here, and nobody will think of looking for him in our flat."

"But ..." she stammered. "If these friends of his find out ... You know what happened to Stephen Armitage."

"They wouldn't try that again," he said though more to reassure her than out of conviction. Already, Fisher's staff had probably covered up two murders and were doubtless hunting for their master. And this last flight pointed to some crime or another. He had never believed that a gorilla like Wade had murdered Armitage on his own initiative. Someone had planned the accident and might repeat the procedure for him. It was a risk he had to accept if he wanted to crack open the only problem that interested him – what had happened to kink Fisher's mind and personality. Was he an amnesiac? Either a true amnesiac who remembered nothing at all? Or a hysterical amnesiac who blotted out painful or threatening situations and fled to avoid them? Was he a Jekyll and Hyde character, perhaps with other personalities thrown in? Or a split personality with paranoid delusions? Or just what he acted and looked – a straight psychopath who killed in cold blood and showed neither guilt nor remorse, nor any other normal human reaction?

With Deirdre back in bed, he sat for several minutes studying the sleeping face. Not even in repose did it lose that hard, impassive set. In Maclean's experience, culled from his own case-histories, what happened in the human mind leaked by some sort of psychic and physical osmosis into the face to be read by anyone with enough insight or intuition. This man had not acquired that mask yesterday, or five months ago when something or someone like Elaine Dancy roused his dormant instincts. To uncover the events that had frozen Fisher's mind and emotions, he might have to dig into his youth or boyhood – or even farther back into his parental background. This man fitted into no classic pattern. Then who did, exactly? In anybody's book he was a fascinating case. In case Fisher woke and panicked, he left the bedroom light burning; he switched on his slow-running tape-machine which would record any sound or speech for three ˙ hours. Before enveloping himself in blankets and stretching out on the sofa, he locked the bedroom door. With a suspected murderer in the house nobody could afford to take risks.

Next morning he walked to the tube station to return with a pile of newspapers. "He's still out," Deirdre said, indicating the bedroom. "Let him sleep," Maclean replied, dosing his coffee with milk and sugar and helping himself to toast and marmalade. One by one he scanned the morning papers while Deirdre tidied the flat. He was searching for two things: any reference to Laurence Hallam Fisher's disappearance, and any crime committed in the past days which might resemble the two previous murders or those he had picked out in the morgues. Not a hint in any of the half-dozen morning papers. Nor did the eight o'clock London news mention any new murder. It was Saturday. If Fisher had gone missing yesterday, no-one would get alarmed until Monday morning. Furthermore, everything went into abeyance over the week-end and whatever crime Fisher might have committed would go undiscovered for a day or two.

"How many patients on our books for next week, mavournin?"

"I've already cut them down to twelve."

"Ring round and say I've got flu, or anything infectious enough to scare them off."

"They'll go along the street to our competitors."

"Most of them have been all the way along the street, That's why they came to me in the first place."

Deirdre shrugged. He had an answer for everything. But he was right; the Freudians, Jungians, Adlerians, existentialists, transcendentalists and all the others sent him their hard cases and somehow he always managed to straighten them out a little. "I'll tell them the truth," she snorted. "You've gone off your head."

"Careful," he grinned. "That's infectious too – and it'll keep them away for good."

Fisher slept solidly until late that afternoon. When he opened his eyes Maclean was sitting by his bedside watching for the first reactions before the other man's mind could seize the situation and he could begin acting a part. However, this man had blank eyes and gave no inkling of recognizing him or remembering who he, himself, was. "Where am I?" he said, finally.

"My name's Maclean. I'm a psychiatrist."

Fisher digested this information then said, cryptically, "So, they decided to have me treated."

"Don't you know me?" Maclean asked and Fisher shook his head and affirmed that he recalled nothing of their previous meeting. "Do you know who you are?" Again, the slow rotation of the head. Maclean gave him no clues that might help him identify himself and thus falsify his examination. First, he had to establish if Fisher were a real amnesiac. "Would you mind if the police interrogated you?" he asked.

"The police? Why the police?"

"In the past couple of days there has been a rather bad crime committed in this district. In fact there's been a series of terrible murders of women and the police are looking for somebody they think has lost his memory. I should inform them with your permission."

"Go ahead. I've nothing to do with their crimes."

Normally, such an ultimatum brought the wiliest of amnesiacs back to reality, or frightened them; either Fisher was bluffing, or he genuinely had no recollection of what he had done or where he had been on this and previous occasions. Not many people, whether amnesiac or in full possession of their memories, could place their hand on their hearts and say they didn't mind submitting to a police inquiry. Yet he was sure Fisher was not a true amnesiac. They were like the dodo – everybody talked about them and nobody had seen one. If genuine, they remembered nothing; how to dress, use their knives and forks, how to speak. This man seemed too defensive, too leery for an amnesiac. Yet it was no pose. But he could be a psychopath, cold and homicidal, or a schizophrenic with that congealed mind and body. A funny mixture.

Fisher asked for a jug of water, seized it and emptied the two pints down his throat, then gestured for more.

"How do you feel?" Maclean asked.

"What do you mean?"

"Do you feel your normal self?"

"How would I know when I don't know what is my normal self." Fisher turned those lifeless eyes on him – they recalled every punchy boxer Maclean had ever seen and a whole wardful of terminal alcoholics – and said, "I don't know who I am or where I am or what I'm doing."

"You had no papers to identify you when you collapsed. What did you do with them?"

"I don't know. I didn't even know I'd collapsed."

"You seemed to be running away from something or someone. Do you remember what?"

Fisher reflected for a moment. "I had a nightmare. I dreamt I was murdering someone."

"Who? A woman?"

"No. Myself."

From his case-notes, Maclean recalled that Fisher often imagined himself pursued by his younger double, a man dressed in uniform. "Did you kill yourself as you are now – or your younger self?" For a moment he thought Fisher was going to refuse to reply, that he sensed a pitfall, then he muttered in that flat, droning voice, "The body was that of a young man."

With that statement, Fisher clamped his mouth shut and behaved as though he didn't even hear the psychiatrist's questions; his ice-blue eyes stared at a point on the opposite wall. In a few minutes he had lapsed into sleep. But he had let one clue drop: when he killed, either in fact or fancy, he felt he was acting out of self-preservation. Maclean could also see why Armitage had mistaken him for a rare case of multiple personality – several Jekylls and Hydes rolled into one. During their interview which had lasted just over an hour, Fisher had created the impression that he was another man and elsewhere in spirit. But Maclean had the advantage over Armitage of having already encountered Fisher and knew that he used the same voice and gestures. A genuine multiple personality would have acted in character with each of his roles. However, this man really seemed to feel he was not himself. He was searching for a missing past as if realizing that a man with no past had no future. But how to help him?

"You should hand him over to the police," Deirdre said.

"Perhaps I should."

"No perhaps about it. You're making yourself an accessory after the fact."

"What fact? Fisher's a psychiatric casualty who has turned up on our doorstep. Nobody has proved anything against him, or even put out a missing or wanted report on him."

"But if he murdered two women."

"That's only my guess."

They took turns to keep vigil by his bedside; he slept round the clock and until Sunday morning just after nine. Maclean once more bought all the Sunday newspapers and culled every crime paragraph and read every missing-person report. Not a thing he could connect with Fisher. Their patient still drank a lot of water and accepted sweet coffee but rejected the food Deirdre made and offered him. In mid-morning he was persuaded to get up and walk round the room in a dressing-gown. He glanced dull-eyed across the park and watched the double-decker buses and traffic along Bayswater Road; but for all the interest he showed it might have been somewhere in Siberia. He asked no questions, volunteered nothing. Maclean found that teasing information out of him was harder than pulling teeth.

"Don't you think your family might be worried about you?" he asked.

"Family? What family?"

"All right then, your workmates. You must have had a job."

"I don't remember workmates or doing any job."

He appeared to recollect nothing of his past. From one of the popular magazines, Maclean had unearthed a picture of Fisher's house at Sutton. Even a sight of that did nothing to take the stiff, unyielding expression off his face. Surely, Maclean thought, he would react to the photographs of the two murdered girls; they must mean something. But no. A stare, a shrug and a shake of his head.

"Do you know this man?" Maclean asked, handing him the pictures he had collected of Fisher himself. Among them, the photograph taken at Liverpool Street station walking behind his mother's coffin placed on a railway trolley. That evoked no more response than the older pictures of Fisher with his wife, with his whole family, with Anne and Roger and even with Elaine.

But those pictures and their caption which Fisher read as though for the first time, did they really mean nothing? Maclean noticed that when he had studied each series of pictures or cuttings, Fisher closed his eyes and in a few minutes had gone to sleep. As if unwilling to face the truth, or seeking refuge by flight into sleep. Sitting during those long hours by his bedside, Maclean juggled with the reasons for this man's behaviour. At nine he had lost his father and probably transferred all his affection to his mother. Did she domineer him? Did she inculcate such a dread of women in him that they became monsters threatening his personality, even his existence? Or did he dote so much on his mother that he equated his love for any other woman with incest, or violation of his own mother? What had blunted his emotions and given him that zombie look? That, too, might form part of his defence against women. Or against people, like psychiatrists and others, who pried too deeply into his inner life, who touched the quick of his mind. He seemed like a person with a complete mental block. That had probably begun with a shock. What was the most traumatic thing that had happened to Fisher? His accident and his mother's death without a doubt. Did he blame himself for killing the one person he loved? Maclean made a note to get hold of fuller reports of that accident and find out exactly how it occurred.

For most of Sunday he tried to engage Fisher in small-talk, probing for that word or phrase that might strike the right mental node or combination and set his memory going. For, judging by Armitage's experience, he had only a couple of days left before this man rose, dressed, picked up any incriminating evidence he might have left lying around and fled back to his family to resume his normal life. Somehow, Maclean felt he must dredge up other clues to this man's secret thoughts.

"Why don't you ask Anne to come over?" Deirdre suggested. "He might recognize her." Deirdre and Anne had taken to each other after their hospital meeting. Both had done ward nursing and had other things in common.

Maclean agreed. If Fisher did not recognize his daughter it would prove some sort of amnesia or an acting *tour de force* worthy of the Royal Shakespeare Company. At the same time, Anne would observe her father and appreciate how serious his mental condition was. He rang the number of her flat in South Kensington.

Ten

Anne Fisher put down the phone and turned to take Peter Hamlin's hand. "It's my father," she said. Drawing her down on to the sofa, he put an arm round her shoulder to comfort her and tried to keep his voice neutral as he asked, "What's happened this time?"

"You know he disappeared on Friday night. That is, he didn't come home from the office, and he didn't stay in our town flat as he said he would."

"But nobody was worried," Hamlin said. Nobody, he might have added, but Max Anderson and Laxton who had lost Fisher somewhere between the boundaries of the City of London and Westminster. It had meant a week-end of overtime for him with Anne, who, they thought, would be one of the first to learn where and when her father broke surface again. Hamlin had known worse jobs and less pretty girls. Not that he'd ever admit it to Max, but he'd have spent his week-end with Anne without any orders.

"No, he's vanished before," Anne said. "But he's always turned up after a day or two."

"Where is he now?"

"With that psychiatrist I told you about. The one who broke into the garage and found that our driver, Wade, had knocked down and killed one of his colleagues."

"What was his name – Maclean, wasn't it?"

Anne nodded. "He's just rung to say that my father's with him and he's no idea who he is where he is and what he's been doing over the past two days."

"Amnesia?"

"It could be," Anne said. "Dr Maclean wants me to go over to his flat and see if my father recognizes me, if I can help him get his memory back." She squeezed Hamlin's hand. "Would you come with me, Peter?"

"Sorry, darling," he said, thinking quickly how he could avoid a face-to-face meeting with Fisher. "I don't want to get involved with your father when he's in this state." He smiled at her. "He might forever hold it against me if I ever have to ask him a favour." He cupped her face in his hands and kissed her. "But I'll run you over to your trick-cyclist and stay on the end of a phone in case I can help."

"It's spoiled our evening," she complained.

"There'll be other days, other evenings," he whispered, helping her into her coat. "Your father's more important than our date."

"I didn't think men were so understanding," she murmured and kissed him back.

"As long as you let me know if there's anything I can do when you've seen him," he said as he led the way downstairs to his car. Driving through the thin Sunday traffic, he cursed Max Anderson for landing him with this assignment where he had to deceive a girl he was fond of. It gave him that crawly feeling along his spine when he imagined how she'd react if she ever found out her father was a spy. And what would she do if she discovered that he, Hamlin, who acted as though he loved her, was one of the people who were keeping her father in business.

He had followed orders – but only up to a point. He had shadowed Anne and for weeks had eaten his meals in the small South Kensington restaurant where she sometimes had dinner. Inevitably they had got to know and like each other. She believed he was working as a special writer for an international magazine that allowed him to pick and choose his own assignments. At the moment he was researching a series of articles about racial tension and the growth of a multiracial society in Britain. He felt badly about lying to someone as innocent. But he had also lied to his boss, Max

Anderson, saying he had slept with Fisher's daughter to keep him from asking the perpetual question. When he analyzed his own emotions, he realized that he could not bring himself to seduce this girl and cheat her two ways. Her ignorance of this rotten racket in which he and her father had become embroiled and her own lack of guile rendered her so vulnerable that he could not exploit her. Week after week he promised to quit this job, to beg a transfer away from London, or even abroad. Otherwise, he'd wind up like the other cynical hard-skinned characters in the spying game. Morons like Boulder and Laxton. Or curdled, worm-ridden beings like Max Anderson, living for second-hand sexual thrills by picking up titbits from him and others like a tramp collecting fag-ends. He would have packed it in long ago had it not, ironically enough, been for Anne. He felt protective about her.

"Shall I wait for you?" he said when they had arrived outside the flat.

"No, I may be hours." She looked at him, her corn-flower-blue eyes misting with anxiety. "When can we see each other again?"

"I don't know. If I don't hear from you before then I'll ring you tomorrow."

"I'll be thinking of you." She brushed his cheek with her lips, opened the door and ran into the flat entrance.

Maclean led her into the bedroom for a brusque face-to-face with her father. For a moment they stared at each other, she looking for recognition in his eyes and he regarding her as some stranger who had burst into his private world. Anne swivelled round and brushed past Maclean into the living-room where she sat down and cried. Deirdre comforted her and she wiped her eyes. "I didn't realize," she sobbed. "He's lost everything."

"No, not everything," Maclean said. "He'll get his memory back, probably in a day or two." Patiently, he explained what had happened on the two previous occasions with Armitage; he kept his own suspicions about the crimes her father had committed to himself. "The trouble is that these episodes conceal and camouflage his real trouble like the scab over an ulcer," he said. "Unless we can knock the scab off and drain that ulcer ..."

When he halted before completing his thought, she looked at him. "What will happen if we can't?"

"These disappearances and mental flights will become more frequent and longer until they dominate his life."

"You know, I always thought my father was harbouring some great secret that he did not want even to think about himself," she said.

"Maybe you're right," he said. "Maybe it's because he's bringing it into the open that he's running away like this. Maybe we shouldn't try to find out what's going on inside him and stop him from trying to find out." He caught her gazing, puzzled, at him and went on, "Sometimes a person's secrets are the most important thing he possesses. Take them away and he's left with nothing. I spend half my life attempting to cure neuroses when privately I feel they're the most interesting part of my patients."

"But we must find out," Anne said. "We can't let him go on this way."

Maclean nodded agreement. She listened while he outlined how he had attempted to bring back her father's memory — by prompting gently with questions, photographs, newspaper cuttings and her own presence.

"I was saving this to the end," he said, holding up the tape cassette like the one she had seen her father play back in his study the night the psychiatrist had broken into the garage. "You told me how he cried when he heard it. Shall we see how he takes it now?" She nodded.

He would have preferred to watch Fisher's reaction to the tape undisturbed by anyone in the room, but had no way of doing this. Anne and Deirdre took seats on either side of the bed as he placed the tape-machine on the chest of drawers and switched on.

As Armitage's voice came through, then Fisher's responses when he described how he and his girl, Jane, would slip out of the theatre to make love and how this love was obliterated by someone or something, all three watchers noticed that the man in the bed tensed and his eyes moved as though tracking a mental scene. He listened intently to his own eulogy of Jane followed by the grave recital of Goethe's poem. As the tape ended, he relaxed, then fixed Maclean's face with eyes that had a dead, sterile glitter. He said nothing.

"You recognized that voice on the tape-recorder?" Maclean asked.

"Yes."

"It's your own voice, isn't it."

"My voice! Never."

"But, Daddy, it is your voice," Anne cried.

Fisher gazed at her. "Who are you?" he muttered. "It is not my voice."

Maclean motioned Anne to keep quiet. "But since you recognized the voice, whose is it?"

"A friend."

"Where is this friend?"

"I don't know. Dead, most likely."

"When did you know him?"

"Long, long ago."

"Where did you know him?"

"Where else but in Germany!"

"Which part of Germany?"

"Berlin."

"West Berlin or East Berlin?"

"I can't remember that."

"Can you remember his name?"

"His name was Miller."

"Not Müller?"

"No, Miller."

"His first name?"

"William."

"Was William Miller a friend of Jane?"

"Of course he was."

"What was Jane's surname?"

Fisher did not answer; he had closed his eyes and they realized he had gone to sleep, behaving for all the world like a person who had answered questions under some truth drug. Back in the living-room, they all gazed at each other, mystified by what they had heard. "Miller – that was the name Roger saw him write all over his blotter the day he celebrated with champagne," Deirdre said.

"Yes, and he is Miller – at least one of him is," Maclean commented.

"You mean my father may be more than one person," Anne asked, and Maclean signified Yes. "But if he is can you do something for him?" she said.

"Only if we can discover what caused his personality to split in the first place," he replied. "And that means taking him back into his past and exorcizing his ... well, whatever's troubling him."

"Do you have any idea of what that is?" Anne asked.

Maclean pointed to the tape-recorder, saying that it seemed their most vital clue since it had provoked some reaction from her father. "What was the most dramatic or traumatic thing in his life?" he asked.

"I don't know." She reflected for a moment. "His son's death by drowning perhaps."

"No, he wouldn't blame himself for that," Maclean said, shaking his head. "But he might feel guilty about driving the car that his mother died in."

"Then he's never once spoken about it."

"Because it's too painful," Maclean said. He looked at her. Fisher's blue eyes must at one time have had that same vital sheen instead of their yellow glitter like sterile, reflected moonlight; he must have had something of that naive gaze and shy smile and quick gesture. Where had all that gone? To Anne he said, "Did your mother ever learn if your father was driving at the moment of the accident that killed his mother?" She shook her head.

"Pity. It would be interesting to know if the authorities

blamed him. Or if he blamed himself."

"How can we find out?"

"Not by asking him directly. I'll see what I can unearth."

"What do we do about my father now?"

Maclean pondered for a moment. In a couple of days, if Fisher repeated his previous behaviour pattern, he would begin to recover his own identity. He would have given much to observe that process, to gain another insight into this curious on-off amnesia or multiple personality. But what if Inspector Wormwood or John Pearson picked up the trail to the nursing-home and then his flat? What if Fisher had perpetrated some crime? To come nearer home, what if Deirdre carried out her threat to catch the next Irish boat if he did not spend some time by his couch in Harley Street? Sighing, he told Anne to leave her father with him for the night since he was asleep. She could tell her mother a white lie, saying her father had landed at her flat and would be home the following day. She could come and collect him early tomorrow. "Don't worry," he said, showing her downstairs. "When he's in his home surroundings his memory will come back. But keep an eye on him and don't allow him to go on the loose again."

Eleven

While listening with a distracted mind to one of his permanent cripples Maclean was wondering about Fisher who had left that morning after breakfast with his daughter. What was he doing wasting his energy on Deirdre's humdrum types – crack-counting, eyelid-fluttering neurotics, rich soaks or their sex-starved wives, housebound women with phobias about men in general and rapists in particular, others with cat and bird phobias and a puberty case with anorexia nervosa? Not even their names changed, let alone their stories. A puzzle like Fisher landed on his couch once in every decade and now it looked as though he would have to leave it unsolved while he earned his high Harley Street rent. Breaking off early for lunch, he told Deirdre that he had several errands to do. A taxi took him to the German Institute in Prince's Gate where they had a newspaper library.

He gave the archivist the place and date of the accident and file after bulky file of German newspapers piled up in front of him. First he scanned the Berlin evening paper Der Abend for June 17, 1953, the date of the accident. Nothing that day or the two following days. West Berlin papers at that time were giving most of their coverage to the march of East German workers to the seat of the German Democratic Republic in East Berlin to protest about increased work quotas and wages. However on June 18 in two morning papers, Berliner Morgenpost and Der Telegraf he came across similar reports, the first emanating from the correspondent of the press agency, Deutsche Presse-Agentur, the second from a reporter called Johannes Gunther Meyer.

Laurence Fisher had been driving a 1938 Hillman saloon when he hit a lorry on the road between Nauen and Berlin, eighteen kilometres away; driving rain had cut visibility to between fifty and a hundred yards when the accident happened at eight o'clock in the evening just beyond the outskirts of Nauen. Eye-witnesses said the car was a complete wreck which had to be cut away from the lorry chassis to free both passengers. Margery Hallam Fisher was dead before she arrived at the local hospital in Nauen. Her son was reported to be suffering from multiple fractures and internal injuries. Doctors in the casualty unit described his condition as very critical. Within two hours of his arrival they had transferred him to the Charité Hospital just beyond the Brandenburg Gate in East Berlin. With its immense reputation, made by surgeons like Sauerbruch, Fisher could not have chosen better; but Maclean wondered why they had not taken him to one of the modern hospitals in West Berlin which lay nearer; however, the accident had occurred in East Germany and the East Germans might have felt humiliated appealing to West Berlin and possibly British or American doctors; again, the accident might have had legal consequences.

Maclean flipped through the issues of the Communist Party newspaper, Neues Deutschland; it made light of the hunger marches but carried a long agency report on the accident; in its June 19 edition, it spoke of the brilliant surgeons who were fighting to save Herr Fisher's life, then dropped the story until seven weeks later when it reported that he had left Berlin by rail with his mother's body; it recapitulated some of the facts of the accident. West Berlin papers had also run accounts of Fisher's departure.

In fact, several reporters had interviewed Fisher when he came through the Brandenburg Gate to arrange with the British authorities in West Berlin for the transport of his mother's coffin. Maclean had almost forgotten that the Berlin Wall did not then divide the city physically in two, although it obviously existed already in spirit. Replying to questions, Fisher mentioned his injuries – compound leg and arm fractures, broken ribs, internal and facial injuries. He praised the Charité for having wrought two miracles, saving his life and patching him up. (Maclean, you fool! Why didn't you do this homework before and question him about his seven weeks in hospital?) He gleaned little more from the press files, but it seemed that Fisher had returned by rail, through Hamburg to the Hook of Holland and from there to Harwich and London, retracing his outward route.

Maclean spent a good hour noting the names of places and people involved in the accident or who had witnessed it. Everyone had exonerated the lorry-driver from blame; several papers, including Neues Deutschland, hinted strongly that Fisher had been overtaking a small van on a blind corner when he hit the lorry full-on. Why then hadn't they held some form of inquest on Mrs Fisher's death to impute responsibility and clear the lorry-driver officially? Maybe they didn't want to cause the son more distress than he had already suffered.

With a bundle of scribbled notes and several photo-copies in his pocket, he wandered back towards his office, stopping to have a sandwich and coffee in an Oxford Street snack-bar. When he pushed open the door of Deirdre's room, he could sense she was halfway to the Irish boat. "Anything wrong?" he asked.

"One of your patients has been waiting for over an hour and your friend from Scotland Yard's been on the phone twice."

"John Pearson? What does he want?" Maclean had the queasy feeling that the Yard had discovered the truth about Fisher and had tracked him to his flat.

"He didn't say – just that you should ring him." She put him through to Pearson's extension at Metropolitan Police Headquarters; they both listened while the detective-sergeant explained that a cleaning woman had discovered the body of a high-class prostitute in her flat near Kensington High Street. She had been strangled but not violated. "It has all the hallmarks of your man," Pearson said.

Maclean gestured to Deirdre to get rid of his patient and the others for the afternoon. "Can I see her?" he asked Pearson.

"I've an inquiry at Ealing, but if you hurry I'll meet you at Hammersmith morgue on my way," Pearson said.

When Maclean arrived, the detective had already briefed the morgue attendant who had displayed the body for them. "Reddish-blonde hair, fair complexion, blue eyes, sensuous mouth, medium height, good figure," Pearson intoned. At a glance, Maclean saw that she bore some resemblance to the two women he had chosen from the newspaper cuttings. Apart from the hair and other features, she had prominent cheek-bones and an upward tilt to her nose. "What's her name?" he asked.

"Alexandra Georgina Hamilton, aged thirty-three. Hails from Nottingham, but has been doing the streets around Mayfair for eight years. We reckon she was strangled four nights ago – late Friday."

"No clue about the killer?"

"Well, for one thing he behaves like the man you're looking for. And there's a definite link between this and two other crimes."

Maclean did not ask which. He said. "Have they asked you to take part in the investigation?" Pearson shrugged, saying they had detailed him to stand in for Wormwood, who was enjoying a long week-end, so he knew the dossiers. When he had made several notes about the Hamilton murder, Maclean asked if there were any pictures of the dead woman.

"At the Yard. If you don't mind making a detour through Ealing you can have a look on your way back."

As Pearson made his call and they drove back through London, the psychiatrist was deliberating whether to confess that Fisher had disappeared on Friday evening a few hours before Alexandra Hamilton had met her death. When they finally arrested Fisher – and now it could only be a matter of time before he gave himself away or they traced him – Pearson would never forgive him for withholding vital information. Indeed, he could lawfully charge him with failing to assist the police and accessory to murder. When he had decided to keep his mouth shut, Pearson increased his concern and doubt by commenting, almost casually, "We picked up the murderer's fingerprints in the flat. It's the first real clue we've found on this strangler."

On reaching his office in the new block at Scotland Yard, the detective pulled a couple of folders out of a filingcabinet, extracted a wad of pictures which he pushed across the desk to Maclean. A whole series of Alexandra

Hamilton, dead on the bed, with various shots of the bathroom and living-room and two close-ups of a bathroom glass and whisky-glasses. Pearson jabbed a finger at the glasses. "He left his dabs all over those tumblers," he said.

"Have you checked them against all your fingerprint files?" Maclean asked, trying to keep his tone indifferent.

"No luck." Pearson shrugged. "Whoever did this and the other murder jobs had a clean sheet."

"You know this man, Fisher, I'm interested in," Maclean said. "You can check your prints against his when you get them."

"I already have," Pearson came back. "I remembered your suspicions and you can forget any notion that your friend, Fisher, is the Mayfair Strangler."

"So, the prints don't match?"

Pearson motioned the psychiatrist to follow him along the corridor to the projection-room; from the murder dossier he produced two slides which he injected into the machine, throwing their blown-up images on a screen. On the right-hand set, a tented arch stood out clearly on the thumbprints and those of the index and third fingers. On the right index-finger, a cicatrice broke the print pattern. Nothing like this on the left-hand set, which showed conventional whorl and loop configurations. "Those tented arches are fairly uncommon," Pearson observed. "Just one in five on our files. So there's no possibility of error." He paused then pointed to the right-hand set. "Those we picked up all over the Hamilton dame's flat. The left-hand set is Fisher's."

"I didn't know Fisher had anything on his crime-sheet and you had him filed," Maclean said, now having to conceal his bewilderment.

Pearson explained that he had made a routine check, aware of Maclean's suspicions, though he hardly expected to trace any prints; to his surprise, he discovered Fisher had been involved in a car accident near Beaconsfield when he was twenty-two and had been charged with careless driving. Normally they wouldn't have fingerprinted him for that, but the driver of the other car had died and the prosecution had initially indicted Fisher for manslaughter before deciding they could not make this charge stick and dropping it.

"Sorry," Pearson muttered, switching off the projector. "We'll have to go on looking for our man."

Maclean was trying to resolve the puzzle in his mind. Had the Yard's renowned fingerprint experts made a mistake? "I suppose you've double-checked the Fisher prints?" he queried.

"You really are sold on your theory," Pearson grinned. "We matched them with those that the Bucks County force took at the time as well as verifying our own files. No chance of a slip-up."

"Can I have a copy of the prints you found in Miss Hamilton's flat?"

"Help yourself out of the file. But I didn't give them to you."

Maclean could hardly leave the Yard quickly enough. In the nearest call-box, he rang his own consulting-room. "Mavournin, did you wash up the breakfast things this morning?" he asked, nervously.

"Of course not. You know I always put them in the washing-up machine."

"But you didn't switch it on, did you?"

"For three cups and saucers and three plates and a few glasses – and us not earning any money!"

He stifled her complaints about his absence and her revolt when he ordered her to shut shop and come home. "It's important – life or death," he insisted. Deirdre grumbled even more when she arrived at the flat and was told to ferret in the machine and find Fisher's drinking-glass and breakfast cup; she watched, mystified, as he brushed talcum powder on to the glass and cup and stuck bits of cellophane tape on both, removed these and peered at the crockery and tape with a magnifying glass; again and again, he checked his observations against the two sets of photographs Pearson had slipped him. Finally, he turned to her, his face a study of confusion and concern.

"It's incredible," he muttered. "There may be two Laurence Fishers."

"But you said that days ago."

"I was talking then about their mental states. Now I'm saying there may be two physically different people called Laurence Fisher."

"You mean the man who was here this morning is only pretending to be Laurence Fisher."

Step by step, he explained what Pearson had discovered, then showed her the fingerprints they had found in the Hamilton flat and those left by Fisher on their glass and cup; every detail of the two sets of prints corresponded, down to the cicatrice on the index-finger.

"When he was lying in bed, did you notice any suture marks on an arm or a leg – or any scarring?"

"I didn't look."

"Pity!" he muttered. Fisher could not change his fingerprints; nor could he fake the scars and stitches of those compound breaks from his accident.

Deirdre had finally got the significance of the matched fingerprints. "You mean ... he killed this ... this woman before he turned up at the clinic on Friday night then landed here," she gasped.

"No doubt about it. And little doubt about the other two prostitutes I suspected he had murdered."

"And the other Fisher?" she mused. "He probably killed him as well to take his place."

"I don't know about that."

"But you do know enough to inform the police," she said.

"I suppose so," he muttered.

"You suppose so! He's a murderer. He might disappear again and murder some other poor woman."

"Anne's looking after him," he said. "And he's not likely to break out again before he's recovered."

"If you don't ring Pearson, I shall," she declared.

"Mavournin, give me a couple of days," he pleaded. "I'd like to see him when he's got his memory back to find out why he's two different people and runs amok like this."

"All right – two days."

He thanked her, though he himself felt dubious about concealing such crimes. He had proof of murder, triple murder. As a good citizen he should alert the authorities. But the part of the puzzle that had interested him initially remained unsolved. What made Fisher act like a combination of an amnesiac, a psychopath, a schizophrenic? What motive had he for murdering these women who resembled his ideal creature, Jane? Now he had another mystery? If this man was not Laurence Hallam Fisher who was he? And what had he done with the real Laurence Fisher? Those secrets had cost at least three women their lives, and one psychiatrist. He doubted if detectives like Pearson would penetrate them. He wondered if he would, even given enough time.

Twelve

Norman Blount scrutinized every sentence written in half a dozen morning papers about the Kensington strangling; he had no need to glance twice at the statements made by local detective-inspector, Robert Savage that they were dealing with a maniac who had murdered two other women that he named; Blount had already made his own deductions. Fisher had gone adrift on Friday night and this Hamilton strumpet with her titian hair was his kind of woman. Thank God that Ruth had rung to say Fisher had managed to return home and stay there. Blount poured himself another cup of tarry coffee from his electric percolator and lit a cigarette off the one he had smoked down to his liver lips. If the Scotland Yard men had linked this crime to the two previous murders, they might soon have a description of the Mayfair Strangler. And Fisher would buckle under interrogation and land them all in it up to their eyeballs. It was going to be one of those days.

Before leaving, he tidied his two-roomed flat and washed up. Blount did everything for himself; his own housework, his own laundry and mending, his own cooking and shopping. And his own thinking. He believed all this made him his own man. He had no wife, no girlfriend, no close friends, no clubs, no pubs, no hobbies and few pastimes. That way nobody could ever nail him. In his book, friends spelled as much danger as the professional opposition. A Judas instinct lay no more than skin-deep in everybody, man and woman. He had more than enough human contact in his furtive meetings with his controller from the embassy just along the road in Belgrave Square and through the messages he and others left in dead-letter holes throughout London.

Then somebody like Fisher is hung round his neck like an albatross, or planted on him like a time-bomb set to detonate God knew when. However, he had to admit Fisher had done more than a hundred undercover men or their cloak-and-dagger spies; their organization provided the background to dozens of defence and commercial secrets and processes. In hobnobbing with prominent politicians, aristocrats and business leaders, Fisher gleaned internal and foreign policy secrets that no-one else could have obtained. Their masters were overjoyed that soon he would become a peer of the realm with access to even higher and mightier sources of information and influence. Little did they understand of his odd behaviour and the risks he was creating for all of them. Before those Yard men came round asking questions he had to get Fisher out of it.

How? Where? His mind sparked with notions. A

business trip to the Continent to meet their agents? A tour of Canada to discuss newsprint supplies for their various magazines? He'd think of something. A quick call to Ruth to say he was driving out to visit Laurence and he ran downstairs to the underground garage of the block of flats in Belgravia. As he eased his Mini out into the King's Road traffic he was still mulling over his schemes.

Ruth and Anne were waiting for him in the living-room. Briefly, Anne explained what had happened, although omitting any reference to Maclean; her father had wandered out of his office on Friday night and had stumbled into her flat not knowing where he had been and hardly realizing where he was.

"How did he remember where you lived if he'd lost his memory?" Blount asked.

"I've no idea. I think he just passed the flat and it looked familiar." Anne watched Blount's cheeks puff out as he digested this statement. Of all her father's senior collaborators, she liked this man least; with his pebble-lens glasses and pebble-dash skin and scruffy clothes he looked sly, shifty and mean. Too mean even to share anything with anybody.

"Where is he now?" he asked.

"In his bedroom, asleep, I think," Ruth said.

"Is he back to normal?"

Anne shrugged. "He's still a bit peculiar. His memory comes and goes. I think this time he's lost more than two days."

"He needs a holiday, a long holiday," Blount said. "Maybe a cruise, somewhere away from magazines and everything connected with them. And away from this town."

"He'll never agree to go," Ruth said. "I've been telling him for years he works too hard and he should take a holiday."

"Let me have a word with him on my own," Blount said and walked upstairs towards the bedroom. When he entered, Fisher was sitting in a dressing-gown gazing through the window dreamily over the grounds of his small estate. Blount took a seat beside him. "Laurence, you'll get us all hanged," he said softly.

"I couldn't help it," Fisher replied in a hollow voice.

"I know that," Blount said with surprising gentleness. "Do you remember where you went, or anything you did?" Fisher shook his head, sadly, then glanced at the copy of the Daily Express Blount was opening in front of them.

"Recognize her?" he queried. Fisher cast a distracted look at the picture of Sandy Hamilton and shrugged. "She's dead," Blount muttered. "Strangled, by the man who murdered two other women who looked a bit like her."

"It means nothing to me," Fisher murmured.

"I thought not. But it means that you'll probably have to take a trip abroad."

"Abroad?" Fisher's eyes showed interest. "Funny, I was thinking the same thing. I'd like to take a bit of a break."

"Any idea where?"

"No, not really."

Blount's eye fell on the German guide-book and several maps that covered the small gueridon table in the bedroom. Fisher followed his gaze. "Anne brought me those from the library," he said.

"Did she mention Germany?" Blount asked, his suspicions sharpening.

"No, I asked her for them," Fisher said.

"Were you thinking of any particular part of Germany?" Blount insisted.

"I had the idea of maybe spending a couple of days in Hamburg," Fisher replied. "And then my mother and I never did get to see Berlin all those years ago."

"Good idea," Blount said. "I'll come with you." He caught his boss looking curiously at him as though weighing every aspect of this offer. "You'll need somebody with you who speaks the language, won't you?"

"I suppose so," Fisher muttered. "Give me a couple of

days to make up my mind exactly where I want to go and I'll let you know."

"No, we've got to move quicker than that," Blount snapped. "We've got to be away by tomorrow at the latest, you understand why?" Fisher nodded, dumbly, as his collaborator pointed to the newspaper picture and story.

As soon as Blount had gone, Anne came up with coffee and biscuits and handed him a cup which they drank sitting by the window. In the raw morning light, she noticed how grey his features appeared. Ever since his return the previous morning, Anne had watched her father; on the surface, he seemed himself and acted normally, but those washy blue eyes had a distant, infinite look and several times while they chatted he would stop abruptly as if his mind were short-circuiting across some memory gap.

"Did you find anything in the guide-books?" she prompted.

"Guide-books," he grunted. "They only take you over well-trodden ground." However, he rose and went to the table where he had left the guide-book and maps of West and East Germany. "More than twenty years ago, I took my mother with me to Hamburg where I was covering an aeronautical conference ... She didn't get many holidays or much fun out of life ... We had a week in Hamburg in a splendid hotel ... She'd always wanted to see Berlin, Potsdam and Brandenburg, those sort of places ... On an impulse I rang my office and got two weeks' leave so that we could both go there ..." He paused for a full minute staring at nothing in particular before continuing. "We drove through the East German frontier ... it was easier then ... and down to Berlin." Again a long pause, then, "Only ... only my dear mother never got there."

Despite listening intently for any new detail, any sign of emotion, Anne found the voice droning over the facts, not even changing its rhythm or pitch when her father mentioned his mother's death. He might have been reading off a column of figures. Odd, she reflected that the fragment of taped conversation in Maclean's flat appeared to have stimulated his interest in Germany and that accident. While he lay in his bedroom and his memory had begun to return, he had asked first for a biography that he was reading, then as an afterthought shouted for her to bring a volume of Goethe's poems in an English translation with the guide-book and maps.

She poured him another cup of coffee. "And you've never gone back?" she said. "I mean, to Germany?"

"It was something I hardly dared think about."

"Oh! Why?"

"I don't know. Probably I didn't want to relive an old nightmare."

"You mean the accident," she said. "That wasn't your fault."

"What do you know about it?" he muttered, a slight edge to his tone.

"Only what you told Mummy and she told Roger and myself."

"Nobody knows what happened," he said. "But my mother died – that was enough for me to know."

"Well, don't think about it," she said.

"I can't help it."

Fisher sipped his coffee slowly, reflecting on that strange instrument, the human mind: how it could inspire so many thoughts and memories and trick the body into believing them real; how it could create emotions that the senses had never experienced; how it could paint strip-cartoon images that had never existed even in its own structure. That whole Berlin episode seemed like a badly-told tale in his mind, a blurred and garbled account with no beginning, very little middle and no end. One thing he desperately wanted to know at this moment: Had he really lived through that accident or had they planted that in his mind with so much else? How much of him was somebody else and how much Fisher? Anne sat there, believing that he dreaded making a trip to Germany because of the accident. No, he was using the accident as his launching-point, his pretext. He only dreaded what he might find if he started a proper quest for his own identity. And for the identity of the one creature he had loved: Jane. More and more, instinct told him that immense tracts of his mind and personality had somehow vanished and unless he traced and resurrected those missing experiences he would go slowly but surely mad. He could begin in Hamburg and track over the route to Berlin to try to sift and separate the true from the false; he would grope and feel his way back like some old hound reliving its past through its sense of smell.

Anne looked at her watch and packed the cups back on the tray. "Will you be all right for an hour?" she asked. "I promised to run Mummy to the hairdresser in Sutton and do some shopping for her."

"Off you go, darling," he said. "I'll be fine until lunch-time. Just tell Moore and the others not to bother me."

When she had gone, he paced up and down for several moments to check through the sequence of actions he had already meditated, then rose and began to dress; in the wardrobe he ferreted out a small holdall into which he threw a change of clothing, a waterproof and his toilet things. At the window, he waited until Anne had brought the Renault from the garage and had driven off with Ruth before walking into his study. From there he called the local bank manager, ordering a thousand pounds in notes and as much again in international traveller's cheques; he picked up his passport from the desk and shoved this into his holdall with the guide-book and maps. He rang the car-hire firm he used in Sutton to arrange for a cab at the entrance to his drive in five minutes. In his heavy overcoat and hat, he slipped out the side-entrance, made a wide sweep behind the shrubs to emerge at the front gate.

"Where to?" the minicab driver asked.

"Barclays Bank in Sutton, then London Airport," he ordered.

An hour later, Anne returned with her mother and went straight to her father's bedroom to see how he was. She did not panic or alarm her mother, but verified first that he had gone. It reassured her somewhat that this time he had planned his disappearance; he had taken clothing and toilet articles, even the guide-book; she searched the pigeonhole of his desk and saw he had also got his passport. Obviously, he intended to go abroad, probably to Germany. Neither Moore nor any of the staff had spotted him leave, and all their cars still sat in the garage. He'd hardly have marched the mile into town. Anne phoned the hire firm they used and the girl there disclosed that her father had ordered a car just over an hour ago. No, it had no two-way radio, so they'd have to wait for the driver's return before knowing where his fare had gone.

When Anne had informed her mother she rang Maclean to explain what had happened. He advised her to keep contacting the hire firm. Her father had probably made for London Airport. Did he have money in the house? Not much. Then she should telephone his office and bank to ascertain how much cash he drew; she should also check with London Airport to find out if he boarded one of the Lufthansa, British Airways or international flights to Hamburg, Hanover or Berlin. Anne noted all these instructions, then said, "Should I tell the police?"

"No – on no account tell the police. They might frighten him, make him do something desperate." How could he reveal that her father had left his fingerprints in a murdered prostitute's flat and probably in two other police murder files? Indeed, it struck Maclean that he might have remembered this last crime and decided to flee before the police arrested him; or someone might have urged him to leave the country until the trail went cold.

"I was thinking," Anne said. "Somebody must go after him and bring him back."

"Once we've an idea where to start looking."

"Dr Maclean, I wondered ... would it be too much to ask if you would help us find him? Of course we'd meet all your expenses and pay whatever fee you thought reasonable."

"We'll talk about the cost later," Maclean said. "Deirdre and I shall be with you in an hour."

While she waited by the phone for information and Maclean's arrival, she phoned Peter Hamlin to cancel their date and tell him that her father had gone missing. Immediately, he offered any assistance she needed. His office owed him a month of overtime and week-end stints and wouldn't crib if he cashed them in now.

When Maclean and Deirdre reached the house, she was able to inform them her father had taken the cab to London Airport. There, the information desk had the names of half a dozen passengers who had booked late on the midday flight to Hamburg. But nobody called Laurence Hallam Fisher. Maclean seized the list she had noted and scanned it, his eye halting at one name. "Miller ... William Miller," he muttered. "That was the name he mentioned the other day when we quizzed him after we played the tape."

"He's gone to Hamburg where he started that trip with his mother more than twenty years ago," Anne exclaimed and recounted the chat she had with her father a few hours before.

"It looks as if you're right," Maclean conceded, though he wondered why a fake Laurence Fisher should worry about a trip he'd never made and an accident he'd never had. If he were really a fake ... "But judging by your talk with him, he's probably making for Berlin eventually, covering his former tracks." He reflected for several minutes, then continued, "It means we'll have to split up to try to catch him at both places."

"I've decided to go myself," Anne said. "Where do you think I should start looking."

"Hamburg," Maclean said. "But you can't go alone. Haven't you got one of your father's staff you can take with you. Or a servant?"

Anne shook her head, conjuring up the image of Blount with his puff-cheeked face and shifty eyes. "There's nobody I trust," she said. Then an idea struck her. "I've a close friend, a young man called Peter Hamlin. He's a journalist and he's just said he'd give me any help he can."

"Take him with you," Maclean said. "And the quicker we all get moving the better."

Within half an hour he had made a plan that Anne and Hamlin could follow; he gave them the number of the official information centre in West Berlin where they could leave messages for him and arrange a rendezvous if her father's trail led them to Berlin. He and Deirdre would fly straight to Berlin and backtrack along the route if necessary. To Anne's surprise he handed her a sheet on which he had noted details of her father's accident including the name of the hospital in Nauen and La Charité in East Berlin. Then he and Deirdre got into her tiny car and headed for London Airport to try for the afternoon flight to West Berlin.

Deirdre could not drive quickly enough for him; she could sense him counting the minutes. After a while, she broke the silence. "I was wondering what would happen to Anne when she finds out her father isn't Fisher."

"More important, what'll happen to Fisher himself when he finds out he's not Fisher?"

"But he knows that, surely."

"Some of the time maybe. And even then he's not too sure."

"So you think it might be dangerous for him to search too deeply into his past."

"It could be." He did not want to elaborate since his own mind hadn't resolved the problem. Fisher was obviously going back to unearth his past, to find himself again. Long ago something had happened to him in Berlin. But had it happened to Fisher? Or Miller? Or whoever he really was? In one sense he hoped Fisher would discover the truth, but another voice whispered it might be better if he didn't. Some secrets were better left where they were. Buried in the mind. It was too painful to disinter them. In his case-book, Fisher's amnesiac bouts might have acted as a defence mechanism to prevent the mind recalling and thus revealing dangerous secrets. If Fisher succeeded in reopening some old wound that had scarred over years ago, it might prove fatal.

"Get a move on, mavournin," he muttered.

Another man was making arrangements to fly to Berlin. By calling her father's office, Anne had alerted Norman Blount to the fact that his master had bolted once more. Ruth did not hide the details from him; he had taken his passport, two thousand pounds, clean clothing, and had probably flown to Hamburg. Blount also learned that Maclean, the psychiatrist, and his secretary were already on the way to the airport and Berlin. Anne, with her boyfriend, Peter Hamlin, was catching a plane later that night for Hamburg.

It took Blount a couple of hours to collect his things, fix enough funds and book his flight on a different line from the doctor and his secretary. Fisher, he felt sure, would not waste much time in Hamburg. Whether his boss knew it or not, his real destination was Berlin. And there he would find Blount blocking his way, waiting to shepherd him back home. If he refused to return and do the job they'd trained him for, too bad for him.

Thirteen

Fisher took a taxi from Hamburg airport to the Hotel Vier Jahreszeiten and booked a suite, observing they still did things with old-world elegance. Kaiser Wilhelm tables and writing-desk, hand-worked tapestry on the bedhead, and Empire chairs. Several years before when setting up his Hamburg office he had stayed there and he chose it now

because it would impress his agent. He had used the name
George Bleane to sign the register, though he had no idea
why that name flickered through his mind as he entered the
baroque foyer.

From his suite he rang Walter Rasch, his correspondent
and agent for North Germany, inviting him for a drink in
just over an hour's time at five o'clock; he wished to discuss
certain changes in the West German operation. But in the
meantime would Rasch hire him a car, something ordinary
like a VW, an Opel or a Taunus? He'd like to drive through
East Germany to Berlin where he had some business.

"You got a visa in London, I suppose?" Rasch asked
with his teutonic flair for detail.

"No, but you can fix me a transit visa for two or three
days," Fisher replied. "I went that way years ago and it's
something of a sentimental trip, you understand?"

"Hmm," Rasch muttered as though far from understanding what sentiment or nostalgia had come over his
impassive boss. "I'll do what I can."

"Just one thing, Rasch, I want to travel as an ordinary
tourist, so don't make a fuss with the East German
authorities."

An hour later, Rasch reported with the car papers and
insurance certificate. Fisher would find the VW 'beetle' in
the hotel garage in half an hour. Rasch had used a little
discreet persuasion on the West German frontier police at
the Lauenburg crossing-point and they'd know Herr Fisher
when he arrived tomorrow. "They're more friendly with the
other side than you think," he said, wrapping banana
fingers round the double Scotch Fisher handed him.
"You'll get your visa for a week when you get to Horst, the
East German side of the frontier." Holding out his glass for
a refill, he went on to say that the other Germany was more
concerned about whether people could pay than about their
politics.

Fisher discussed one or two minor changes he was
making in the Tekpress set-up in Germany, then brought a

deeper flush to Rasch's florid features by the magnanimity with which he augmented his salary.

"Are you dining in the hotel tonight?" the German asked and when Fisher shook his head he proposed taking him home or to one of the more fashionable restaurants along the inner port.

"No, I think I'll wander round on my own and have a look at things," Fisher murmured.

"Not the Reeperbahn," Rasch suggested with a grin at his mention of Hamburg's notorious red-light district where they trafficked in every form of sexual practice, every vice, every human aberration.

"Not me. I'll bed early. I want to get off fairly smartly in the morning." As he and Rasch parted company at the hotel entrance, he gripped the German by the arm. "One thing I must insist on. I don't want anybody to know where I am for a week. Understand? That goes for my family, my friends and even people like Norman Blount. Understand?" Rasch nodded then disappeared along the quayside.

In the garage, Fisher checked the keys and papers of the VW – an ordinary hump-backed version which did not look conspicuous. Rasch had hired it in his own name from the Selbstfahrer Union Hire Company in the town. If Anne or Blount followed his trail here they'd lose time picking up his hotel booking and car under two different names. Blount must have received orders to track him down at any cost and bring him to heel as he had done so often in the past. Eventually, he would worm the details out of Rasch, or perhaps prove clever enough to guess where he was going.

A chill wind was blowing from the Elbe estuary but Fisher marched along the Alster quay without coat or hat; even here, in the chic district among the fashionable restaurants and shops, Hamburg smelled like a working port; a tang of tar and salt water and diesel oil mingled with the odour of a dozen varieties of sausage and sauerkraut and mashed potatoes and peas. Almost despite himself,

Fisher put his nose in the air like some leery old hound and savoured the atmosphere. That meant something. Crossing the market square, he went through the gate into the botanic gardens; there, he could not resist stopping at a stall and ordering a Frankfurter which he dunked in mustard and ate on the hoof; at the bar in the gardens he washed it down with a stein of beer though refusing the small schnapps the kellner suggested.

"*Ausländer?*" the man queried as he wiped the counter.

"*Ja, ich bin Engländer.*"

"*Sie sprechen sehr gut deutsch.*"

Fisher drained his stein hurriedly and quit the bar before his embarrassment showed. Never to his knowledge had he spoken German before, even rejecting suggestions that it was his voice on that tape; yet he had ordered a sausage and beer in the language without giving it a thought. It troubled him, compelling him to question his identity. For more than twenty-five years he must have acted like Laurence Hallam Fisher without being aware of the fact that he could be someone else. Until Roger's girlfriend recalled a past love from what seemed like another incarnation. Only at moments like this one with the German waiter did he become conscious of the fact that he was Fisher – and another person.

As he left the botanic gardens and wandered back to the town hall, he tried to recall his visit to this town twenty-five years before. Surely he should have remembered this great pile of a city hall, longer than its tower, and that was three hundred and fifty feet high with a platoon of patron saints guarding its façade. However, he remembered nothing. Not the town hall, nor the Bismarck monument, nor the churches or museums. If his mother and he had stayed here a week they would have visited some of those! Curiously, he did have a flashback of one thing: changing trains at the Hauptbahnhof, standing amid clouds of steam and the stench of stale oil to watch them transfer the coffin to the Dutch express. Why remember that? At times he seemed to be thinking like Fisher and at others like this stranger.

He imagined what he and his mother must have done and repeated their actions. He drank one glass of wine in the Ratsweinkeller below the town hall. It stirred nothing in him. No more than the solitary meal he ate in the Alster-pavillon across from the hotel on the edge of the small harbour with its pleasure-boats riding on the lights from a thousand buildings, colliding and splintering on the water. Eel soup and Vierländer duck washed down with local beer did not evoke a single emotion. Whatever German he knew had deserted him. It must come in bursts as familiar things impinged on certain mental pathways, he reflected.

A young man of thirty, surely he'd have had a fling on his own along the Reeperbahn! A taxi dropped him at the eastern end of the half-mile parade of sin and vice. Its night spots and strip clubs with their strident music and sweaty nudes left him unmoved; their obscene posturing and seamy language revolted him. In one smoke-laden strip club, a negress and a blond German girl offered a display of sexual contortion, then joined him at his table; he was inveigled into buying these two lesbians two bottles of champagne, then the negress whispered that he could have them both for five hundred deutschmarks. He fled. No, he neither remembered nor wanted to remember that sordid boulevard. Striding back to the hotel through the keen wind seemed to cleanse him. After a nightcap of Scotch and soda, he undressed, got into bed and in a few minutes had fallen into a profound and dreamless sleep.

Next morning he put himself on the road early, his VW furrowing through the milky haze rising from the Elbe Valley. He ignored the new motorway which had not existed during his last visit; at nine-thirty he had passed both check-points at Lauenburg and Horst with a new visa; as the sun skinned away the mist he made better time, bumbling at the speed limit of ninety kilometres an hour along the arterial road that carried nothing like the traffic in the other Germany: several times he involuntarily gravitated to the left-hand side and had to warn himself to drive on the right. East German villages had nothing like the clean and opulent look of those in the federal republic; at Pritzier he drank a coffee in the drab state restaurant in the town centre and that bitter mixture touched some chord in his memory; just after midday he reached Ludwigslust, a pile of old buildings stippled with new blocks of workers' flats, a vast park with a baroque castle in the middle. He seemed to have met that fancy architecture before – stone ornaments sticking like scabs to the turrets and growing like mushrooms from its pillars. In the state restaurant he chomped solidly through two perspiring knackwurst sausages and a hillock of tired sauerkraut, black bread and apfelstrudel all of it so insipid that he would certainly have remembered eating here. To crown it, the waiter twisted his arm to make him pay in West deutschmarks and when he refused whipped away his bottle of Radeberger Pils saying it was '*Polizeilich verboten*' to drink when driving in East Germany.

Sipping his coffee, he studied the guide-book and maps. His mother and he must have kept to the main Hamburg–Berlin road all those years ago, although his recollection was hazy. Anne would know that. So would Blount. He had to get them off his back by finding a place to stay the night away from his old route. His eye lighted on the town of Stendal; although the guide-book listed no tourist hotel he had surely to find a bed among 40,000 people. Next day he'd fumble back through the secondary roads to the main road and Nauen where he meant to locate the exact spot that his Hillman had met that Mercedes truck a quarter of a century before.

Back on the road, he filled up at the Intertank pump on the edge of town as a precaution, having noticed that sometimes thirty miles separated these state petrol stations. A few miles down the road, he felt suddenly overcome with fatigue. Was it the car heater or the monotonous drumming of the engine? Even when he twisted the scoop round to blow air into his face and rubbed his ears, he still had to give the road his full concentration to stay awake. An hour later, he bore right to run along a river valley before crossing the Elbe at Wittenberge by a curious railway bridge on which they had placed planks for cars and trucks. This country now looked familiar, a chequered pattern of ploughed fields and grazing land stippled with Friesian cattle and broken now and again with beech, ash and pine forests; as the rolling land unfolded before him, he sensed that he could trace the outline of the succeeding horizons before actually seeing them. Probably a mirage effect, he thought, rubbing his eyes. At Osterburg, an hour before Stendal, he had to stop and drink a pint of bitter coffee to enable him to continue. Somehow he got to Stendal, found the state Goldbroiler restaurant and ordered a meal. While he ate his roast chicken four soldiers entered, sat two tables away and shouted for vodka. With a start, Fisher realized from their bottle-green tunics and gorget patches that they were Soviet officers. He had almost forgotten that he was in the Soviet Zone.

"Von wo kommen die russische Soldaten?" he found himself whispering to the surly manager of the state restaurant.

"There's a camp and firing range fifteen kilometres away on Lezlinger Heide," the man replied.

Lezlinger Heide! That name resonated in his mind like some distant trumpet note; he could even attach mental images to it, an expanse of heather and moss and gorse, pitted by shells and gouged deep by tanks; he could see and even smell burnt-out tanks with bodies scattered around them and a pall of black smoke ascending over the vehicle depot. But like those last, flickering pictures before sleep, the scene blurred over. He felt dog-weary.

"Haben Sie ein Zimmer für eine Nacht?" he asked the manager.

"Yes, I can let you have a room," – he lowered his voice

and flicked a glance at the officers — "if you pay in Westmarks."

Fisher nodded. Humping his holdall, he followed the man up narrow stairs to the rooms above the dining-room. A single iron bed, rough table, chair and a wash-basin furnished his room under the eaves. Fisher hardly noticed them. As soon as the manager had collected payment in advance and gone, he lay down on the bed and fell asleep, still in his clothes.

At seven-thirty he woke to find the landlord placing a tray on the table with hot, sliced sausage, cheese, black bread and butter, coffee and milk. Without being conscious of it, he must have risen in the night and undressed, for his clothes hung over a chair. At that early hour he could not face such a meal but drank the coffee and ate a slice of pumpernickel; he then sluiced his face and body in the wash-basin and dressed. At eight o'clock he was back on the road. Although he had slept well, he felt slightly woozy as though he had drunk too much last night instead of two glasses of a nameless Hungarian white wine.

On the road west from Stendal nothing much moved. Nevertheless, he drove carefully against the low sun and slight morning mist. At Rathenow he stretched his legs and drank a coffee; his map told him he would branch right to bring him back to the main road above Nauen where he intended to spend the night.

Now his landscape was changing character and he was driving through marshland incised with streams and canals. Once through this, he hit wooded country with a few villages and farms dotted along the road. Just after eleven, he saw the smoke of a small town in a valley a mile or two farther on and decided he would lunch there if it had a restaurant. He must have had his mind on something else when he passed the town sign, for he looked at it without registering the name; for some reason, he reversed the VW and had a second look. Schonebrücke. It signified something but what he did not know. Anyway, there must be half a hundred towns called Schonebrücke in both German states. Yet Fisher had an eerie sensation that someone, or something, beyond his control had drawn him to this sleepy market town in this fertile valley forty kilometres west of Berlin.

Cruising slowly along the main street, he observed that half the houses and small blocks of flats looked fairly new, as though Schonebrücke had suffered during the war from the Allied or Russian advance; most of the shops, too, dated from the past thirty years. In the centre, a new town hall and police headquarters sat on the edge of a square shaded by linden-trees. Fisher parked there and strolled down the side-streets radiating from the square. Here, the war had spared quite a few old houses and these did look like remembered things; but he had the sensation of regarding a surrealist painting or film where strange objects had intruded into familiar settings. Bewildered, he wandered back to the centre where he had spotted a small café with several tables at which half a dozen people were eating. Taking a seat by the plate-glass window overlooking the main street, he ordered the menu – lentil soup with two red sausage rings sunk in it like the reflection of his own weary eyes, roast veal and strudel. He chewed slowly through the meal as though loth to finish; as he ate the strudel a couple of boys in suede jackets, short leather pants and knitted stockings went by on bicycles with schoolbags strapped to them. Of course, the school! He had to see that. And the church. That they wouldn't have destroyed. He'd recognize both those buildings.

Idly, he stirred milk into his coffee and sipped the thin beverage. Could anybody go back this far without feeling confused, split-minded? Could anybody go back at all? Was he playing a futile game with no end to it? A click from the heavy metal door short-circuited his thought and, lifting his head, he saw a woman enter the café to buy cigarettes. Her he had seen before – but only because she had already passed the window twice glancing in both times. She looked not unlike his own wife, Ruth, in age and appearance with her blonde hair, aquamarine eyes and strong features; her heavy coat had a cape and hood which dropped on her back but he could see that she was slim and had slender legs under leather calf-boots. Despite himself, he listened as she ordered her cigarettes and small-talked with the café manager. Her voice sounded low-pitched and cultured, her enunciation slow and clear enough for him to catch every word of the gossip about the weather and the town. Several times she turned her head to gaze in his direction. Was he imagining things, or was she staring at him?

Her cigarettes paid, she crossed towards the door, then, as though acting on an impulse, side-stepped to his table.

"*Entschuldigen Sie bitte,*" she said. "*Sie sind Wilhelm Friedrich Müller, nicht wahr?*"

He gazed at her, his eyes scanning her face feature by feature, searching for some clue that would unlock his memory; at the same time he noticed her eyes tracing his own features with the light of recognition in them. He shook his head and said:

"*Nein, ich bin nicht Wilhelm Friedrich Müller.*"

She inclined her head, muttered an apology and had turned on her heel to leave when he rose and stopped her. "Sit down for a moment, madam," he said, pulling up a chair for her. He helped her off with her coat, noting her elegant and shapely figure and the expensive blouse and skirt that would have appeared to come from one of the better Hamburg fashion houses rather than an East German state store. She had fine hands which selected and lit a cigarette. He ordered coffee for her and, when it came, he leaned over to whisper:

"What made you think I was Wilhelm Friedrich Müller? And anyway, what happened to him?"

Fourteen

Maclean followed the messenger through the vast office in which a dozen journalists were working at typewriters and twice as many teleprinters were quivering and clattering with outgoing copy from the Deutsche-Presse-Agentur to its subscribers and incoming reports from a dozen foreign press agencies to be rewritten and processed for German newspapers. At the far end of the newsagency office sat three steel and glass cubicles and the messenger led Maclean to one of these and ushered him inside. Even behind the thick plate glass he heard the printers and type-writers crepitate.

"It never stops," Johannes Gunther Meyer said with a shrug as he motioned the psychiatrist to a chair. "Now, how can I help you, Herr Doktor?" he asked. Meyer had a face like a melon, his chin, cheeks and the crown of his head forming a perfect oval. Maclean explained he had traced the journalist to his office as head of the DPA Berlin bureau through a Reuter correspondent.

"I don't know whether you recall when you worked as a reporter here for Der Telegraf covering an accident to a British journalist and his mother."

"Nauen, about twenty kilometres from here. The mother died in the car and he just got away with it." Meyer scratched his bald head with the end of his ballpoint pen. "Let me see ... June 17, 1953, wasn't it?"

"Right," Maclean said. "But what makes you remember it so exactly and so vividly?"

"I just wondered and still wonder how they ever put him together again," Meyer grunted. Seizing a pad, he wrote the name, Laurence Hallam Fisher, and the date of the accident; he pressed a buzzer and handed these details to the messenger for the newsagency archivist. While they waited for the information, he explained that his and other West Berlin newspapers had truncated the story for two reasons: at that moment workers in East Berlin and several other big cities in the Soviet Zone had rebelled against working conditions, low wages and food shortages and this had eclipsed every other event; secondly, papers generally had very little newsprint and thus rationed news items. Before Meyer had completed his story, two cassettes had arrived from the agency library. Meyer clipped this microfilm into his machine, consulted the key code and a few seconds later he and Maclean were reading what the DPA and other agencies and papers had reported on Fisher's accident.

"Seems it was his fault."

"No doubt about that at all," Meyer said. "Two witnesses saw him pull out to overtake on a rising bend. The Mercedes truckdriver couldn't do a thing."

"When did you see Fisher?"

"I didn't really see him. I got there too late, but I interviewed a surgeon and a physician who were in the casualty unit at Nauen hospital. Both of them were categoric – he was too badly smashed to survive. Secretly, they weren't bothered when the Charité hospital in East Berlin took him off their hands. His lungs had been punctured by broken ribs and his spleen had ruptured and he had a dozen broken bones. They wouldn't have known where to start at Nauen."

"They obviously did at the Charité, but that's a good hospital," Maclean said.

"It's a great hospital," Meyer corrected. "What a job they must have done! I remember the Nauen people saying that not even Sauerbruch at his zenith could do much for the Englishman." He ran the microfilm forward and they read his and other interviews with Fisher when he entered West Berlin two months after the accident.

"Do you know if he remembered what had happened at the time of the accident?" Maclean asked.

"Meyer shook his head. "We asked him that. In fact he remembered nothing about the accident and for days before it happened. And I'm sure he wasn't pretending."

"Did other newspapermen think he might have been acting as though he had amnesia?"

"Why should he?" Meyer said, then held up a finger. "I see what you mean – to avoid answering incriminating questions." He shook his head. "No, he was genuine though we wondered why the East Germans had let him off so lightly when they could have given him two years in jail. Maybe they thought he'd been punished enough by losing his mother." From a box on his desk he pulled out a cigar, lit it, then looked sharply at Maclean. "If I'm not being too inquisitive has it caught up with him – the accident, I mean?"

Maclean nodded. "He's been blaming himself for his mother's death and came to me suffering from depression," he lied.

"Then he did remember something of the accident."

"I don't really know," Maclean said. "And I don't think he does either, but I'll be able to confirm that with the details you've given me." Without giving the German journalist time to ask any more pertinent questions, he rose and held out his hand. "You've been a great help and I'm deeply indebted," he said.

Outside, he walked on to the Kurfürstendamm and turned right towards the zoo. Meyer had given him quite a few leads – all of them pointing across the Berlin Wall into East Berlin. It was, none the less, a good start. Deirdre and he had arrived in Berlin two hours before and Meyer was his first call. He had dumped his baggage at the Lichtburg Hotel and left Deirdre there by their room telephone to keep contact with the two city airports, Tegel and Tempelhof, in case they spotted Fisher's or Miller's name on their passenger list; she was also waiting for word from Anne and Hamlin via the Berlin information centre.

Maclean passed the shattered hulk of the Kaiser Wilhelm Memorial Church at the head of the Ku'damm and listened to its five o'clock carillon, almost drowned by the traffic din. No-one could think clearly in this stampede of vehicles and people, so he headed for the relative calm of the Tiergarten park and strolled to a lakeside seat; on the lake two four-men crews were sculling through a flotilla of swans and multicoloured ducks.

Fisher was evidently heading for Berlin where his life had taken that mysterious turn; but so far as Maclean knew he had not yet penetrated any of the city check-points; when he did, he might lose himself for days or weeks in West or East Berlin. However, Maclean imagined that he would make for his old haunts – if he could remember where they were. Somehow they had to put themselves in his path and halt him; for unless they forestalled him he might do something desperate to himself or some luckless woman.

So he, Deirdre, Anne and her boyfriend had to act quickly, if warily. A hint to anyone that Laurence Hallam Fisher, the prominent magazine publisher, was missing in East Germany of Berlin and they'd have an army of newspaper and TV reporters on their necks. To say nothing of the police. Long before meeting Meyer, he had suspected that some or perhaps most of the answers to Fisher's problem lay beyond that immense wall dividing the city, a kilometre from where he now sat. But before penetrating into East Berlin he had to know roughly where he – and Fisher – were going. And why. A man had to grope his way inch by inch in this town, the most sensitive and explosive spot in East-West politics with the two hostile systems separated physically. However, he had to pick someone here – a man he knew he could trust and who might help him discover what had happened to Fisher.

When he had reviewed the whole problem, he sauntered out of the Tiergarten and risked his skin crossing the street to the enormous Europa-center, a cosmopolis in steel and concrete. From a coin-box he called the Free University Clinic in the south-western Dahlem suburb; in 1969, soon after the great teaching hospital opened, he had given a lecture at a conference on psychological medicine and had struck up a friendship with one of its leading psychiatrists, Professor Ernst Linder. Now Linder was booming at him over the line.

"Maclean ... Gregor Maclean! Where are you?"

"At the top of the Ku'damm. I'm here on a private trip but I have a problem and I'd like to meet you. I need your help."

"Can it wait until dinner at my place. Mitzi would be delighted to cook for you."

"No, Ernst – it's urgent." Maclean could overhear Linder muttering to himself then to his secretary before he said, "I'll finish here in a few minutes and meet you – say at Kranzler's – in twenty minutes."

"Not Kranzler's," Maclean said. Who knew how many East German and West German undercover operators mingled with chic Berlin society in that elegant coffee-house? "Isn't there somewhere we can talk privately?"

Linder paused for a second or two then gave him the address of a bierstübe off the Lietzenburgerstrasse, five minutes' walk away from the top of the Ku'damm. Maclean arrived to find a cellar with vast oak tables and benches dented with the banging of steins; in the close atmosphere his head nearly turned with the smell of fermenting hops and steamy odour of hot sausage and mustard. Linder strode in, shook his hand numb, then led him to a cubicle in a dark corner, his tall, bulky figure stooping under the oak beams; for himself he ordered a bottle of Rhine wine, for Maclean a pot of coffee. Under a thatch of white hair, Linder had a boyish face and a boisterous manner concealing a kind mind which Maclean knew from reading his contributions to psychiatric literature had unravelled some complex cases. Now he listened to the conundrum of Fisher which Maclean outlined without revealing anything of the three murders or the difference in fingerprints.

"What brings him back here?"

"Part of his story's here. An important part – the accident. But he's doing what we're all doing one way or another – searching for ourselves. Only he's that bit more lost."

"Sounds like a dual personality," Linder said.

Maclean let him think so. What interested him and had brought him here was Fisher's accident, he told Linder tongue-in-cheek. He wondered what psychic trauma the Charité Hospital psychiatrists in East Berlin might have discovered when Fisher was recovering. Now if he could only have a word with the surgeons and doctors ...

"Twenty-five years ago," Linder muttered. "Most of them will have gone." He puffed on his cigar, gulped his third glass of wine and glanced at his watch. "I've a friend there – Eisler, the head of medical admin. I might just catch him and he might know who handled the case ... when did you say he went in ... June 17, 1953."

"Can you call East Berlin direct?" Maclean asked.

"On the emergency line," Linder grunted. "It suits them when they need help or drugs they don't have and can't get from their Russian friends." Disappearing into the phone-box in the corner of the cellar, he spent ten minutes there. When he returned, he gulped the remains of his glass of wine, then sat down, a puzzled look on his face. "Your friend, Fisher, never went to the Charité on June 17 or any other day."

"But he said so himself," Maclean countered.

"Coming from East Berlin and having a motoring offence hanging over him and a dead mother to transport home he might have had his good reasons," Linder said.

"Where did he go?"

"Dr Eisler's trying to find out. There are only three or

four hospitals in that sector where he could have gone with his injuries. Give him half an hour and he'll ring us here."

They sat and chatted while the bierkeller filled up with local Berliners and its atmosphere thickened with tobacco smoke and talk of football, and lottery winners. Maclean quizzed his friend about the Wall. As a foreigner he could come and go as he wished, but they'd tab him at the checkpoint and might shadow him wherever he went. For West Germans like himself they put on a show of letting through a few thousand a week; but anybody making a practice of using the check-points without good cause found the *Sicherheitdienst* behind him; to discourage those the other side, the *Vopos* still shot a few who tried burrowing or barging through the Wall. To keep themselves updated on the latest progress, they let a few doctors and scientists and medical researchers cross the zone boundaries to attend conferences in West Berlin; but these men they hand-picked not only for their talent but the size of their family who remained as hostages in East Germany. "They could give Hitler and his thugs a lesson in fascism," Linder snorted.

A *kellner* pushed between the tables to tell Linder that someone was waiting on the line. In a few minutes he came back, shrugging his broad shoulders. "No trace of your problem patient," he said. "Eisler checked with the casualty and surgical departments of half a dozen hospitals and even phoned Nauen to verify their side of the story. He left there with an ambulance on June 17 for East Berlin, but he seems to have disappeared en route. Eisler doesn't know what to make of it."

Maclean shook his head as though he, too, felt bewildered. But his suspicions were hardening that Laurence Hallam Fisher had either died on the way to hospital. Or they had taken him outside East Berlin for treatment. Whatever happened THAT Fisher did not return through the Brandenburg Gate two months later. Someone else had. Linder was looking quizzically at him.

"Well, Dr Mac, what do you make of it?" he said finally.

Maclean did not reply directly. West Berliners had sharp antennae for anything touching espionage and, whatever he did, he had not to reveal his notion that the hated East Germans had switched one of their nationals for Fisher and sent him back through the Brandenburg Gate; it might stretch Linder's friendship too far to ask him to keep that secret.

"I was thinking back to that conference you held at the Clinic at the end of '69. What was the name of that man who gave the fascinating talk on brain-washing by aversion therapy, who used jargon like Revulsion Therapy and Elation Conditioning and Affective Homeostasis and so on?"

Linder poured the dregs of the wine-bottle into his glass and looked over its rim at Maclean as he drank them. "What are you thinking – that they might have brain-washed this man, Fisher, before sending him back?" he said. "To do what – spy for them in Britain?"

"I don't know. It's just one of the possibilities."

"Now that I remember, they were supposed to have a training centre somewhere on the outskirts of East Berlin," Linder mused.

"What was his name – the psychiatrist who gave the lecture on brain-washing?" Maclean insisted.

"Gaedmann ... Dr Werner Gaedmann. He'd done some work preparing reports on conditioning men for General Gehlen's counter-espionage centre near Munich. He had to get top clearance to give that paper at our meeting."

"But wasn't he quoting somebody else, somebody who'd defected across the Wall?"

"That's right, he was."

"It's the man he was quoting I'd like to see if it can be arranged."

Linder shook his head. "If I know anything he'll be planked somewhere safe under another name with a life-pension from the Federal Republic for his services to its security organization and probably a Swiss bank account stuffed with CIA money."

"Can we try, Ernst?" Maclean pleaded.

"If it's for a patient and not for you-know-what."

"It's for a patient – Fisher. You have my word."

Linder looked at the empty Niersteiner bottle with regret and hoisted himself up. Maclean followed him outside to his BMW and marvelled at the skill with which he jinked through the dense traffic and kept the needle edging the hundred-kilometre mark along the south-west highway. They caught his secretary as she was leaving the Free University Clinic and within minutes they had traced Gaedmann in the medical directory and official register. "He's still in Munich," Linder muttered.

"I can fly down," Maclean said. "It's what – just over an hour?"

"If he'll help," Linder remarked. "Some of them are scared even of their own side." He put three calls through the switchboard – to Gaedmann's Munich consulting-rooms, to his hospital and his home in Thalkirchen. His consulting-room answered, then Linder replaced the receiver. "He'll ring back in five minutes. He says he's busy. He's so cagey that he's probably checking that I'm who I say I am even though he must know my voice."

In five minutes the phone rang. Linder explained what he wanted Gaedmann to do, listened for a moment or two, then let loose with a stream of imperative German that made Maclean sit up; it reminded him why people like Linder had twice in thirty years knocked the world off its tack. Even with his imperfect knowledge of German he realized that Linder was leaning very heavily on Gaedmann, invoking loyalty, friendship, sense of vocation, and hinting that any lack of assistance would be repaid a thousandfold which would do Gaedmann's professional reputation and bank balance no good at all. By timing Linder's verbal salvoes and Gaedmann's replies, Maclean put the issue in no doubt. After ten minutes Linder cradled the receiver gave a broad grin with a flash of gold inlay. "Of course he has agreed to co-operate," he said. "There's a plane at nine o'clock from Tegel and he'll meet it himself at Munich airport."

"Does he know what it's about?"

"He has enough of an idea. If he gives any trouble ring me and I'll knock the kinks out of him." Going to a cupboard stuffed with drug samples and medicaments, he rummaged to emerge with a bottle of Scotch and one beaker. "Sorry you don't use your national drink," he said, pouring himself a double ration to make up for his abstemious guest. "You and your secretary will dine with us tonight. My girl has already told Mitzi and she'll make us something special."

Another wild slalom through the rush-hour traffic and they retrieved Deirdre who had no messages, either from the airports or Anne Fisher. Maclean explained that she would have to stay in Berlin tomorrow to keep the connection open while he flew to Munich. She gave a resigned shrug. If it hastened the end of this case and their return to London she'd do anything.

Mitzi, a well-cushioned blonde in her forties, met them at the door of Linder's flat near Charlottenburg castle. She chided her husband for overlooking the fact that they had already invited two friends and their wives; but she assured them they had enough food and drink for everybody.

Enough! Eyes popping, Maclean watched them prepare their bacchanalia with libations of schnapps; irrigate their crayfish, smoked salmon, their sausage meats and other hors-d'oeuvres with draughts of white wine and the odd schnapps; attack roast chicken or Wiener schnitzel or both and wash this down with more wine; finish with a dozen varieties of French and German cheeses, strudel and pastries. They seemed to have no heads, no legs, no liver, no organ that gourmandizing or boozing could touch. What made them gorge like this? Berlin with its siege mentality? Was it just another Teutonic custom? Beside them he felt like an ascetic, or somebody deficient in a vital metabolic element. Or sadly out of training. He felt relieved when eleven o'clock chimed from the carriage clock and the coffee and liqueurs were drying up.

Back in their hotel he phoned the information centre. Yes, they had a message for Dr Maclean from Miss Fisher. She and her companion were catching the late-night flight from London to Hamburg, arriving at two-thirty in the morning and had booked at the Alster-Hof. Anne had ended her message by saying that Norman Blount had also decided to help in the search and had probably flown to Berlin.

Maclean replaced the phone. Ten hours behind Fisher, Anne and Hamlin would probably get to Hamburg too late to check the hotels to discover if he had stayed in the city. They would have to wait until morning to pick up his trail. Why had she mentioned this man Blount?

"Do we know anything about a Norman Blount?" he asked Deirdre.

"Anne doesn't like him," she replied. "But he's her father's closest friend and has been with him since he started publishing magazines."

Maclean wondered where Fisher had gone to ground that night. Wherever it was, he hoped they would get to him before he committed any rash action, and before this associate, Blount, caught and led him back home. Having travelled this far back along the fork he had taken a quarter of a century before, Fisher should surely be allowed to go the whole way. It might shock Anne and her boyfriend, Hamlin, and Ruth Fisher to have to face the fact that Fisher was not Fisher but someone who had played the part so well for a third of a lifetime that he had deceived everybody – himself included. But a man's mind and his identity meant more than the susceptibilities of his family. Fisher had a right to recover his true Self. He might even trace Jane, the girl he had loved all those years ago. Maclean crossed his fingers that he would – even if it did cause a stir.

Fifteen

Anne felt someone nudge her and looked up, bewildered for a moment until she heard the drone and whine of jet engines. "We'll be there in a few minutes, darling," Peter Hamlin whispered, pointing out of the Trident porthole. Beneath her, in the darkness the twisted skein of the Elbe estuary and Hamburg glittered like a handful of brilliant stones thrown on a jeweller's cloth; they tracked the river through the huge sprawl of the city as they lost height and came in to land.

At the terminal building a man was holding up a board with Hamlin's name on it; he handed them the keys of the car they had hired from London airport. Before leaving the building, Hamlin checked with the information desk. No, there was no record of a Herr Fisher or Herr Miller boarding a flight from Hamburg to Berlin or anywhere else ten or so hours ago. Nor had he booked a hotel from the airport. Hamlin collected every scrap of tourist and other literature on Hamburg before they got into the Taunus for the twenty-minute drive to the city.

Anne passed him a cigarette and held the lighter while he peered, his face tense, at the signposts for Hamburg. "I feel more and more guilty," she murmured.

"What about?"

"Getting you involved in something that doesn't really concern you."

"Anything that you do or want to do concerns me as well," he replied, reaching out his right hand to take hers and squeeze it. Did his own guilt show through? If only this girl who trusted him knew the irony of her remark and his situation. Only yesterday he had been keeping watch outside Maclean's consulting-room when Max had summoned him to the office. One of his airport spies had informed him that Fisher had just walked into the departure lounge with a ticket for Hamburg. They had to pick up his trail and follow it. In no circumstances had he to get to Berlin. If he did their whole operation would crack wide open. Years of work would go for waste paper and they'd all have to run for cover. He had called Hamlin because the girl would obviously know what had happened to compel her father to flee the country. At first Hamlin had jibbed at involving the daughter. But just then Anne had called him at the office to reveal that her father had vanished and she was trying to locate him. "Tell her you'll help," Max had whispered. He had made the offer which she accepted. Now his conscience about tricking her was tempered by the fact that she did not have to make this trip on her own, that he could at least protect her as well as doing his job.

"Anyway, it's more important than listening to blacks and whites in London airing their race hate," he said.

"Where do you think my father is?" Anne asked.

"It's anybody's guess," Hamlin replied. He refused to look farther than the next move. Not only because he considered this good practice, but he did not like to envisage what a psychopathic individual like Fisher might do on the loose. As far as Max and his own job went, it was another assignment; his next one would probably confront him with just as many problems. For this girl sitting beside him it was different. What would she do when the scandal of her father's real purpose in life broke over her head? He tried to put himself in her place, to imagine how she would feel before he pulled himself up. In a minute he'd be thinking like her then commiserating with her and finally admitting he really loved her. And maybe he did. Maybe that was why he injected so much emotion into the lying tales he spun to Max about having slept with her; otherwise Max, with his nose for fiction, would have hit on the truth.

They had reached the Alster-Hof hotel on the corner of the small, inner harbour. There the night porter had their room ready and handed them a note with Maclean's Berlin hotel number and room on it. Hamlin had ordered a double room since, as he remarked, they wouldn't have much time for sleep.

"The police don't ask you for a report on foreigners any more?" he queried with the porter.

"Sometimes they come and have a look over the list," the man said. "But only when they feel like it." His hand went through the motions of raising a glass to his mouth. Hamlin handed him a list of hotels that he had discovered at the airport; he wanted the switchboard to ring every one and put their reception desk or porter through to their room; he ordered a gallon of coffee and sandwiches and shoved the Hamburg telephone directories and personal and professional index for the town under his arm as they took the lift to the second floor.

When they had dumped their two valises he sat Anne down with the hotel list. She would ask each hotel porter if anybody had booked a room the previous afternoon or evening under the two names her father was using – his own and Miller. If they said No, she should get a list of the English people who had taken rooms from yesterday afternoon. "But there are more than a hundred hotels," she complained.

"Do the luxury ones and don't bother about anything under two stars," he said.

He himself began by ringing several of the hotels, then the police. Anne stopped for a moment to listen to him, then said, "But I never knew you spoke perfect German."

"I did ten years on it, right up through Oxford and I've used it quite a bit as a newspaperman," he said.

"Come to think of it, I don't really know much about you, Peter," she said.

"When we've time I'll take an hour or two off and bore

you off your feet with my life story," he grinned. "Where have we got?"

"The *Vier Jahreszeiten*," she said. "They have three Englishmen – Messrs Dixon, Enderby and Bleane."

"Bleane? ... Bleane? That's a funny English name."

"I queried it and they assured me it was English."

They toiled steadily through the hotels listing all the British visitors. By six o'clock they had finished all but the smallest hotels and had noted thirty-seven names, but nothing resembling Fisher or Miller. Hamlin rang the airport to check on passengers who had flown out since their arrival; he rang the customs and immigration posts for both road and railway where they crossed into East Germany; he thought better of trying the East German side. In every inquiry he drew a blank. He might have changed names again or left by car for Berlin. If he had, Maclean or Blount would catch him at the end of his run. He hoped Maclean would lay hands on him first, for he only knew half the story and could no more than suspect an espionage link; as a psychiatrist he had an inkling of how to defuse a time-bomb like Fisher. Blount on the other hand might make a balls of the whole thing by going through the Wall and bringing the whole of the East German *Staat-sicherheitdienst* hierarchy down about their heads.

Burying his cigarette end in the small mountain on his ashtray, he picked up the list they had compiled. They could hardly take a picture of Fisher round the eleven hotels where thirty-seven British visitors were staying and ask the staff to identify him as a client. Anne poured their umpteenth cup of coffee from the flask and they sat discussing what they might do to narrow their inquiries. "Does your father know anybody in Hamburg?" he asked.

"He has an office here – at least Tekpress has, I think."

Hamlin was already leafing through the town's personal and professional index. "Tekpress ... 14bis Hansa-strasse ... Korrespondent, Herr Walter Rasch." He flipped over the pages of the telephone directory. "His home number's 243010." He had already seized the phone when she took it out of his hand.

"You can't get him out of bed at six o'clock," she said. "Anyway, you've had enough for the day. We both have."

"You're right," he conceded. "We might have to get back on the road in a couple of hours. I'll ring him in just over an hour." He pointed to the bed. "You get in there and I'll take the sofa."

Anne took his hand and looked wistfully at him. "Peter," she murmured. "For months I've had my own thoughts and my own feelings about our first night together ... it was nothing like this."

"I know – a freezing April night in Hamburg working our tongue muscles to the bone and drinking black coffee to keep awake. It's crazy."

She stood on tiptoe to put her arms round his neck and kiss him. "Don't think I wanted some Mediterranean tourist palace, all moonlight and magnolias. I'm not all that schmaltzy."

"Well, I am," he grinned.

"I can be, too, if needs must."

"But it'll have to wait until we catch up with your old man."

"Peter," she whispered in his ear. "Do you love me a little?"

"You don't have to ask that. And you know what questions like that lead to." He kissed her, then gently thrust her away before he weakened. Pointing to the turned-down bedsheet, he mimed sleep. "We'll need all our energy," he said. She shrugged but complied.

Had Max witnessed that little scene he would have booted him out on the spot. Passing up a chance like that! If they'd been any young couple, if he'd met her casually, he would have needed no persuasion. But, thrown together like this, how could he take advantage of her mental and emotional confusion about her father's flight? Moreover, she would soon know that he, Hamlin, had tricked her, lied to her, manipulated her – but at least he had not used her body.

He watched her take off her jacket, blouse and skirt and climb between the sheets in her slip; within minutes she had gone to sleep and he gazed at her face, white with fatigue, and her arm, drooping lax by the side of the bed. Before he settled on the sofa and pulled the blanket over himself, he ordered the night porter to call him at seven-thirty.

When the alarm call woke him he let Anne sleep on while he showered and drank some of the coffee from the flask and ate a roll. He had already planned his moves for the day by the time he had dressed. He shook Anne awake. "I'm going to phone your father's agent, Rasch, and he might want to speak to you."

Rasch took some convincing that he was speaking to Fisher's daughter and her friend; at first he denied emphatically that he had seen his employer or spoken to him. So far as he knew, Herr Fisher was not in Hamburg. Had he visited the town he would have informed him, his agent, as he normally did.

"Herr Rasch, this is a matter of life and death," Hamlin said. "Mr Fisher has been seriously ill from overwork and is not himself. If you have seen him and he has sworn you to say nothing, forget that promise."

"I made no promise."

"Look," Hamlin shouted. "You may cost Mr Fisher his life if you refuse to tell us what you know. And it'll cost you your job."

"I will not be threatened," Rasch shouted back.

"All right, we'll have to do it the hard way by checking with the police and railway authorities and the car-hire firms since you're so pig-headed."

"Where are you staying?" Rasch said, his voice milder. He noted the hotel and declared that he would have to come and identify them before making a decision. Hamlin paced up and down, fuming, until Rasch puffed into the room. He demanded to see their passports, then apologized.

"Herr Fisher made me pledge my word to say nothing."

"Where is he staying?"

"The *Vier Jahreszeiten*."

"But the hotel was the first one we rang," Anne exclaimed.

"He was using another name – Bleane, I think it was."

Hamlin yelled at the switchboard operator to get him the *Vier Jahreszeiten* while he noted the type and number of the car Fisher had hired in Rasch's name. In a few seconds he was talking to the hotel receptionist who revealed that Mr Bleane had paid his bill and had left just before seven-thirty – forty-five minutes ago."

"How far to the frontier?" Hamlin asked Rasch.

"Half an hour on the autobahn – just over an hour on the state road. Depends how you drive."

When the German had departed, Hamlin and Anne packed and he sent her to the kiosk downstairs to buy the best map and guide-book of East Germany. Fisher was obviously repeating the trip he had made with his mother a quarter of a century ago and would choose the state road. Even taking the autobahn, they would not stop him at the frontier; but at least they knew his route and might over-take him the other side of the frontier. While he had the room to himself he called Max Anderson, rousing him and having to apologize for the hour since German time was an hour ahead of London time. Anderson listened to the briefing about Fisher then transmitted his information. Maclean was still in Berlin and Hamlin had to keep contact with him. Blount had flown direct to West Berlin and had gone through the Wall the previous evening. "If Fisher does anything stupid – and you know what I mean – don't try to cover it up. Even if your playmate asks you on her benders." Hamlin banged the receiver back into its cradle. As if he could cover up anything here! Blount evidently had no doubts that Fisher would follow him into East Berlin to meet the bosses who had taken him as a young technical journalist more than a quarter of a century before and converted him to a Communist spy. Would they thank him for making this sentimental journey? Anne came through the door and he grabbed the maps from her to show her how to map-read them out of Hamburg then to the frontier and down the main road to Berlin.

"We'll have to stop at all the state petrol stations and ask if he filled up."

"All of them!"

"There aren't too many stations or too many VWs with a Hamburg registration."

"You'd make a very good detective," she said with that serious smile.

"My newspaper training," he grinned.

"Dr Maclean," she exclaimed. "We'd better tell him what's happening."

They called Maclean's Berlin number and caught him as he was leaving the hotel for Tegel airport. Briefly, they explained that Fisher had spent the night in Hamburg under the name of Bleane, that he was now on the way by road through East Germany and might arrive in Berlin either that night or the next day; they were pursuing him and would probably arrive tomorrow morning.

They made good time to the frontier and had no trouble at Horst on the East German side. He dismissed her suggestion of making enquiries, fearing that he might rouse suspicion among the Communist authorities. On the empty roads he still had to hold the Taunus down to the speed limit of ninety kilometres an hour to avoid trouble with the police; Anne slept on his shoulder, waking only at the Inter-tank stations, spaced at about thirty kilometres along the road. Several garage attendants had spotted Fisher's car and at Ludwigslust where they stopped for a Hamburger and fried eggs they found the station where Anne's father had bought petrol no more than an hour before. Some quick mental arithmetic told Hamlin that the VW had enough petrol to reach Berlin. And if he were sticking to the speed limit like them he'd therefore get there an hour ahead.

"Yes, but he'll stop at Nauen," Anne objected when he voiced these thoughts. "That's where he had his accident and he's always promised to check on his mother's death."

"Where would he go?" Hamlin said. "The hospital, the police? No, not the police." He bit on his tongue.

"The accident happened just the other side of the town," Anne said. "He'd probably stop there if he recognized the place."

"We must find him before he gets to Berlin. If we lose him in that place we might never pick up his trail."

"But Norman Blount's in Berlin and he's sure to pick him up if Dr Maclean misses him."

"Yes, Blount'll catch him," Hamlin muttered. Little did Anne know that Blount was probably carrying a gun which he had been told to use if Fisher disobeyed his order to return with him. That thought pushed his speedometer up to well over a hundred kilometres an hour and he braked and went back to ninety. When he pulled up for petrol beyond Perleberg, he asked casually if a Hamburg VW had gone by but the pump-man shook his head. At the next three stations he got the same response. "Your father has gone off the road somewhere," he said.

"No, they've been looking the other way, that's all," she said.

But at Nauen, when they made enquiries at the hospital where Fisher had entered casualty in 1953, no-one had either seen or heard anything of him; nor had the Inter-tank station and the café in the main square of the town. They pressed on to Berlin, mystified. There, at the Heerestrasse checkpoint between East Germany and West Berlin, Hamlin quizzed the city frontier police and the British sergeant on duty at the guard-post about the friend he had lost on the way. No, they had not seen a Hamburg VW with anyone answering Fisher's description in the past several hours.

Where had Fisher gone? He would scarcely have doubled

south all the way round the Havel lakes and entered by the Hanover and Munich road. No, he'd run to earth somewhere between Ludwigslust and Berlin. And he might come into the east or west sector of the city by any one of half a dozen checkpoints. Was he playing hide-and-seek with them? They continued their journey down Heerestrasse, across the causeway and the northern tip of Grunewald forest. At the Lichtburg Hotel, Deirdre had booked them two rooms beside theirs. Maclean, she explained, had flown out to Munich that morning to make some mysterious inquiry, but had left no contact address or number.

"I only hope he has more idea than we have how to pick up Anne's father," Hamlin groaned. For the moment he had run out of ideas and could only wait for a lead from the psychiatrist.

Norman Blount might have flown direct to Schönefeld airport in East Berlin, but that might have aroused suspicions; therefore he flew into Tegel, took the underground to the Ku'damm and wandered along the broad avenue and into Kranzler's Kaffeehaus; there he took a seat under the red-and-white striped awnings on the first floor at a point where he could watch the surge of humanity on the pavements and offer himself for observation as he sipped his coffee. A minute or two before five o'clock, he spotted a familiar figure with bulky outline and crumpled suit, walking towards the bombed ruin of the Gedächtniskirche; he wondered where Dr Gregor Maclean had been and where he was heading. His contacts had informed him that the psychiatrist and his secretary had arrived several hours before him in Berlin and Fisher's daughter and Hamlin were waiting in London for the next Hamburg flight. However, not one of them would begin to guess where to look and by the time they did he would have collared Fisher and put him back on the London plane.

A scrawny young man took the seat beside him and ordered a beer, drank it quickly and left. Blount glanced at the copy of that morning's Bild Zeitung that he had forgotten on his chair, hidden by the table. Picking it up, he looked around. At that moment, he noticed the scrawny man watching him from the corner of Joachimstaler-strasse, then nod. Blount ran an eye over the headlines and turned to page two. Half the simple crossword had been done, but without reference to the clues. He read the words PLANTERWALD ACHT UHR. It gave him two and a half hours to cross into East Berlin and meet his contact. But before he kept that rendezvous he had his own small pilgrimage to make. Leaving the café, he strolled up and down the broad avenue of the Ku'damm window-shopping, rubber-necking buildings like the Europa-center and the Memorial Church. Nobody appeared to be tailing him. But in West Berlin who could say that for certain? To reassure himself, he caught the underground to Charlottenburg and made two changes before boarding the S-Bahn elevated railway to take him across the Friedrichstrasse check-point. At that station, his British passport took him past the *Vopos* without difficulty. He got down a few minutes later at Unter den Linden.

As he walked up towards the Wall, a platoon of East German guards goose-stepped past him halting at a memorial for Nazi victims to leave sentinels there. He watched them, perplexed. How like the SS he had seen parade along the same splendid thoroughfare! On the Wall, the miradors flared in the twilight, their stilts appearing to march against the background of moving clouds; in their dun-grey uniforms, *Volkspolizei* patrolled the dead area between the Wall and houses, machine-pistols in one hand and the leash of an Alsatian in the other. Blount turned away and strolled down the dismal avenue – once the heart and soul of old Berlin – hurrying past the white façade of the Soviet Embassy, then the faceless glass-and-concrete Palace of the Republic at the bottom.

Blount had not seen East Berlin for thirty years, since the day he had passed through the Brandenburg Gate and flown to Britain with a Canadian passport and a whole new background that they had invented for him month after month. So much so that he believed himself a Canadian citizen, although he had spent no more than nine months in Canada. No-one in Toronto had questioned the pedigree of a small-town Canadian of German origin who had trained as a printer in Edmonton, Alberta, and who had come to work as a compositor on the Globe and Mail. He had all the right skills and papers, including a valid union card. Eventually, he would have gravitated across the border to his real job in Washington had they not recalled him for special duty in England. Fisher had just arrived there and needed somebody they could trust to act as go-between as well as help him build up his magazine organization. Over the years, Blount realized that he could have had worse assignments, even if Fisher did prove a handful at times.

Now back in Berlin, he recalled his last weeks there as a soldier at the end of the war. Hardly a house intact and anybody walking through the rubble, the bomb and shell craters, stepped warily lest a wall toppled on them. Or a forsaken land-mine exploded and added them to the debris still stinking of death. What a difference these days! He looked up at the long sunlight spangling from the tops of tall blocks of flat, hotels and shops around Alexanderplatz, the centre of East Berlin. Those spelled progress. Like the wide sweep of Karl-Marx Allee and other boulevards radiating from the series of squares and showplaces. A slight regret though, that it had nothing of the organized panic of West Berlin, nothing of its colour and movement, nothing of its variety. People here looked as serious and dull as those great Marxist-Leninist tomes like museum-pieces in glass cases by the entrance to the square.

A quarter of a century had tempered Blount's idealism, his worship of such doctrines. A pragmatist, he observed that these people were not only less affluent and less happy but also less free. In Britain, that freedom had allowed him and Fisher to act as spies for more than a quarter of a century; at first he had considered it as laxity, as spineless decadence in the capitalist democracies; now he realized it formed part of their strength and their vitality. Build walls round people and preach one doctrine and you finished with a race of robots or slaves. Intelligent and shrewd, Blount realized that the Soviet Bloc had emerged from the war with none of its great inventions to its credit – the atom bomb, radar, the jet engine, the rocket, the electronic calculator, the tape-recorder and other things. Why? Because of the high fences Stalin had erected round the Soviet Union and its researchers for more than twenty years. It was to make good all this lost ground that men like himself and Fisher had been recruited and trained to spy. Yet he acknowledged that, without such barriers sustained by an élite party and buttressed by its secret police, the Communist system would have eroded and crumpled.

Blount ruminated all this as he walked north-west, away from his rendezvous point towards the Pankov district. Boarding a bus, he rode half a dozen stops, dismounting at Breitestrasse, then walking west through familiar territory. No fluorescence here. No modern buildings as in Alexplatz or Marx-Engelsplatz. No aura of opulence. Just a murky light to show the slums of the working-class sector. Heiner-strasse stood as he always remembered it with a shudder. A terrace of burned and blasted brick, patched after the blitz but still disclosing peeling doors and grimy curtains. He'd been born there and had left primary school when the war broke out. Had he returned, he'd have finished like these people, toiling in the foundry machine-shop, making cylinder blocks or castings for tractors or trucks. Or some other cretinous task. But the Party – God bless it! – had reached out and rescued him after the war, given him free education in the Karl-Marx University, Leipzig, teaching him their version of history and languages. Only when they posted him to the SSD (*Staatsicherheitdienst*) spy school near Dresden did he appreciate why they'd chosen those subjects.

Number Nineteen Heinerstrasse matched his recollection of it. In the past five years they'd given the doors and windows a lick of paint; in the front room, giving on to the narrow pavement, a blue electric glow shone and a TV accent resonated. Memory filled Blount's nostrils with the smell of lung and noodle soup and the damp reek of wet clothing drying by a coal fire and the week-end tang of beer on his father's breath and the yeasty, heady smell of napfküchen at Christmas and other feast days.

He marched on quickly. Too quickly. At the end of the street he turned and headed south. His parents had died in the bombing or the invasion of Berlin and all his past links had gone with them. However, he felt glad he had performed that small pilgrimage; it taught him how lucky he had been to serve his time in easy circumstances and decent surroundings instead of rotting away in murky streets like these. He had no wish whatever to resurrect his past.

If Fisher had only thought and felt the same way! Blount did not understand what could happen to make a man who had everything – a lovely wife, a son and daughter, a big house and a fat bank account – suddenly want to plunge back into a personal history probably no better than his own. If the man experienced qualms like himself surely he could suppress them, bottle them up! He wondered what sort of training they'd given Fisher. His indoctrination must have been faulty somewhere.

By the underground and *S-bahn* stations at Schonhauser Allee, he entered a state restaurant, dingy, ill-lit room redolent of the astringent odour of sauerkraut; they served the menu, a vegetable soup with a greasy iridescence, a pork chop with an inedible crust of hard fat, and flabby strudel. After this, he took the elevated line to Ostkreuz and crossed the bridge to Treptower Park. A ruby aircraft-warning light blazed on the massive monument to the Soviet dead during the Battle of Berlin giving him his direction. He marched quickly down the main track to the Planterwald Restaurant.

As he entered, a man rose from a table near the door. Although he had not seen him for thirty years, Blount recognized Bartels who had trained with him at Karlshorst, a couple of miles away. Following him upstairs, he wondered if he'd worn half as badly as this grey-haired SSD chief with a face like a burnt-out cinder. They entered a small, private dining-room panelled in pine; on the bench seats at its massive table sat two other men. Bartels introduced Blount without naming him, as their man from London; he did not name either of the strangers. A waiter wheeled in a trolley with bottles of beer, slivovic, vodka and schnapps and locked the door behind him. Blount had a few moments to study the two men. About the younger one he had no doubt – a die-stamped product of the SSD school of recent date. He must have suffered from alopecia totalis, for his hairless head shone like a ball-bearing; his blue eyes had a curious albino transparency as they seemed to stare through Blount. Their immobile, half-closed lids gave them a sinister glare. As for the second man, he must have measured nearly two metres judging by the level of his head against the panelling. He had grizzling hair, a thick moustache with brown snuff-marks on it and an impassive look on his broad face. He looked much too serene for an SSD man and Blount would have reckoned him a doctor or a technician.

"Tell us everything about Fisher, leaving nothing out," Bartels said. "Start from the beginning of his crisis."

Blount went back six months to the moment he himself had noticed Fisher go off the rails. Every few minutes, either the bald-headed young man with the hatchet face, or the older man would halt him to put a question or clarify a point.

"These two women you say he murdered," the older man said. "Describe them." And he noted minutely details of their face, hair, figure, age and background; he cross-examined Blount like a prosecuting counsel about Fisher's circle of friends, about Roger's girlfriend, about Fisher's disappearances and his spells of amnesia. As much as

Blount knew or could assume about Fisher's family history went into the notebook. This big man gave him the impression that Fisher was some rare lab specimen rather than a human being, a fine piece of mechanism that might have seized up temporarily with sand or grit. When they had spent more than two hours quizzing him he felt wrung out like a floor-cloth.

They poured him half a tumbler of brandy, then ignored him; the older man immersed himself in his notes, reading and annotating, murmuring to himself while the younger one fixed a beer stain on the table with his dead eyes. Finally, Bartels said to the tall man, "Well, Herr Doktor, what do you think?"

"I hardly think it's serious enough to worry people at headquarters. He's had a lapse in his conditioning and some of his mental blocks have been breached. But we can reinforce his conditioning and reinstate the blocks before sending him back."

"But if he finds out who he really is," the younger, bald-headed man put in.

"We'll have to convince him he's wrong."

"How?"

"By the same psychological methods that we used before and which I needn't elaborate here." He glanced over his spectacles at Blount as he made the statement.

"And if he still won't be convinced?"

"I don't think you need worry," the doctor said.

"I am. Let's say he resists your methods."

"Then that would be up to you and your organization." He shrugged his shoulders. "It would cease to be a medico-psychological problem."

Bartels interrupted their discussion to put a question to the doctor. "Do you think he can find his way back to where he started?" he said.

"I doubt it. He'll be the first of that intake if he does." He grinned, fished in his pocket for a snuffbox and took a pinch, then grinned. "Or any other intake for that matter."

"But we'll have to watch him," Bartels said and the doctor nodded.

Blount wanted to ask what exactly they had done to Fisher to train and indoctrinate him; it sounded highly scientific and somewhat inhuman; but from the faces of the two SSD men and the doctor he knew better than to betray inquisitiveness, so he held his tongue.

"I wonder what would happen if he did," Bartels mused aloud.

"Simple," the younger man murmured. "We'd have to take care of him." That hard edge to his voice and its low pitch made his meaning clear to everybody.

Sixteen

She drank her coffee, wrapping the fingers of both hands round the cup as though to warm them and looked at Fisher, the corners of her eyes crazing slightly with the effort of framing an answer to his question. "Why did I think you were Wilhelm Friedrich Müller?" she repeated. "Because, except for one thing, you look exactly like an older version of him."

"And what was that one thing?" Fisher said.

"He smiled a lot ... in fact he laughed."

"Young people laugh too easily," he replied.

She burst out laughing. "That's what I meant," she said. "What's your name?"

"Glaser ... Ursel Glaser." She glanced at him quizzically. "It doesn't mean a thing to you, does it?"

He studied her face meticulously, straining for some focal

point of remembrance, then shook his head and said, "No, and I don't see how it could. I've spent no more than a few months in Germany and haven't been here since 1953."

"But you speak excellent German – even with a bit of our Brandenburg accent."

Unconsciously he must have lapsed into German. "I had a German mother," he lied, warning himself to watch what he said. "I prefer to speak English."

"Well, I can try," she smiled. "I used to teach it at the local school."

Her intrusion and her questions had disturbed him, knocked him slightly off balance, and he almost blurted out that he had known a William Miller who might be the same man. But the coincidence seemed too far-fetched, so he checked his tongue. Yet he had begun to ponder whether in studying the map his subconscious eye had lighted on the name Schonebrücke and that word matched some latent memory; then almost despite himself he had turned off the road, lured by that name. It gave him an eerie feeling in his stomach. Ursel finished her cigarette, drank another mouthful of coffee, murmured an excuse for having badgered him and was rising to leave when he stopped her. "Look," he stammered, "you've got me interested in your Wilhelm Müller and you haven't answered my second question – what happened to him?"

"He left here as a soldier in 1944 at the age of eighteen and he was reported missing, believed killed, on the Russian front."

"But you obviously believed just the missing bit," he said.

"Stranger things happened during that war," she muttered gravely. "I just had the feeling that he was alive somewhere and might come back home one day to see what changes had taken place." She smiled wistfully. "I thought perhaps he might have been badly wounded, or ..."

"That he'd lost his memory," he prompted and she nodded.

"How old were you when he left?"

"Nearly fourteen," she said, her face creasing sadly.

That made her forty-seven or forty-eight, he calculated. At that age she looked well-preserved, her skin had a healthy bloom and her eyes sparkled and had an opalescent fleck in their irises that intrigued him. And her voice had that low, throaty quality that he liked. She was talking again.

"Willi used to deliver our papers and morning bread when he was on his way to school ... and he'd carry my schoolbag," she said. "Then he went to work in the saw-mill just outside the town. I used to cycle that way to school and we'd wave to each other." She glanced at him, smiling. "I suppose you think remembering things like that is very foolish."

"No," he said, solemnly. "Memory's the only thing that really counts."

"When he left for the army I cried for days," she whispered. "And I couldn't tell anybody why. They'd have laughed at me, a schoolgirl with a crush on a young soldier. That's why when I saw you ..." Her flecked eyes travelled over his face, pensive. "Maybe I just wanted to believe you were Willi, though you could be his twin brother."

Ironic, Fisher thought. Her past clung to her like a ball and chain she could never sever while he had no history that he could remember clearly, or even feel with his five senses. Not even a shadow. Here they sat in a German village that he had stumbled on – or had he? – and was creating strange resonances in his mind as they chatted about a man named Müller.

"Are you married?" he asked.

She nodded. "Glaser's my own name. My husband's called Sänger and he has a law practice in the town."

"Children?"

"Two – a son and a daughter."

"Like me," he said. He introduced himself, filling in his background and the reasons for his trip through East Germany.

"But this is well out of your way," she exclaimed. "How

did you manage to land in Schonebrücke?"

"I must have lost my way and taken a wrong turning," he replied. But his excuse lacked conviction and she sensed this. When he reconsidered it, his statement had symbolic overtones for his own life. "Anyway, now that I'm here I wouldn't mind having a closer look at the place."

"There's not much to see."

"Would it be imposing too much on you to ask you to be my guide?"

"No, I'd love to." She explained that her husband had a case to plead in Tangermünde and her children were both away, the son studying medicine in Humboldt University, Berlin, and the daughter doing art school in Brandenburg. "Where shall we start?" she asked. "At the school?" A sort of tacit complicity had developed between them; she would indulge her nostalgia by showing him what she wanted him to see and guessing what he himself wanted to see – the Schonebrücke of Wilhelm Friedrich Müller. Following her directions, he drove the half-mile to the school but she suddenly stopped him on the way. "That's the sawmill I told you about," she said. To him it looked like any other small sawmill with planks and pitprops and trimmed logs in criss-crossed piles and an open hangar echoing with the whine and rip of the saw. "Herr Pohlmann who used to own it died not long after the community took it over," she commented.

Pohlmann? Pohlmann? He was dying to ask if the name fitted a red face, a pot-belly and a ham fist that had left its mark on his cheeks and ribs more times than he could count. Somehow that name had pervaded his mind with the resinous smell of new-cut pine logs. Banging home the gear-lever, he accelerated away so fast that he jolted Ursel back in her seat.

Only one part of the school remained from before the war; new chrome-and-concrete classrooms had burgeoned round the original primary school, a grey sandstone building with a bell-shaped tower. "I taught there until my first child came," Ursel said, pointing to the turreted structure. She led the way inside, saying it was a half-holiday.

In each classroom, Fisher stopped for several minutes, studying the desks and the dais and blackboard, even feeling them with his fingertips; from each window he scanned the landscape. Every room had that smell, familiar in every school he had known, an indefinable odour of carbolic soap and lysol disinfectant and powdered ink and chalk. Through one tall window he gazed at the skyline with its beech and birch copses and, to the left, a curious land pattern formed by three hills. "They call it The Sleeping Beauty locally," Ursel said. He saw it did have the shape of a naked woman, asleep. Casually, he sat down at one of the desks to see how the horizon appeared from there. He could swear that he had already seen that outline, framed as it was in the window. Another notion struck him. He could not possibly have come this way all those years ago! Ursel approached the desk in front of his, running a pointed nail over three letters gouged on the lid. W-F M. "Willi had this desk," she said.

"What age would he be in this class?"

"Between ten and eleven."

They returned to the town. He had to admire the monument to Kapitän Johannes Webel, local hero of the Franco-Prussian War, visit the oldest timber-framed house, step inside the baroque town hall, its seventeenth-century paintings replaced by portraits of Lenin flanked by Walther Ulbricht and Leonid Brezhnev. "Are you a communist?" he asked.

"As much as I was a Nazi," she replied.

On the way to the church she halted the car. "That's where the Müllers lived," she muttered. He looked at the cottage with a main door bracketed by two windows and a small garden patch surrounded by a wooden railing. He felt her scrutinize him and wondered if his face betrayed his confusion, or the fact that he could have described the interior of that house – yes, down to the ornate, white porcelain stove with its kinked pipe and the old-fashioned kitchen-range and the flower-patterned wallpaper in the mansard room overhead where he had slept until he had volunteered to try to save the Fatherland. His eyes pricked with tears and he fumbled in his pocket for a cigarette. Ursel handed him one of hers. Only when he felt the rasp of the tobacco on his throat did he realize that he had never smoked before. He tossed the cigarette out of the window. "When did they die, Müller's folk?" he said, keeping his tone conversational.

"His father ten years ago and the mother eight, but I don't know the exact dates. If you're interested you'll find them in the churchyard where we're going next."

Fisher drove on. "Did you know the Müllers?" he asked.

"I used to visit them about weekly," Ursel replied. "They never got over the loss of their son."

"He didn't write from the Eastern Front?"

"Yes – regularly until January 1945. His last letter came from Insterburg in East Prussia a few days before it was overrun by the Russians. Then they heard he was missing, presumed dead."

Her voice had a slight catch and he asked no more questions until they turned into the forecourt of the church; of its red-sandstone façade, tower and spire he remembered nothing; its plain interior looked like any Lutheran church he had ever visited. Ursel led him to the graveyard where a marble headstone bore the names of Walther Friedrich Müller and Ilse Becker Müller; in front it had rose-bushes and a fresh bunch of cut carnations. "I put flowers there when I tend my own parents' grave," Ursel said.

Fisher was making an effort of will to recall the two people who lay under that headstone; but his mind would not concentrate, switching on and off like some accident warning beacon. In rapid flashes he saw his father in worker's smock, chopping wood, smoking his pipe and reading the newspaper; then both his father and mother in black Sunday best in church; a glimpse of her with a shawl over her shoulders fetching him from school as an infant, or bending over the old kitchen-range or weeding among her vegetables in the back garden. They both seemed cerebral abstractions of human beings. But, if they were, why should this deep, nameless sadness fill his mind, compress his chest and tighten his throat as though in a vice? He must have slipped, staggered and begun to lose his balance, for suddenly Ursel was gripping one arm and supporting his body with her shoulder and other hand. "Do you feel all right?" she said, lapsing into German.

"Yes, I'll be all right," he replied in German before he could stop himself. "I've had a long day, that's all."

Ursel pointed across the valley to a villa on the hill about a mile away. "I live over there. I can make you some tea before you have to continue your route." He hesitated, wondering if he could trust himself to accept, then nodded. She took his hand and led him to the car which she now drove.

Her house, a modern bungalow built three or four years ago, had six rooms, two of them in its steeply-pitched roof; its elegant but comfortable pinewood and upholstered furniture reflected Ursel's appearance and character. She sat Fisher on a sofa and went to the kitchen to make tea. When she returned, he saw that she had removed her costume jacket as well as her coat and boots; in that blouse and flared skirt and fashionable shoes, she looked very pretty; she had the sort of slender and lissom figure that appealed to him ... His mind was still attempting to recapitulate what he had observed and sensed that afternoon; yet the harder he tried to distinguish reality from his reverie, the more bewildered he became. His perplexity must have been inscribed on his face, for Ursel deflected the talk away from the Müllers into chit-chat about the village as she poured and handed him a cup of tea. As he drank the tea, almost involuntarily he blurted out, "Do you have a picture?"

Ursel rose and disappeared into what looked like a study

to return with an album. She took a seat beside him on the sofa and opened it. "This belonged to the Müllers," she explained. It contained the sort of portraits people had commissioned for their weddings and other big occasions, serious and posed studies under artificial lighting and snapshots in black and white and colour. Neither of Müller's parents coincided with Fisher's recollection of them in the graveyard, although in some snaps he seemed to identify a feature or two and an attitude.

But when Ursel flipped over the leaves he saw instantly why she had accosted him in the café. His own face seemed to stare out at him – through schoolboy eyes, then in the Hitler Youth uniform, then that of the Wehrmacht. He laughed, as Ursel said. That apart, some things about the face had not changed; the ears, the slight chin cleft, the nose and set of the eyes looked like his. "I wonder what really happened to him," he said finally.

"I'd give anything to know," she murmured. "I used to lie awake at night wondering how much he had suffered and if he had died, how he had died, or whether he had been taken prisoner and had gone astray somewhere in Russia after the war."

"You loved him very much, didn't you?"

She gave an almost imperceptible nod. "I loved him when I was young enough to know what pure love is."

"It doesn't wear off or alter."

"No, it hardens with the years."

"Nothing can stand against it."

"No, nothing."

They might have been talking about the remembered image of the dead as well as pure love, he thought. "And yet, if you could go back and start all over again ..."

"Nobody can go back and start again and, if they could, I wonder if it would be wise." Her voice had an infinitely sad ring.

Twilight was filling the valley but they sat there, side by side, as though loth to break the spell by moving.

Eventually, Ursel put out her hand to grasp his and he turned to gaze at her and, even through the dusk, saw that her cheeks glistened with tears. Instinctively, he placed an arm round her to comfort her and felt it tingle as it brushed her neck. At that moment he realized how much he desired this woman, even though she bore little resemblance to his ideal, Jane. Reacting to the pull of his arm, her head came to rest on his shoulder and she began to caress his hand with the pads of her fingers. Abruptly, that physiological fear gripped him, that primordial panic that cancelled every other feeling in him. It was the sort of dread that a drowning man must feel when going down for the third time, knowing that he will never break surface again. And yet his hand was undoing the button of her blouse as though he were daring himself to go through with an act of love that would send pleasure surging over him, too.

Her breast felt firm, its flesh swelling, its point hardening under his touch, while her body yielded. He felt the blood pulsing in his temples and behind his eyeballs and his heart hammering so hard that it seemed likely to burst his chest as he brought her head round with his other hand and kissed her. Then he thrust her back on the sofa, pinning her head with one hand and tugging frantically at her blouse and skirt with the other.

Ursel had remained passive, lulled into compliance by the mental shift that her meeting with this man had provoked; she could almost imagine that the man she had loved as a girl had returned when he put his arm round her and began to fondle her. But the brutal force with which he twisted her neck round the crude kiss ended her romantic reverie. The Willi Müller she loved could never have done this. When he rammed her down into the sofa and crushed her with his body, she knew he was going to rape her. And, looking at his eyes even in the half-light of the room, she saw something else – the lethal glitter of a predatory animal at the moment of its kill. Summoning all her strength, she tore at his arm which encircled her neck and began to flail with her other arm at his face and kick with her legs. He had ripped her skirt away, but she managed to lever his other hand and arm away from her throat. Enough to draw a breath and scream at the top of her voice in German, "Nein, Willi Müller. Nein, Nein, Nein!" Her shout seemed to take a second or two to penetrate before she felt his body slacken against hers; then she saw him shake his head, like a dog coming out of the water.

"I'm sorry, Urssi," he muttered in German. He pushed himself off the sofa and stood up. "Forgive me. I didn't know what I was doing." He leaned over and kissed her on the cheek, then groped and blundered through the dusk-filled room and out the front door.

Ursel listened to the sound of the VW racketing away from the house and fading down the valley. For about twenty minutes she lay on the sofa in the darkness, still shaking off the nightmare and wondering what demon had possessed that quiet man to make him try to rape and probably murder her. What had stopped him? He had reacted to the name, Willi Müller. Then he had called her by the diminutive of Ursel, something she had not heard for thirty years. When she had recovered, she rose, switched on the light and fixed her clothing. Fisher had departed so abruptly that he had left behind some of his notes. They meant little, a few English jottings about the village and what he had seen and done. But the writing struck her as familiar; only a German brought up on Gothic script would have formed the letters K and H like those. Stepping into the study, she found the packet of Willi Müller's letters that his parents had left her with other belongings. As she scanned the notes and the letters, comparing the writing, she had no doubt that they had been written by the same hand, even if maturity had altered and refined the writing of the man who had just driven away. So, he must be Willi Müller – even though he himself appeared to doubt his whole identity. Sadly, she put the things away. Well, there was no going back, not when a whole world of time and space had separated two people like them.

Fisher cursed himself as he drove back through the village and regained his route. Had he kept his head, he might have found out so much more about Müller. Even now, so soon after the events, he had difficulty recalling just what he had done and seen. For half an hour he drove like a robot, his eyes fixed no farther than the yellow light fanning ahead of him on the empty road. But soon he felt so weary that his eyes began to lose their focus and several times he literally had to pluck the left-hand front wheel out of the verge – on the wrong side, the British side, of the road. Long before he reached the main road he had abandoned earlier that day, he drew the car to a halt in the middle of a forest, found a clearing and drove into it. He snapped the front seat back, pulled his heavy coat over himself and in a few seconds had fallen into a sleep so profound that he appeared drugged.

Seventeen

As soon as Maclean stepped into the terminal building at Munich airport, he recognized Dr Werner Gaedmann as the man who had given the conference paper on The Rôle of Operant Conditioning, Programmed Learning and Environmental Factors in Behaviour Control. Only a Teuton would have constructed such a title. Yet Gaedmann seemed the antithesis of the blond Aryan; he had a short, squat body and a square face with muddy, brown eyes, a snub nose and oily hair. His palm squelched with nervous perspiration when Maclean shook his hand. Gaedmann looked scared. "I don't like this," he muttered. "I don't like it." Maclean quick-stepped after him to the car-park and the beige Mercedes which he drove like somebody fleeing from his own exhaust fumes. "If they found out," he mumbled several times, more to himself than Maclean.

"They?"

"Either side. You don't understand."

"That's why I'm here," Maclean snapped.

"I don't know if he'll say anything, or even see you." Gaedmann mopped his sweaty cheeks with stubby fingers that fingerprinted the wheel of the Merc as he swung down Lindwurmstrasse and took the road south-west. Evidently he did not feel like conversing, for he tuned into a pop-music programme on the radio and boosted the volume. So Maclean watched the farming country flash by before they began to climb into low, wooded hills. On the southern horizon, the snow-capped Bavarian Alps scalloped the blue sky. After half an hour they entered a valley filled by a vast lake which Maclean identified as the Starnberger See; a steamer was making for a jetty halfway along the shore. Gaedmann turned left along the road running due south by the lakeside; for perhaps fifteen kilometres he continued before braking to a halt and switching off the radio. "He has made one condition," he muttered. "If you want to talk to him you must do the last kilometre blindfolded."

"I'm willing."

Gaedmann did the job professionally, binding a cotton cloth round Maclean's eyes and head, then fixing this with strips of surgical tape so that he had no chance of peering out of the corners. From the gear changes, the car note and its rolling motion, he assumed they were climbing a winding road. Quarter of an hour and they stopped. Gaedmann came round, helped Maclean descend and guided him over three steps and a gravel path, then through a door, along a corridor and into a room where he removed the bandage.

Maclean blinked in the artificial light. They had closed the wooden shutters on both windows to prevent him from remembering or identifying any of the countryside; nothing in the room gave him a clue about the occupants of the house; it was a nondescript study with a kneehole desk, three chairs, two wooden filing-cabinets and bookshelves cladding three of its walls. Behind him the door opened and Gaedmann reappeared with another man who wore tinted glasses and had covered his head with a Basque beret. "This is Dr Maclean, the friend of Professor Ernst Linder that I spoke to you about," Gaedmann said. Neither man made any attempt to complete the introduction. Maclean placed the man in his early fifties; he had an undershot chin and a pronounced neck twitch and moist, bloodshot eyes. Not the first psychiatrist Maclean had met who found it difficult to live with his neurosis.

"I must thank you for allowing me to see you," he said. "In fact to consult you."

"I only agreed because I was interested in this – what would you call him? – patient of yours," the German replied in guttural but good English. "Can you explain what has happened to him?"

Maclean produced his case-notes, reduced to a couple of typed folios, from his leather folder and handed them to the German psychiatrist, who sat down at the desk and read them carefully three times before returning them. "It is as I imagined," he murmured. "One of their men who is trying to find his way back and recover his identity."

"What happened to his own identity?"

"It was simply erased from his mind and replaced by another man's," the German replied in matter-of-fact tones.

"I realized they had made a switch."

"How? This man, Fisher, did not tell you, did he?"

"No," Maclean replied. He explained that he had discovered discrepancies when comparing the present Fisher's fingerprints with some taken more than thirty years ago from the original Fisher.

"You may have proved the difference, doctor. But can your patient? That is the question."

From his leather wallet, Maclean produced a blown-up passport photograph of Laurence Hallam Fisher taken in 1953, the newspaper pictures of the same year and some more recent ones. These he spread on the table to point out the small, physical disparities between the pictures of the original Fisher and the man who was now masquerading as him. "I'm not really interested much in the physical side," the German psychiatrist said. "Anyway, 1953 was a long way before my time."

Maclean pointed to the original passport photo. "This man was carried dying into East Berlin in the middle of June 1953 and two months later another man" – he indicated a recent picture – "this one, appears in his place not only acting and talking like Fisher but actually believing himself to be Fisher. How did they do it?"

"It's no miracle. Fisher was a technical and scientific journalist and therefore listed on their files as someone to be watched and possibly subverted and used. By coincidence, the *Staatsicherheitdienst* happens to be training someone who resembles him closely enough to fool people. Fisher, you say, has no family except his mother. Then he obliges them by running into a lorry and killing his mother and himself."

"But to condition a man to replace another one in two months – that's surely something of a miracle, isn't it?"

To answer the question, the defector rose and ran a finger along one of the bookshelves; Maclean saw that he had collected editions of the works of Pavlov, the first man to analyze conditioned reflexes, the American J D Watson, who invented the science of behaviourism, and almost everyone who had contributed to behaviourist science and philosophy, everyone who had written about the techniques of conditioning human action. "You know all these techniques yourself," the German said. "Your man was probably under training for a year or more before the accident. All they had to do was brainwash him in everything about the background and personality of Fisher, the man he was going to impersonate. He already knew all the ideology, all the espionage techniques."

"So, Fisher's a spy!"

"Didn't you know that?" the German asked shooting a puzzled glance at Gaedmann who merely shrugged and looked worried.

"I suspected as much, but never confirmed it since it made no difference to me," Maclean replied. "I look on Fisher as a patient and all I want to do is get him back to England in one piece and treat him there."

For several minutes the German psychiatrist sat bent over his desk folding a bit of paper into a small square and tearing bits off the corners to produce an intricate and artistic pattern which he smoothed out and scrutinized as though it might contain the answer to his problem. At last he looked up at Maclean. "I hope he makes it," he muttered.

"Why shouldn't he?"

Again the German hesitated and went through his paper-tearing ritual. "You've seen aversion therapy at work, haven't you?"

"Worse still, I've had it myself."

"Oh! What for?"

"I was a drunk."

"So, they left a full whisky-bottle and no water in your cell and when you'd emptied the bottle and got drunk they shot you full of apomorphine or antabuse and you spewed rings round yourself and thought you were dying a thousand deaths, and they left you in your own vomit and filth and repeated the procedure for two or three weeks until you couldn't see a whisky ad in a newspaper without feeling sick. Right?"

Maclean nodded. It seemed a crude but fair summing-up.

"Well, multiply that by a hundred and you can imagine the aversion techniques they used in order to teach their spies to avoid traps like liquor and women. When I was at the East Berlin school they had a man called Reiner Eberhardt – a giant all of six foot six or more – who'd been a behaviourist psychologist at one of the biggest mental institutions in pre-war Berlin. He devised dozens of aversion techniques and their opposite for the school."

"Their opposite?"

"Reward techniques. Punishment and reward – as you know, these are the twin pillars of behaviourism. So, the recruits at Eberhardt's school had sickness tablets when they were sinning against the spy manuals and they had happiness pills – what he called Elation Conditioning – when they were doing the right thing."

"And he was turning out not men and women, but robots," Maclean grunted, remembering Fisher's zombie face.

"He had his own term for that – and everything else. It was Affective Homeostasis, a sort of emotional neutrality." He spread his paper pattern on the table and smoothed it with scrawny, yellow-stained fingers. To his astonishment, Maclean noticed that he had fashioned two identical profiles facing each other on either side of what looked like a Grecian urn. Did that hint at the German's thinking – two identical men sharing the same space? He was speaking once more.

"But he was brilliant, our Dr Eberhardt. Probably his Pavlovian training. To test whether his aversion or elation tricks were working he'd put on special film shows. I've seen young men and women vomiting at the sight of Garbo or Harlow being kissed, or fainting, and I've seen the same people walking with their heads hitting the ceiling out of films showing good Communists dying on Nazi bayonets for the Party and Mother Russia. Borge, the Russian spy who operated in Japan, was a big hero."

"Didn't he put on plays, too?" Maclean asked, recalling

those tape-recordings where Fisher mentioned Jane and rehearsals, and the ranks of plays at Sutton.

"Oh, he did better. He put them through rehearsals of the sort of situations they might meet in England or America or France – wherever they might operate."

Now Maclean had the answer to something that had bothered him during his flight that morning. Bleane! The name Fisher had used to book into the Hamburg hotel the previous night and Hamlin had mentioned as he was leaving for the airport. Lord Bleane, one of the characters in Somerset Maugham's Our Betters, his play about upper-crust adultery among the leisured and moneyed classes.

"What did they do – use plays from the London and New York theatre and get their students to act them?"

"No, they took situations from a dozen authors and had one of their tame Marxist writers who'd lived in England and America to rewrite them and bring them up to date. That way they learned the customs and how to handle situations."

"They used quite a bit of Priestley," Maclean suggested.

"That's right. An Inspector Calls and I Have Been Here Before and others." He shrugged and added, "I think they appealed to Eberhardt because they had a sort of schizoid quality, you know characters were there and weren't there and they were stepping out of their context in time and space." Gesturing towards the editions of Priestley and other authors above his head, he said that to make the retouched scenes more realistic they drafted in several actors from the Berlin Schauspielhaus, the national theatre. They took over a big country house with an English look and built real houses for the other sets. When they finished they had the makings of an English village.

Maclean produced a map of both sectors of Berlin and asked the defector to point out where the spy school was. After hesitating for several minutes, the man reluctantly ringed a spot at Schönerheide in the north-east corner of the city. "But you'll be wasting your time if you go there," he muttered. "Since ... well, since my time they've moved it well away from Berlin eastwards and I wouldn't know where."

Maclean realized they had moved the school because of this man's defection. "I'm not interested in the school or where they've moved it. Just describe the place and give me the address." He noted the nearest *S-bahn* station at Buch and the streets leading to the former training camp, then insisted that the psychiatrist give details of the camp itself. From his leathern wallet, he produced the rest of the papers he had compiled on Fisher and the pictures of the dead prostitutes and Elaine Dancy. One by one, the German psychiatrists studied them, then the composite picture Maclean had built from all the others. He shook his head, saying the pictures meant nothing. He had seen no-one like them either inside or outside Eberhardt's school. Yet he lifted the portraits of Elaine Dancy who had triggered off Fisher's breakdown. "I don't know where or when, but I seem to have met somebody like this one," he muttered.

"I believe that this man, Fisher, murdered three women because of some girl he had once loved and who looked like her," Maclean said, pointing to the Dancy portraits.

"He murdered them because he loved someone!" Gaedmann put in. "That sounds a bit fantastic, doesn't it?"

"I mean," Maclean said, "he went searching for women like her thinking they were his ideal woman, his old love. And when he found out they weren't he strangled them."

Both he and Gaedmann turned to the man who had served several years in the spy school; he finished his latest paper pattern, raised his head and shook it slowly. "No, it didn't happen quite like that," he said.

"What made him strangle those women, then?"

"Fear."

"Fear of what?"

"Of being betrayed, or betraying himself."

"I don't follow," Maclean said.

"They considered – Eberhardt and his political bosses who ran the spy school – that the biggest pitfall for the spy was love. Any agent who fell in love not only didn't perform his job properly but he became a danger to himself and his whole network. Love was the greatest threat to his self-preservation. So they used aversion techniques and operant conditioning to build in mental and sensory blocks against love."

"Conditioning powerful enough to make a man kill if he thought he were falling victim to love or making real love," Maclean breathed. He remembered those fragments of comment Fisher made on that tape, saying that his and Jane's love could not resist their tricks and had died. "But they didn't produce this conditioning and mental blocks just with aversion techniques. They must have used something more."

"The same thing that they used to make your patient forget his past, assume the background of another man and really believe he was that man."

"You mean – hypnosis?"

"Hypnosis – but reinforced by drugs and aversion techniques. Electric shocks, deep insulin therapy, horror films, everything that could inspire the fear of death and associate it with love."

"So a person like this man, Fisher, finished by identifying death – his own death – with love."

"That was the idea."

Maclean had wondered about hypnosis in connection with Fisher. He realized that by using hypnosis you could instruct the mind to reject what it had learned and even what the senses had felt; you could inject reams of new mental and sensory data into the mind quickly. And hypnosis, reinforced by behaviourist techniques, would enable them to equip a man with a complete new personality in a few months. That was the 'miracle' they had wrought with Fisher. "It's diabolical," Maclean exclaimed.

"It works," the defector muttered, pointing to the pictures of the three dead prostitutes.

"It works – but it destroyed Fisher, too."

"They'd salve their conscience by arguing that he volunteered for training, motivated by Communist ideology to fight against and eradicate capitalist society."

"But say he changes his mind ... say he's attracted and absorbed by the society he's been instructed to destroy ... say his conditioning begins to break down."

"It shouldn't," countered the German psychiatrist.

"How do you, or anybody else, know when the controls built into him no longer function? How do you know when those hypnotic suggestions or post-hypnotic suggestions will begin to wear off?"

"We don't. But some post-hypnotic suggestions have lasted a lifetime. And I do know that the two men and a woman who tried to break their mental controls and change their way of thought and their allegance finished up in madhouses." He shrugged. "They don't give any of them a return ticket and their way back is booby-trapped with self-destruct mechanisms everywhere."

"And you believe that's what's going to happen to my patient, Fisher."

"It's the only prognosis," the psychiatrist answered drily. He scooped together all the paper patterns, crumpled them into a ball and tossed this into the wastepaper-basket. As though to himself he murmured, "They're caught young, full of idealistic pap and anger ... too young to know what they're giving away ... too young to realize they can't take their own life back and there's no second time round."

Maclean pointed to the photographs of Elaine Dancy. "She started the whole thing because she looked like a character in one of these Communist and capitalist morality plays of yours – a character called Jane. Do you remember anybody of that name?"

"No."

"I believe Fisher came to Berlin to search for this woman

he knew as Jane and whom he still loves."

"If I were you I'd turn him round and go back with him," the psychiatrist said. "He won't find her, and I doubt if he'll even remember her real name."

"Love can't win in this game, you mean?"

His question met with a shrug that made Maclean wonder if they were talking about the same phenomenon. Love wasn't something you practised in bed for half an hour every night and people who thought so were in love only with sex. Love was like faith, either you had it or you didn't. If you did, you accepted the things you loved for what they were. Deirdre had it or she would never have trailed after him into situations like this. Fisher had it, too, for this girl Jane. And he would go through fire, water and any other obstacle to prove his love. This German psychiatrist didn't begin to understand that sort of love.

Gaedmann had begun to fidget and look at his watch. They had talked for more than an hour, but Maclean still wanted to ask the defector so many questions about their methods of indoctrination in their ersatz bourgeois towns and villages and aristocratic country houses; he wanted to ask this man what had induced him to lend his art and experience to such inhuman experiments. However, he knew such questions would remain unanswered, for the West German security services and probably the American CIA had obviously ordered him to hold his tongue. Who knew? Perhaps they used the same methods and did not want them broadcast to less advanced or sophisticated countries!

Once again he submitted to being blindfolded before Gaedmann steered him through the small study door. At his elbow he felt the other man who accompanied them to the front door. There, he heard his voice for the last time whispered, "I'm sorry, doctor, but you're wasting your time ... there's no solution for your man."

Gaedmann drove back with his radio blaring as though Maclean had some hidden microphone to pick up an indiscretion he might make. In Munich airport cafeteria he ate a sandwich and washed it down with coffee while waiting for his flight. He rang Deirdre to inform her he would arrive around 6.30.

She was waiting for him at Tegel when the Boeing 727 touched down. Anne and Hamlin had come with her. "Good trip?" Hamlin asked and Maclean gave a non-committal grunt. Fisher was a patient and on those grounds he did not wish to divulge more than he need. Moreover, he had to think of Anne and the shock she would get if she knew how her father had been programmed like some computer to calculate and behave as a good agent for a potential enemy. But he had a third reason: he did not altogether trust Hamlin and wondered exactly what he was doing taking time off to track Anne's father.

"We missed him along the road," Hamlin said and explained how they had spent the whole of that day from the time they landed in Hamburg. "We've just checked the entry-points and don't think he's crossed any of them into the city yet."

"I hope not."

"Why do you say that?"

"Because I think I know where he's heading."

"Where's that?"

"Somewhere in East Berlin."

"Then hadn't we better watch the check-points across the Berlin Wall?"

"I've already made arrangements with the West Germans on the two main entry-points to let us know."

"But we should stop him," Hamlin protested. "He could get lost in this place."

"He is lost," Maclean said. "And I think we should let him try to find his own way."

"Isn't that dangerous?" Anne asked.

"I suppose so," Maclean admitted, then shrugged. "But your father has a rendezvous with himself in East Berlin, a rendezvous he thinks he must keep. And unless he does his amnesia might get worse until he loses the place completely." He caught Hamlin throwing him a curious glance as they entered the hotel. "I've had enough for one day," he said. "I'm going to eat in my room and go to bed. I'll see you at breakfast tomorrow."

Eighteen

Maclean spent no more than ten minutes in his room. Time merely to study the plans of the underground and elevated railways that traversed West and East Berlin and to scan the street map of that area the German psychiatrist had ringed four hours before. If Fisher did begin to think for himself, he would surely make tracks for his old training school. And he, Maclean, had to get there before him and try to prevent the drama when the man who had become a robot recognized his true identity.

Slipping out of his hotel, he strode along the Ku'damm, crowded at that early evening hour, to the S-bahn station at the zoo. Beyond the ticket barrier after he had bought his ticket for East Berlin, something prompted him to pause and look over his shoulder. There at the ticket office he spotted Hamlin. His coat collar hid part of his face, dark glasses another part, and on his head he wore a cap. As he came through the barrier, he glanced right and left then sauntered to a refuge on the platform.

Maclean kept his head down on his street map, feigning not to see the other man. He had wondered where the men who had followed him everywhere in London had gone. Now he knew why. Clever of them to attach their man to

Anne so that he could keep tabs on all of them. However, it did mean that the East Germans would probably leave Hamlin to take care of him and only step in if he got too troublesome. Better to have somebody you knew than a faceless *Staatsicherheitdienst* agent. He boarded the train and noticed that Hamlin was strap-hanging on the swaying, jolting carriage behind. At the East-West control point in Friedrichstrasse station, Hamlin kept well back. Two policemen gave no more than a look at Maclean and his passport and he boarded the train going east. Once more, he noted Hamlin sprinting for the same train. Changing at Ostkreuz, Maclean took the *S-bahn* to the Pankow where he had to change. Walking along Berlinerstrasse, lit as much by the moon as the street lights, he could hear the other man no more than thirty yards behind.

As the urban-line train took him into the north-east corner of the city, the houses began to thin, broken by parks and new blocks of flats surrounded by playgrounds and gardens. Five stations he counted. At the last stop before the boundary between East Berlin and East Germany, he got down and marched north and west, picking up the streets indicated by the German psychiatrist until he reached the fringe of Schöneheide; here, he cut left to cross a broad road and butt against the railings round a section of open ground. A gate with a sign above it read: Marx-Engels Park of Rest and Culture. According to the notice, it had closed at sunset two and a half hours ago and opened at nine in the morning. Maclean's torch lit a plaque revealing that Walther Ulbricht, secretary-general of the Communist Party of the German Democratic Republic, had inaugurated the park and its People's Palace of Culture and the Becher Museum on May 1, 1965.

So they had turned it into a museum and recreation area. Irony of ironies for someone like Fisher, or the German psychiatrist who knew the real purpose of that building inside the iron railing in the past. Moonlight threw the main drive and two small buildings into relief; but trees screened the central building. Fifty yards to his left, Maclean spotted the tall, tiered façade of a block of flats, its front facing the park. He made for this, but halfway there he stopped to listen. Hamlin was no longer following him! He had certainly left the *S-bahn* station at Karow. Obviously, he had gone to report to his bosses in East Berlin what he knew about the Munich trip and this little excursion into their territory. Maclean wondered if they'd be lying in wait at the checkpoints to detain him in East Berlin until they had grabbed Fisher. He continued his way. In the flat entrance he met no-one so he hoisted his fifteen stone to the sixth floor, crossed to the small window and looked out.

No doubt about it, that building in front of the small lake, and the smaller constructions round it, had once formed the spy school Fisher had attended. With its pillared portico, twin turrets and mansard roof, it vaguely reminded him of Fisher's Sutton house, although that he had only glimpsed in the dark. It also answered the defector's description. A light burned in one of the second-floor windows where, he assumed, the caretaker lived.

When he had seen enough, he retraced his route to the *S-bahn* station. Still no sign of Hamlin. Arriving at the Friedrichstrasse check-point, he presented his passport and visa to the two policemen; they gave him the same impassive stare and gestured him through. He could hardly believe those were West Berlin chimneys flashing past the *S-bahn* window a minute or two later.

Hamlin had returned at eleven o'clock, half an hour before, the night porter told him. Ordering a pot of coffee, Maclean sat down to record the notes on his trip through the Wall and decide calmly what to do about the traitor on their side. If his guess proved right, Fisher must have spent two nights on the road and would reach Berlin next morning; he might drive straight through this sector into East Berlin with his British passport; but he also had a valid visa and might make a detour and enter East Berlin from the East German side. Now that Hamlin knew they had discovered the old spy school, he might have to catch Fisher before he got through the Wall and try to warn him somehow. These thoughts were competing with each other in his head as he finished his coffee and went to the lift.

It took Hamlin several minutes to answer his knock and he came to his door on the fourth floor blinking and rubbing his eyes. "Something up?" he mumbled and Maclean nodded, following him into the bedroom. "What's happened – Fisher come through the check-point?"

"No – but you just have."

"Me!"

"You followed me all the way to Schönerheide, then doubled back to tell your bosses." Hamlin's mouth dropped open and he made to utter something when Maclean cut him short. "It's no good denying it."

"I wasn't going to deny it," Hamlin said. "I was going to explain why."

"You're a spy, aren't you?"

Hamlin shrugged. "I suppose you could say that ... I'm really a special branch detective, but they conscripted me into this business, which, if you want the truth, I don't much care for."

"You mean, you're working for the British secret service!"

"Who did you think?"

"The people the other side of the Wall."

"Shows how good we are," Hamlin grinned. "We wanted it to look that way to everybody, especially Fisher." Crossing the room, he took and lit a cigarette, dragging deeply on it for several moments and studying Maclean's face. "This is breaking every rule in the book, but, since you know Fisher's a spy and you've rumbled me, you'd probably jump to all the wrong notions and wreck the operation." He paused for a moment, then went on, "There's another reason why I'm trusting you to keep your mouth shut."

"What's that?"

"Anne ... she mustn't get hurt."

"I don't see how she can avoid it if people discover the truth about her father."

"All right ... but I meant she mustn't find out everything."

"Everything being that you were using her for your little racket," Maclean muttered.

"That was the worst part of the job, believe me," Hamlin said. "If Fisher hadn't started acting crazy, then disappeared, I'd have turned the whole thing in and asked for my old job back."

"Anne's in love with you, isn't she?"

"I think so ... but it's not one-sided," Hamlin said. "And if she rumbled me I know she'd never forgive me and we'd both wind up among the walking wounded."

"You'd better start from the beginning and tell me everything," Maclean said.

Hamlin pointed him to a chair and sat himself on the edge of the bed. It began, he said, five years after Fisher had arrived back from Germany with his dead mother and started the first of his magazines. An East German agent crossed the West Berlin boundary and sought asylum. Among the spies he had betrayed was a man called Blount – Norman Blount.

"That's Fisher's closest friend and business ally."

Hamlin nodded. He, Hamlin, hadn't joined the game at that moment when the SIS had picked up Blount in London; two counter-intelligence men, helped by a couple of members from Scotland Yard's special branch and the Royal Canadian Mounted Police, marked the whole of Blount's card; they tracked him every step he took in Britain and followed his trail back across Canada. There was a Norman Blount in the Canadian villages and towns with the parents their man claimed as his. Only they were all dead. Blount had been planted in his namesake's dead shoes by the East Germans to operate in North America before they suddenly found more urgent work in Britain. From tagging Blount, they realized he amounted to nothing more than a go-between, a courier who protected the real spy by doing the most dangerous job in the espionage game – keeping contact and passing information.

"The real spy being Fisher?"

"He was the big mystery," Hamlin said. "Not one of us over the years could ever figure how and why an unremarkable, small-time journalist had gone Communist without some close friend or acquaintance knowing or guessing. His mother's background, his own background, his devotion to his mother, his whole story just didn't square with spying for the East Germans and, through them, the Soviet Union. It baffled everyone in the SIS, and still does. But there he was, primed by his masters and a changed man, coming back from Germany to start his magazines with his new wife's money and Communist funds and assistance."

"Why didn't you reach out and nail him then?"

At first they wanted to see how far his operation would go, what contacts he had and what new twist he'd give the oldest racket in the world. They had another motive. With his magazines, Fisher had to establish a network of correspondents, some of them spies. Journalism had always provided one of the best covers for intelligence men and one by one they picked up the half dozen men in the Fisher organization who were not just providing copy for his technical journals but information on everything from swing-wing aircraft, missiles, laser beams and nuclear technology, civil and military, to medical research.

"And you let all this go on!" Maclean gasped.

"There are probably half a hundred spies like Fisher operating in Britain and the USA that we know nothing about," Hamlin said. "If we'd knocked him off, tried and jailed him another two would have sprouted in his place. A known spy who doesn't know he's known can be a priceless asset to his enemies."

"So, you used him."

Without giving the game away to him or anybody in his organization, Hamlin said. They had even set up a technical newsagency to provide copy for newspapers and magazines as a cover; they had trained their own men as journalists to do the job of Disinformation as they put it. In this way, they had succeeded in running double-agents from this press agency, men who acted as informants and part-time spies for the half dozen spies in the Fisher network.

"You were selling them secrets that didn't exist," Maclean said.

"So that they didn't believe the ones that did," Hamlin grinned. "We mixed in a few genuine titbits of information to keep them on the boil."

"When did you come into this business?"

"Just under three years ago. I hadn't been long transferred to the special branch when they called for somebody to help with their surveillance. I didn't like the job much, but at least I learned a bit of rough journalism."

"And Fisher hadn't been in trouble with women until about six months ago?" Maclean asked.

Hamlin shook his head. It had mystified them when he had first cut loose in Mayfair. Higher policy had ordered them to keep quiet about his links with dead prostitutes. Without sharpening the point too finely, they had decided that two or three callgirls could not be allowed to compromise such an important operation. Had the Yard's murder squad arrested Fisher and had he broken down under interrogation it would have ruined years of SIS work. And the intelligence chiefs did not want that.

"You sacrificed not only the dead women, but Fisher," Maclean snapped.

Hamlin objected that he only obeyed orders. For him, the whole Fisher episode had become a complete enigma; a man who acted like a typical English gentleman, who was quiet, dignified, who looked as though a dangerous game like spying was the last thing he'd play, suddenly erupts like a dormant volcano. It floored him. Why? Did Maclean and his psychiatry have any clues or explanation?

"Maybe he suddenly saw through the stupid game he was playing," Maclean suggested, tongue-in-cheek.

"No, there's a lot more to him than that," Hamlin declared. "Something that none of us know and we'll probably never find out."

Not if I can help it, Maclean thought. Only he and a handful of others who were either the wrong side of the Wall or in hiding could give Hamlin and his bosses the answer to their riddle. What they did not realize – and he hoped they never would – was that Fisher, the original one, had ceased to exist, that some nameless volunteer had taken his place.

"What makes you think he'll make for that public park in East Berlin?" Hamlin asked suddenly.

"I don't know," Maclean lied, then almost sub-consciously added, "Why does a hurt animal head for its stamping-ground? Or a salmon swim three thousand miles to its spawning-ground?" As he made the statement, he realized that Fisher was obeying the same sort of instinct in response to his obsession for Jane. Another thought lit up his mind. Love and sickness, didn't they have the same name? Affection. Perhaps that explained some of Fisher's actions.

"I had a word with London before you got back," Hamlin said. "You know who's waiting for Fisher the other side of the Wall – his good friend, Norman Blount. He went through last night."

"With orders to bring Fisher back, no doubt."

"Or kill him."

"Would they do that?" Maclean asked.

Hamlin nodded. "The point is, what do we do?"

Maclean thought for a minute or two. "You and Anne had better keep in touch with the check-points into West Berlin and pick Fisher up if he comes through and let me know the moment he enters East Berlin."

"Where will you be?"

Maclean gave him a boyish grin. "My secretary and myself have decided to make good our lack of knowledge of natural history, or the history of the East German Communist Party, or whatever else they have in that museum I saw tonight."

"Is that where he's making for?"

"If he can find his way back." Maclean turned at the door. "His bosses think he has as much chance of getting there as a man with a white stick in a minefield."

"What do you think?"

"I think they underestimate the man and the instinct that has brought him this far," Maclean said and left Hamlin to ponder that cryptic utterance.

Nineteen

In the forest clearing where he had slept the night, Fisher woke and wound down the VW window. Through the tracery of birch-trees, the fireball of the sun seemed adrift on the morning mist – a red blotch like a bloodstain through a gauze bandage. For several minutes he gazed at the dawn scene that he must have witnessed a thousand times; yet now he felt he was seeing it with a pristine eye. Shafts of sunlight tinted the mist pink and a million sequins glittered from the dew on a spider's web. His eye wandered over the burgeoning branches of birch- and ash-trees and the tall firs; even the snail trails had a beauty that caught and held his gaze. He breathed the pure air and let the breeze caress his face. A magpie was chucking and a black-bird was clearing its throat not a dozen yards away; he felt at one with them and his surroundings. His day augured well. Never could he remember feeling so good; he looked at the scene like a lover regarding his loved one.

Searching in his holdall he found soap, a towel and a safety razor, then plunged through the dripping trees to search for water. Fifty yards away he came on a stream and even in the raw April morning he stripped to the waist and sluiced himself in the icy water that seemed to cleanse him of everything. As he soaped his face he stared at his reflection, observing forgotten or half-remembered things in his face. Had that light returned to his eyes, or had it shone there, unnoticed, for years? It might be the moving mirror, but his brow had a furrow and his lips a quirk that he did not recall having seen recently. He felt hungry. Not social hunger ordained by habit, but the famished sensation of someone who earned his bread by toiling all day. Scooping water into his hand, he drank copiously. Finally, he dressed and made his way back to the car. And as he went, he whispered over and over again to himself: You are Wilhelm Friedrich Müller from Schonebrücke. He could not recollect all that clearly selling his real identity for an ideal and a new name and rôle all these years ago; but surely all this could return to his memory now that he remembered who he really was. He hadn't sold his soul, like Faust! They'd listen on the other side and give him credit for long years of service.

Back behind the wheel, he regained the road and drove east. Several times he halted at a familiar landmark or building to consolidate his new identity. Within an hour he had passed through Nauen without slackening speed, unaware that yesterday he had intended to stop there and make inquiries about the accident in 1953. Another half-hour and he stopped at the Heerestrasse check-point on the West Berlin boundary; he passed the East German guards without difficulty, but curiously the West Germans detained him for half an hour before raising the boom. He could not guess that they were ringing Maclean who had alerted Hamlin to pick up the VW when it passed the check-point. Maclean and Deirdre were leaving for the Schönerheide museum. For a moment they toyed with the notion of shadowing Fisher, but concluded that four people on his tail might arouse his suspicion and alert his masters. Instead, they made arrangements with Hamlin to ring them at the museum with news of Fisher's movements.

Unaware of the fuss he was creating, Fisher drove along the Havel causeway with Hamlin and his daughter behind in their Taunus. Forking right on to the Ku'damm he found a side-street and parked the VW; he wandered to the open-air café at the corner of Uhlandstrasse and ordered a pot of coffee, rolls, croissants, pretzels, butter and honey; these he ate slowly, relishing each mouthful of warm roll or croissant and washing it down with mouthfuls of coffee. When he had finished and paid, he strolled through the early-morning crowd on its way to work, stopping to gawp at the Europa-center and other high buildings that he had never seen, to stare at the traffic surge then halt at the war-riven stump of the memorial church, a reminder of Hitler as well as Kaiser Wilhelm. Its nine o'clock tune chimed. That he had never heard. Jane and he had slipped twice through the Branden-burg Gate to have a look at the forbidden sights of West Berlin; they'd both felt like a schoolboy and schoolgirl playing hooky as they savoured what their commissars in the school dismissed as the Sodom and Gomorrah of the degenerate West. To Jane and himself, its decadence seemed all the sweeter for having been tasted in stolen hours. Love, too, the commissars considered as something depraved; but to Jane and him it seemed pure and clear, like that carillon from the blackened spire.

Until something had poisoned their minds, or someone had driven a stake through their hearts and they had come to hate each other. What had happened to turn everything sour for them? For months after their break he had wondered about that question; he had heard antiphonal dialogue between an insistent voice saying love destroyed what it touched and another voice – his own? – arguing that no-one could really exist without love. But his moral whisper had faded into silence beside the booming, mesmeric tones of his masters. He had willingly yielded himself to them, sacrificing his name and past; he did not realize that he would also forego love and happiness. Until too late.

"*Entschuldigen Sie, bitte.*" Someone barged into him and it took him several bewildered minutes to realize where he was standing amid the swirling crowd on the pavement. After several moments of effort, he remembered leaving his car in Franklinstrasse and he strode back to it. His guide-book told him he must cross the Wall at Checkpoint Charlie. Fumbling and inching across the Ku'damm traffic, he drove to Friedrichstrasse where he joined the queue of cars traversing the barrier. His eye absorbed the sandbags on either side of the allied guardhouse where armed sentries and West Berlin officials were verifying car and personal papers. Planing overhead, the three flags of the USA, France and Britain and a notice warning him that he was leaving the allied sector. Between the booms he saw the watchtower, its open windows framing the faces of two *Vopos* armed with machine-pistols. For a moment, a sort of mindless panic possessed him and his hands sub-consciously jerked at the steering-wheel as though his inner self wanted to turn and flee. But a guard in green tunic was already examining his passport and car papers, the boom swung aloft and he was crossing the dead area between West and East Berlin. On the other side, they gave no more than a cursory glance at him and his papers and raised their red and white pole.

Fisher drove down Friedrichstrasse. He remembered it like a row of rotten teeth, agape with bomb craters and crumbling buildings. At Unter den Linden he turned right. Everything had changed. His skyline filled with curious shapes – chrome-and-concrete cages for people to work and live, a gigantic concrete pencil all of 900 feet high, topped with a striped TV transmitter, to his right the square clock-tower of what he took for the council chambers. One thing alone struck a chord, the stepped and pillared spire of St Mary's Church. Thank God he had not lost the place again!

But, once more, the centre of East Berlin knocked his mind askew. Marx-Engels Platz with its cluster of museums and ministry buildings, Alexanderplatz with its shops and hotels and high-rise flats. He needed something, a touch-stone, a reference point that would orientate his mind and convince him he was on the right track.

At traffic lights it came to him suddenly. The Pieta. Jane and he had come to gaze at it time after time, that painting of Christ's mother holding her dead son on her lap when they had brought him down from the Cross. Didn't the Virgin's expression have something of Jane's sad innocence? Where was it? He drew the car into a side-street beyond the Spree bridge and behind the town hall while he thought. It had to be a gallery on Museum Isle. Which one? They had visited them all. He ruled out the Pergamon, which specialized in oriental art. It had to be the National Gallery, or the Old Museum. He walked back and tried the National but its serried ranks of German painters would never have admitted an anonymous Italian Pieta! Neither the Old nor the New Museums had anything like it. He was about to give up when he saw the old Kaiser Friedrich Museum, its baroque façade like a ship's prow at the confluence of the Spree and its canal. From the moment he entered he knew he had struck the right place. Yet when he bounded upstairs where they kept the Renaissance masters he searched vainly. It had gone. Again he cursed his fickle memory before hitting on the idea of seeking out the curator. That old man scratched his silvery thatch and said, "A Pieta, did you say? In the renaissance gallery? Who by?"

"I don't know ... I mean, I don't think it was signed ... But it was there in 1952 ... I know that for a fact." Impatience and apprehension brought him out in a sweat as the curator bent over his catalogues checking on the various versions of the Pieta they had.

"This one perhaps. A Pieta ascribed to Perugino or to the young Raphael, his pupil. Is that it?"

"I don't know. Can I see it?" A dubious look crossed the curator's features. "It's very important ... it's to help me find someone," Fisher pleaded.

"Wait outside the office," the man whispered and a moment later he joined Fisher in the corridor. "It's very irregular," he said, but thrust aside the Deutschmarks offered him. He led down-stairs to a locked cellar filled with pictures. It took quarter of an hour to locate the painting.

Even in the oily, yellow light from the single bulb, the colours of the anonymous Quattrocento painter glowed. Christ lay slack and heavy across his mother's knees, his mouth a black hole; against the livid flesh and white loin-cloth, the crimson slash on his ribs and marks on his hands and feet seemed to move, to pulsate. If the artist had imagined Christ, he had chosen some nameless Florentine or Umbrian woman to pose the Virgin; she had none of the idealized beauty conventional religious painters sought, but the features and hands of a peasant rendered beautiful by sorrow. Fisher gazed at the face, blanched by the dark hood concealing the hair, the dark gown and indigo sky behind. It had halted him in his stride when he first saw it, and still did. For the Madonna had a face like Jane.

"How long has it been in this cellar?" he asked.

"It hasn't been hung in my time and I've been here twenty years," the man replied.

Buried for more than twenty years. Like his own recollection of it. Yet the wonder was that he had unearthed it at all, after what they had done to erase those memories of clandestine visits to this museum and others with Jane. Above all, to prevent him from remembering her, or even thinking of her. With that Madonna expression surely he could reconstruct her, bit by bit, in his mind and recall everything. Yes, even her name. For her own name wasn't Jane any more than his was Fisher.

However, his masters seemed to have conspired with architects and builders to render his task impossible. Hardly anything he observed as he walked round the city centre seemed the same. He sat for a while in the familiar odour of plush and incense and molten wax of St Mary's church and that reassured him. But, outside, he grimaced at the immense concrete needle of the TV tower, the broad avenue of Karl-Marx Allee, its flats and houses all stamped by some faceless draughtsman in the same mould. Who could pick his way through a concrete no-man's-land like that!

Why should he break stride at Schillingstrasse and at the giant white U on a blue background? Did that underground line lead somewhere? He studied the plan. One way, it ended at the northern suburb of Pankow, the other way at Friedrichsfelde about five kilometres east. Pankow signified nothing and his guide-book told him Friedrichsfelde had a large zoo. That didn't exist in his time, but the name did resonate. He bought a ticket to the end of the line. And like so many signposts from his past the stations reappeared and receded: Strausbergerplatz, Frankfurter Tor, Samariterstrasse, Magdalenenstrasse, Lichtenberg. And finally his stop.

When he stepped out of the tube station he needed no guidance but walked back across the main road to the municipal cemetery on the edge of Friedrichsfelde Park. They had come here, Jane and himself. But why? To visit the Socialist Memorial, that monolith of pink porphyry holding up Marxist heroes? Perhaps. Yet automatically his feet carried him past it and along the rows of stone and marble slabs and headstones decked out with artificial and cut flowers. His eye registered the names, the shape and site of the gravestones. In this vast cemetery with its thousands of graves there had to be one that signified something. But how to stumble on it? For half an hour he prowled round and round before something stirred his memory, pointing him towards the north wall. Scrutinizing each tomb, he finally lighted on it – a white marble headstone capped with a cross inside a circle. There was no mistake. They had chosen the design together from half a dozen standard patterns, and the simple form of words: *Theodor Gerhardt Weber: Geboren 21:5:1889: Gestorben 2:2:1945.*

Jane's real name was Weber. That very surname made his heart leap and brought back other fragments of memory. Jane's father had died in the bombing and artillery bombardment of Berlin during the last months of the war; at that time they could not pay for a headstone, let alone find a sculptor to carve one. They had waited until 1952. Fisher noticed that another name had been chiseled below the father's. *Klara Marie Weber: Geboren 7:9:1895: Gestorben 15:11:1973.* Her mother, whom he had never met. Ivy had crept over the slab and the grave looked neglected. A feeling of sadness overwhelmed him. But this as much as the names and shape of the stone confirmed that he had discovered the right grave.

On his way out of the cemetery, he sought out the care-taker and handed him fifty Westmarks to put some fresh flowers on the grave and trim the ivy. At his insistence, the man sifted through his records which disclosed that the municipality had paid for Klara Weber's burial. "You don't remember if anybody attended the funeral?" Fisher asked. "A young … well, I mean a middle-aged woman?"

"No, but the head gravedigger would." From his office door he bawled to an elderly man in blue overalls. "Hans, do you remember the Weber burial – plot 2348 on the north wall? – Were there any mourners?"

"Only Pfarrer Baumann from the Lutheran Church off Frankfurter Allee with two old men and an old woman." He shrugged. "I mind the day fine … sleet blowing in our faces … Pfarrer Baumann didn't keep us long."

Fisher thanked them and left. Now he had the last address of Jane's mother; he might find the monumental sculptor if he were still alive which might give him Jane's full name and her last address. But perhaps the protestant pastor who had buried Frau Weber knew as much as anybody. When he reached Frankfurter Allee he asked for the Lutheran Church which lay off the broad avenue about a kilometre away. Along his route people were entering the wine- and beer-cellars and the state restaurants. Suddenly he felt hungry. His watch told him it was quarter to one. No good calling on the pastor at that hour. He chose a restaurant called the Deutsches Haus, down a flight of stairs in a cellar with sawdust on the floor. He ate the five-mark menu: potato soup, Wiener schnitzel with fried potatoes and a wedge of insipid cake. Even the beer tasted flat and he had to wait twenty minutes between courses. He did not mind. It gave him time to think without being distracted by the food.

In two days, he had won back some of the past they had stolen, though he still had a long way to go. But he was thinking like Müller just as often as like Fisher. He was sure he could reconstruct all of his past. Especially if he traced Jane. Where and how had he met her? Why did images of a school and a theatre flicker across his mind when he tried to envisage her? Even she appeared in so many different forms that he found it hard to seize on one face, hair style, dress, voice or gesture. Her parents he had never known. Then, he had only a hazy recollection of his own parents. Had they done with Jane what they had done with him – wiped or washed away her past, cut her closest family ties as part of her training to spy? And for what? This greasy, crummy bierkeller and the drab streets and the grim expressionless blocks of flats and showpiece hotels and shops? He would give whatever ideal had compelled him to sacrifice his past, and everything else he possessed, just to know what had happened to her. To meet her and tell her he loved her and hear her say the same of him.

If it cost him everything he would find his way back to where it had all begun. He called for his bill.

Hamlin had followed Fisher into the restaurant to verify that he was ordering a meal. Drinking a beer quickly at the bar, he left and made his way by tube to the town hall and the Berliner Weinstübe where he had arranged to meet Anne. They had considered it too dangerous for her to shadow her father on foot in case he turned and spotted her. Hamlin he had never met.

Anne was eating a hamburger and chips when he joined her and briefly recounted what had happened. "I just don't understand why he's doing all this and why he has this strange meeting with people in East Berlin," she said.

"Dr Maclean thinks it's important for him to go through with this memory test," Hamlin said. "It's obviously something he did or someone he met all these years ago when he had his accident and they brought him into hospital here and he probably thinks he has to clear up something with them." Hamlin cursed himself for dropping too many hints to Anne and changed the subject by asking if she had a number for him to ring Maclean. Yes, she had rung Schönerheide Museum and managed to speak to Dr Maclean, who had given her the name and number of a small cafe a hundred yards from the museum just outside the park. He and Deirdre would eat there and wait for a call between twelve-thirty and two o'clock.

Hamlin noted the number and went to the phone. Maclean listened while he explained Fisher's itinerary and movements, his breakfast and stroll along the Ku'damm, his search through the museums and the long halt at a grave where a family called Weber lay buried.

"What was he looking for in the museum?"

"Some Renaissance painting from what I gathered. Probably something he saw during his convalescence after the accident. They had to ferret about in a cellar for it."

"Nobody has contacted him?"

"No, nobody. They're probably giving him his head. Anyway, why should they if he has a rendezvous your way?"

"True," Maclean admitted. Sometimes he had to remind himself that Hamlin, Anne and everybody except two or three East Germans knew only half the story. To them Fisher was Fisher. "Listen carefully," he told Hamlin. "Don't lose sight of him for a moment. Pick him up at his restaurant and follow him wherever he goes. We'll stay here until closing time."

"When's that?"

"Five o'clock. If he leads you here, park your car to the left of the entrance in front of the first block of flats beyond the main gates and watch the building. We'll join you if we can."

Maclean put down the phone and went back to the table where Deirdre was sipping the muddy concoction they served as coffee. "How's he doing?" she asked.

"Brilliantly – especially in museums and graveyards."

"I wish he'd hurry up and find us," she moaned. "I'm fed up copying meaningless German sentences from the collected works of Lenin and Stalin."

"Give him another two or three hours," he said, helping her to her feet. "Come on, mavournin, we've got to keep those window-seats before they're grabbed by the real proletarians doing real work."

They walked through the iron gates and up the drive to the museum. On the ground floor they had displayed the whole gamut of natural history from protozoa through prehistoric mammals and reptiles to man. By its side beyond the office they had created an agriculture and science museum. Upstairs where Maclean and Deirdre were working they had housed their collection of archives of the German and other Communist Parties with two rooms devoted to the destruction wrought by the Nazis and the allies and the resurrection of the German Democratic Republic. A reading-room with 200,000 volumes completed the museum. In ostensibly searching for the toilets, Maclean had quietly reconnoitred the left wing of the mansion; there, a locked door blocked the passage with a sign reading: Private, Staff Only. He had a suspicion what lay beyond.

As he regained his seat by the window overlooking the main drive, he wondered if Fisher would succeed in leaping or scrambling over those mental barriers to reach this point where they had split off his past and provided him with a new personality and a whole new equipment of knowledge. When Hamlin rang him, he had played with the notion of getting the agent to drop the name Schönerheide in front of Fisher, to hint that his rendezvous lay here. But he ruled out that gambit as cheating. Fisher, or any other man, had to trace his own way back if he wanted to rediscover his real Self. He crossed his fingers that Fisher would.

Twenty

In a side-street where blocks of flats had thrust upwards out of former bomb-holes, Fisher found the Lutheran church with the name of Pfarrer Peter Baumann on the board outside; they had rebuilt it in plum-red brick with an octagonal tower surmounted by a bronze cross replacing the spire. Entering, he walked through the nave, past the simple altar and chancel to the vestry, and rang the bell. A few minutes elapsed before a tall man with a silver blaze in his dark hair came through the door and introduced himself as Pastor Baumann. He offered a chair, apologizing for the clerical robes that cluttered the room. "English, aren't you?" he said.

"How can you tell?" Fisher replied in German which made the minister raise his eyebrows.

"Your shoes and the cut of your suit," Pastor Baumann replied. "You've come looking for someone?"

"Yes, I have," Fisher mumbled, disconcerted by these leading questions. "You held a funeral service for Frau Klara Marie Weber five years ago, didn't you?"

Baumann ran long fingers through the white blaze, thought for a minute, then nodded. "I remember … an old lady who lived alone in one of the homes in Buchholz District, I think. She'd been one of my parishioners until she grew too infirm to attend services. A stroke s'far as I recall. Were you related?"

"No, but I knew her daughter."

"Daughter? Daughter?" He raised his eyes to the slit window. "Yes, you're right. She did often talk about a daughter though I never met her … Paula, wasn't it? … Pretty girl from a picture in her room … Wasn't she studying languages before the war?"

"She had reddish hair, titian hair, didn't she?" Fisher said, interrupting the minister.

"The photo didn't show that … But wait, I think her mother did mention that she and Paula had red hair." He looked curiously at Fisher as though wondering why he should doubt such a thing, then watched him sigh deeply at the answer. "But she died in the Battle of Berlin, I thought … Or was it a road crash?"

"You don't know where she was buried?"

"I see, you're really looking for her grave," the pastor murmured "Sorry, I can't assist. The town hall records would be the best place, wouldn't it?"

"If I had her date of birth," Fisher said.

"From the baptismal records, of course," Baumann said with a smile, clasping his hands together in thanksgiving. "The old ones survived the bomb, praise be." He vanished by a side door to return in several minutes with a thick, leather-bound book. "About what year?" he queried.

"Nineteen twenty-eight," Fisher guessed.

Baumann leafed through the register, running a yellow finger down the names and tut-tutting. "Ah!" he said, raising a finger. "You're wrong. Nineteen twenty-nine. Sixteenth of April."

"And her full baptismal name?"

"I was slightly out. It's Anna Marie Paula Weber."

"Thank you," Fisher said. He rose and put a hand out, but the pastor motioned him to stay.

"I'm beginning to remember something that will save you time," he said. "I don't think there is a grave. I mean, she was never found."

"She went missing during the blitz or the Battle of Berlin, then?"

"That's what they assumed – all except the old lady, that is. She could never believe her daughter was dead. She thought she had been injured and lost her memory, or she'd fled to the Federal Republic and didn't want to cause trouble for her mother by writing or contacting her. So many people just disappeared at that time."

Fisher had fallen silent; he was wondering how long he and Anna Weber, alias Jane, had moved around Berlin on both sides of the sector boundaries without being spotted. "If she had lost her memory and was living here, surely somebody would have recognized her," he said finally.

"Oh, people did say they'd seen her."

"Who? Please try to remember."

Pastor Baumann clutched at a handful of hair, closed his eyes in reflection, then opened them and looked at Fisher. "The mother did tell me a friend had seen someone who looked like her daughter. But it was no more than a glimpse. This man was boarding a train, an *S-bahn* for the city centre, and Fräulein Weber was leaving it."

"Leaving it where?" Fisher almost shouted. "Do you remember where?"

"Blankenberg ... or was it Buch? ... Somewhere in a northern suburb from what I can remember. Near the city limits, I think."

"Nobody made enquiries about her?"

"Yes, I think the old lady did, but she didn't get anywhere. It was difficult a few years after the war."

"What would have happened to Frau Weber's possessions – papers, photographs and that sort of thing?"

Baumann shrugged. "The old lady had virtually nothing when she died ... a few bits of furniture. You know the state paid for her funeral." He thought for a minute. "Papers? I don't really know. They'd go to the municipal records office, but I hardly think they'd keep them."

In the body of the church, somebody had begun to play the organ and its sad, keening notes seemed to echo in Fisher's head like the minister's epilogue on Frau Weber. Thanking Pfarrer Baumann he got up and walked slowly through the church and back towards Frankfurter Allee. Where did he go now? When the concrete pole of the TV tower swung into view, he remembered leaving his car in a side-street near the town hall. A bus took him to the Rathausstrasse and he noticed a policeman standing by the VW; but the man paid no attention as he got into the car and drove off. Pulling into Treptower Park, he stopped to study the guide-book and map of East Berlin and try to plan his next move.

First, he scanned the *S-bahn* line running north-east to the city boundary. Blankenberg signified nothing and Buch not much more. Rosenthal, Blankenfelde, Heinersdorf, Pankow – he let each name of each suburb near that section of the line sink into his head, but vainly. What had the pastor said? Frau Weber's friend was boarding a train from a station on the northern boundary of East Berlin. So, Anna Weber was leaving the train at or near the end of the line. At one of the three stops before the city limits? – Buchholz Junction or Karow or Buchs. Again and again his mind juggled with the names but they might have been Hottentot or Japanese. However, instinct orientated him in that direction. He'd once read that Ysaye, the great Belgian violinist, had forgotten a chunk of a Bach unaccompanied sonata during a performance and, by some muscular reflex, his fingers carried him through the memory lapse; he would do the same, let his senses and old reflexes lead him home.

From where he sat, he reckoned twenty kilometres to Buchs station. But from Pankow station, just down the line from the one the pastor had first mentioned, he had eight kilometres to cover. If he and Jane had frequented that part of the city, surely something would jell in his memory. Turning the car round, he picked up the *S-bahn* line at Ostkreuz and followed it north and north-west into Pankow. At Breitestrasse he should have borne right to pass the old Pankow town hall and follow the railway line; but just before the big crossroads he spotted something that did signify, the signpost to Niederschönhausen Castle. He and Jane had visited that old baroque pile! That signpost pulled him straight on, almost due north. Now the drab streets, the Number Fourteen bus-stops, the crane of a foundry beyond Humboldtstrasse – every one of these features matched his mental pathway as he drove slowly onward.

In the Taunus fifty yards behind him, Hamlin was cursing under his breath, wondering exactly where Fisher was heading. Why hadn't he veered right and aimed directly for Schönerheide? His watch said ten to four. Another hour and Maclean and his secretary would have to quit the museum and park when they shut. And in this ill-lit cemetery of a city they'd probably lose this man at night, if they decided to risk staying this side of the Wall themselves.

Fisher was trail-blazing himself almost unconsciously. Half a kilometre and he'd cross a small bridge, which he did. Another ten minutes and Norden graveyard would heave to on his right. And sharp left he'd see the road leading to Niederschönhausen Castle. However, he wanted to turn north-east into Buchholz district. Would the place still be there? So much had been destroyed and they had built a new school, a police-station and dozens of blocks of flats, hundreds of shops and offices. At Hauptstrasse he turned left. No, thank God! – they'd spared it. Drawing the car up at the iron grill, he dismounted to gaze at the square, two-storey structure with barrack-room proportions between the trees and bushes flanking the main drive. How long had he spent in that billet? A year? Two years? There he had met Anna Weber, alias Jane. Of that he was certain. For how long had they known each other? He could not even guess. It did not worry him how long. A week, a day, even a few minutes would have been enough. Her image flashed across his mind. Her titian hair intensifying the blue of her eyes and her fair skin. And that way she had of wrinkling her eyes and nose and the slight overhang of her upper lip which he could almost feel on his. He could see her plainly, and she was marvellously beautiful.

As he watched, a group of young men in running shorts and vests appeared and jogged towards the rear of the building, the recreation ground in their time; another squad, led by a sergeant-instructor, were doing marching drill by the gable of the building. So they had converted it into a cadet training unit for the East German army!

It hardly mattered. For he could now find his way, blind-fold, to the school. Wheeling the car round, he drove until he met the *S-bahn* line and ran parallel with this for a mile. Beyond Buchs station he turned east and travelled the few hundred yards to the park enclosure. Since he had last seen it, the young chestnut- and birch-trees had matured and hid the buildings inside the grill. He stopped by the information board. Their old headquarters now served the state as a sports centre and a museum – something useful at least. Once through the gate he followed the perimeter road, drawing up where they had constructed part of an English village to lend a more authentic touch to their training. Two cottages, the replica of an English pub and grocery store had converted fairly well into changing-rooms and admin. offices for the soccer, rugby and hockey clubs that used the complex of playing fields. They, too, had learned English games on those surfaces – even cricket and golf. Two Georgian and Victorian houses had gone, their foundations now an indoor swimming-pool and squash court. And they'd knocked together the bank and post-office buildings to use as a gym and indoor athletics track. We played a more sinister game, Fisher reflected, as he looked at all this; but then sport had become a symbol of national prestige and power and ranked possibly with spying.

Amazing how much they had taught him here. How to handle a right-hand drive car on the left side of the road; how to savour tepid beer and discourse on the weather or the league position of Arsenal or Liverpool football clubs; how to wear a bowler hat and carry an umbrella and dance the fox-trot and the Lambeth Walk; how to use the duo-decimal system with its freakish pounds, shillings and pence; he had marvelled then when given English money that a penny bearing Queen Victoria's youthful head (hair done in a bun) could still buy chocolate or sweets or cigarettes or matches at their local store more than a century after being minted. It seemed to symbolize the stability of the English.

On the other side of the main building, the old lodge-house had become several types of church in their day, changing its decor from Anglican, Methodist, Baptist and Presbyterian to teach them about the different sects; sometimes it was transformed into a typical English restaurant with waitresses instead of kellner and English dishes like roast lamb with redcurrant jelly, roast beef and Yorkshire pudding, Cheddar cheese and plum duff by the barrowful. What had they learned about English home-life? Very little, Fisher thought. But then they learned later that their type of spy didn't have a home-life like other people. Or a love-life.

At the bridge over the stream where they had fished vainly, he halted. Anna and he had sauntered along its banks, their shadows tracking them on its sunlit surface. Funny he should remember those quivering reflections. Maybe because they had stripped everything away from him – including his shadow. Like Peter Pan. If he and Anna met now what would they have to say to each other? Hadn't Heracleitus said nobody stepped twice into the same stream? Could anybody – even those lucky people with their minds intact – retrace their way after all these years? Turn your back on the future and it clubbed you over the head or kicked your backside.

By the museum entrance he left his car and mounted the steps. They had changed the entrance hall, but the massive oak staircase remained, its upper half forking to serve both sides of the vast mansion. Upstairs in their day they had lecture rooms and those cubicles where they stuffed English, French and Spanish into you as they might force-feed hunger-strike prisoners or geese, and they initiated you into the techniques of gathering and passing information, of network-building, of establishing yourself in a new country as a model citizen above suspicion.

In the other wing of the mansion lay the first-floor rooms that even at this remove in time provoked an involuntary shudder in him when he recollected his experiences there. *Die Hexenkammern* (Witches' Chambers) they dubbed them. That was where they had confiscated his mind, his personality. There they could make you sing with joy or scream with fear, they could condition you to believe that cherry brandy was cascara and the reverse, that black and white were the same. With their pills and injections and their own secret psychic sorcery they could bend your mind to accept anything. But by that time he and the others seemed no longer aware that they had been programmed like well-oiled, well-drilled computers, like emotional zombies – people who would make the required response to every conceivable situation. He remembered the small cinema and the feeling of ecstasy at the faces of Lenin or Stalin and disgust at Hitler or Churchill or Roosevelt and Truman. Love, too, became a thing of revulsion and old Garbo and Harlow films literally made him sick. They were clever in the Hexenkammern.

Fisher glanced at the rooms giving off the entrance hall,

noting they had become museum exhibition rooms. In his day they had served for their rehearsals. There, they had staged plays which they imagined represented the British or American ways of life; he had acted his way through bits of Somerset Maugham, Eugene O'Neill, Robert Sherwood, J.B. Priestley, Terrence Rattigan, Noël Coward. He could laugh now at their naïve ignorance of Western society, how they mistook stage shows, or their Marxist interpretation of them, for the real thing. Yet he had pleasant recollections of those rehearsals. If his new memory did not betray him, he had first fallen in love with Anna Weber – Jane in one of the plays – when they were acting in Rattigan's The Deep Blue Sea. Or was it in Maugham? He remembered himself and her laughing at the absurd lines written into these plays by some Marxist author who had spent a year in England and six months in the United States. In the Hexenkammern they fancied they had expunged all memory traces of those rehearsals. Yet his own son, Roger, bore the name of a character he had played. And Anne? He had not completely forgotten Anna Weber. And Lord Bleane and Lord Hartman, two other names he had played. Perhaps after all some remote bit of his brain had escaped their dry-cleaning technique, their reprogramming. Didn't his manor-house at Sutton resemble this one a little? When he had finished it, Ruth and others maintained that their living-room, study and master bedroom looked like something out of a film or stage set. Now, he realized he had copied some of the decor of their plays – Our Betters and The Deep Blue Sea. He could even put faces to Kröner and Reinhardt and other actors they had drafted in from the Schauspielhaus to portray some of the older characters in their rehearsals. They had not completely obliterated his past and replaced it with a synthetic version.

Suddenly, from the high cornices of the entrance hall, antiphonal dialogue reached him – lines from one of the lovers'-quarrel scenes from Noël Coward's Private Lives. When the dialogue ended, two voices continued as though during a break in the rehearsal. His own voice and Anna's:

HE: I wonder if we shall miss each other when we leave this place.

SHE: I shall miss you, darling. Just think, in another three months the course will finish and we'll cease to exist for each other. Old Hartman and his wife will stop being Lord and Lady Osborne or whatever and go back to their theatre. I don't know where I shall wind up and you'll probably be sent to England.

HE: It's the country I'd like to work in, so I'll probably land in Indonesia.

SHE: Pity we can't have a reunion every five years. I'll often wonder what has happened to you.

HE: You'll never find out. Anyway, it won't be a left-wing bookshop in Charing Cross Road with a code book and short-wave radio and microdot gear. Something a cut above that.

SHE: I know. You'll do something really splendid, something remarkable. It's a silly thing to say, but all these rehearsals – I used to daydream they were real and I was your fiancée or your wife and we had a country house like Osborne Manor with an English garden and two children and two cars and loads of money. And, above all, that we were happy and in love.

HE: So you don't love me any more.

SHE: I don't know. Please don't ask me.

HE: I almost forgot. The Hexenkammern have taken care of all that, haven't they? I wonder what would happen if I tried to make love to you.

SHE: You know you mustn't.

HE: I know. We'd probably destroy each other if we tried.

When the voices went silent, Fisher walked into the natural history section of the museum – their old stage and auditorium for their masters. He glanced idly at the cases of fossil trilobites and other crustaceans, then at the species of fossil fish and the mounted dinosaur and pterodactyl. As he peered at a stuffed baboon, a door clicked behind him, a reflection quivered in the glass case and a voice whispered in his ear, "Interesting place, isn't it, Laurence?"

Fisher turned to stare into muddy, green eyes adrift behind bottle-lens spectacles; he looked at the puff-cheeked face with its blotchy complexion. So they had sent for his watchdog, Blount, to round him up and fetch him back. "What are you doing here?" he asked.

"A good question for both of us," Blount answered. "Me? I came to help you, Laurence."

"How did you know where?" Fisher asked, then added illogically, "When they've changed everything?"

"They told me. They haven't changed. They're still with us."

"Ah, yes, they told you then." Fisher did something that Blount had never witnessed in nearly thirty years together. He grinned. "So, they thought I might find my way back."

"They hoped you wouldn't." Blount's voice had dropped half an octave and sounded sinister. "But if you did succeed they said you must go back immediately before your presence here makes some people suspicious."

"I'm not going back."

"But think of everything you've built up over a quarter of a century — your magazine empire, your house, your family."

"That's all behind me now."

"But your future! They've even proposed you for the House of Lords," Blount lamented. "You're crazy, Laurence."

"Blame these people here. They drove me crazy."

"But what about Ruth? What'll she do?"

"She's got money so she'll be all right. I never loved Ruth and she knows it."

"But she loves you. And there's Roger and Anne."

"Yes, there's Anne. I love Anne." He stood silent for a moment, then glared at Blount and exclaimed in a voice that vibrated from the walls and the glass cases. "But even for Anne, or anything else, I will never go back and live that lie again. Never!"

"What are you going to do?"

"I'm going to look for Anna."

"Who is Anna?"

"Anna Weber. She was here with me. We loved each other until they stifled and killed our love with their brain-washing techniques."

"But that was nearly thirty years ago," Blount gasped. "You can't hope to find her now."

"Why not? I've made a start – and they'll have to help me, the people who separated us."

Blount gave him a piteous look and was going to say something when, at that moment, the bell rang giving the students five minutes' warning before the five o'clock closing hour. Footsteps clattered on the staircase outside as the students quit the building. Someone tried the door of their exhibition room, but Blount had taken the precaution of locking it. When the building had become quiet again he turned to gaze at his boss, interrogating his face trying to interpret his action. Fisher did not behave like a man obsessed with a woman. Indeed, as the man who had known Fisher longer than anyone else who had worked most closely with him, Blount would have sworn he had never seen him speak and act so normally.

Finally, he shrugged his shoulders. "You know I don't make any decisions. Like you, I just follow orders. So, you'll have to speak to them."

"They're here!"

"Waiting for you."

Blount unlocked the door and led Fisher upstairs, turning left where the steps divided and marching towards that part of the mansion where the doctors had lived and worked – the Hexenkammern. Fisher recognized the long corridor. In his nightmares, it always had a thousand doors, all of them opening on to an abyss. At the end of the corridor, Blount pushed open a door and they entered. Two men rose from seats either side of the desk by the window, those men that Blount had met in Treptower Park the previous evening. He did not introduce the smaller one, with the bald head and eyes like an albino rat. He did not need to present the broad-shouldered giant with the grizzling hair and thick moustache. "I believe you and the doctor have met before."

As Blount retreated from the room, Fisher gazed at the smiling face of Dr Reiner Eberhardt.

Fisher went to the chair they indicated, observing that Dr Eberhardt and the hairless stranger had placed themselves in silhouette against the tall, arched windows of the room. Eberhardt opened a cigarette-box and pushed it across the desk, taking one himself when Fisher refused. He bared stained and crooked teeth in a wintry grin.

"So, you think you've retraced your way back," he said.

"I got here, so I know I have," Fisher replied in German. "Why don't you speak German?"

"I prefer English. Anyway, isn't it polite to speak the language of one's guest?" He pulled on his cigarette, then forced the smoke through his nostrils and his thick moustache. "You recognize me, of course."

"Who wouldn't? Herr Teufelsdoktor we called you."

"The Devil's doctor," Eberhardt grinned. "I didn't know."

"You did, and you earned the title a thousand times," Fisher said. "And you thought you'd knocked it out of our minds with everything else." Fisher did something he remembered doing only once before, with Ursel; he reached out, snapped open the cigarette-box lid, took and lit a cigarette; curiously, his fingers had none of the awkward movements of the novice smoker; he inhaled the smoke, but its rasp on the back of his throat and lungs set him coughing and brought tears to his eyes. It dawned then why Eberhardt had offered cigarettes; he must have smoked before they erected their mental barrier against that and other unideological vices. Herr Teufelsdoktor merely wished to know if that particular control had gone. Cursing himself, he stubbed out the cigarette in the ashtray.

"You don't like German tobacco," Eberhardt murmured, then in a harder voice. "What else have you forgotten to forget?"

"For a start, my own name."

"Which is?"

"Müller. Wilhelm Friedrich Müller."

"How do you know?"

"It came back to me like so many other things. Then I found out where I lived."

"That's interesting," Eberhardt murmured. "Where was that?"

"It was Schonebrücke in Brandenburg." Despite himself, he could hardly suppress a proud, even smug note in his voice as he added, "I even found my parents' house and their grave." And he recited their names, their address, the church and other facts that Eberhardt noted on a pad.

"Did you meet anybody? Did anybody help you in this little quest of yours?"

His voice seemed quiet, conversational. But a cold hand reached down Fisher's back. What if they checked up at Schonebrücke? They might trace Ursel. And since they probably meant to kill him they might dispatch this bloodless executioner with the ballpoint head, sitting glowering at him, to kill Ursel and wipe out every trace of their crime. Whatever happened, he had never to reveal her name.

"Nobody helped me," he said.

"Then how can you prove that you are Müller and these are your parents?"

Fisher gazed at the blurred, shadowed figure of Eberhardt which now seemed flat, two-dimensional. Even his voice appeared to have acquired a hollow resonance as though he were speaking from a tiled bathroom or using a megaphone. This Frankenstein had stolen his mind once; he had not to give him the opportunity to repeat that diabolical trick. "How I prove it is my own business," he shouted, catching the reverberations of his own voice from the walls and high ceiling.

"It is our business," the bald albino growled, speaking for the first time. "You owe us everything you are."

"I owe you nothing," Fisher cried. "You owe me myself, the person you took and twisted for your own ends."

"And we haven't finished," the albino said.

"That's enough argument," Eberhardt snapped, motioning the SSD agent to keep quiet. "Mr Fisher, or Müller as he prefers to call himself, will co-operate, I'm sure, because he knows there's no future for him if he doesn't."

"There's no future for me if I do," Fisher said. Defiantly, he grabbed another cigarette, lit it and drew the smoke deeply into his lungs, suppressing the choking feeling it provoked. "I remembered something else, the other name we had for you," he said to Eberhardt. "Know what it was? Der Führer. We all guessed where you'd learned your trade – at Buchenwald or Auschwitz or some other of Hitler's death camps. But at least there they were humane. They killed the body as well. They didn't leave it walking around with a dead man inside it." With a thrill of satisfaction, he noticed Eberhardt's eyes glitter and his mouth clench; that accusation had really hit him in his crooked teeth. "You only had to change one thing after the war – your uniform and your loyalty," he cried.

"I seem to recall that you served in the Wehrmacht before you came to us to volunteer for special duty," Eberhardt said in that muted voice.

"Volunteered! When we were too young and too ignorant to know what for."

"So now you want to go back and start all over again – you want a second chance, is that it?"

"Yes. And I want to find Anna and, if she doesn't know what you did to us, I'll tell her."

"Who is Anna?"

"You know very well – Anna Weber. She was here with me and all your other so-called recruits."

"What was she like, this woman you call Anna Weber?" Eberhardt reached into a folder and produced half a dozen photographs of women in their early twenties; one by one he proffered them, asking if any of them resembled Anna Weber. He had mixed them carefully. A blonde, two brunettes, a redhead, three with dark hair and all with slightly different hair styles. Their faces too bore little resemblance to each other. Fisher gazed at them. How could he tell which was Anna after a quarter of a century? He felt flummoxed and bit his lip until he tasted the tang of blood.

"None of these is Anna Weber," he muttered.

"And suppose I told you one of them was ..." Eberhardt grinned. "It would seem your memory isn't all you think it is."

"I shall know her when I see her."

"How?"

"We loved each other – that's how."

"Ah! yes. Love, of course. I'd forgotten the oldest panacea."

"The thing you sucked and bled out of us – or thought you did," Fisher shouted. "Nothing you did or could do altered what we felt. Nothing. Nothing." He realized he was trembling with emotion or rage, he did not know which; his voice, too, quavered as he went on. "But I shall find her," he said.

"How do you intend to do that?"

"I've already made a start."

"You mean the museum and the graveyard and the protestant pastor, Baumann. It doesn't really amount to much, does it?"

"I've got time," Fisher countered. "In two days I've remembered more than in thirty years. I've remembered the training barracks and all this. I've remembered you and what you did with your Pavlovian tricks, treating us and training us like animals. I remembered that."

"Let's see how good your memory is," Eberhardt said. In that droning voice which sounded more and more remote, he reeled off the names of a dozen people who, he affirmed, Fisher might know; they meant nothing to Fisher, no more than the half-dozen places that he had visited in East Berlin and beyond; that buzzing voice cited figures and dates, ostensibly from Fisher's personal history, stopping every few seconds to allow Fisher time to seize their significance and comment. They conveyed nothing. He felt depressed and almost desperate about these lapses.

"But surely you must remember this sequence of fifteen numbers," Eberhardt said, as though reading his emotions, aware of his anxiety. He held up a card with the long string of figures then spouted them quickly.

"Yes, I remember those," Fisher cried, relieved to remember something. Without thinking, he rattled off the whole sequence – 357689546783768. On uttering the final figure his head suddenly felt heavy and lolled on his shoulder.

A smug grin on his heavy features, Eberhardt turned to the man with the transparent eyes. "You see – more than twenty-five years ago I gave him a post-hypnotic suggestion, instructing him that when he repeated that series of numbers he would fall into hypnotic sleep. It is almost as if I gave it to him yesterday and means that he'll make no further trouble for us." Rising, he walked round the desk and bent over the sleeping figure. "Who are you?" he asked.

"I am Laurence Hallam Fisher."

"Laurence Hallam Fisher, it is the 14th of August 1953. You recall that date, don't you?"

"Yes, I recall that date – the end of the school."

"You had just completed your training and you had taken an oath. Can you repeat that oath?"

"I Laurence Hallam Fisher promise to pay with my life any breach or betrayal of the pledge I have made to honour the ideals of the German Democratic Republic and the instructions I have received at this school."

"Do you still intend to keep your oath?"

"I intend to keep my oath."

"Repeat after me: Rather than break my oath, I Laurence Hallam Fisher will die."

Eberhardt's voice droned on as he said, "You shall forget this school and every one of the people you met here in the past and in the present."

"I will forget them all."

"You shall forget the woman called Anna Marie Paula Weber."

"I will forget Anna Marie Paula Weber."

"But you shall remember all the principles and training you received here between 1951 and 1953 and you shall comply with that."

"I will remember my training and I will comply."

"Laurence Hallam Fisher, you came to the German Democratic Republic and to Berlin on a sentimental pilgrimage to commemorate your mother's accidental death and for no other reason." Fisher repeated the sentence mechanically.

"Now repeat this," Eberhardt said. "I will forget and put behind me everything that has happened to remind me of my past before 1953 and all my troubles of the past six months."

When Fisher had repeated this, the doctor then asked him to repeat another injunction:

"I will go back to my home and my family in Britain and continue my work there for the ideals and interests of the Deutsches Demokratische Republik." Fisher said this like a robot.

"When you wake up, you will accompany your friend and associate, Mr Norman Blount, to West Berlin and from there you will fly to Britain. Have you understood?"

"I have understood."

Turning to the albino, Eberhardt ordered him to tell Blount to take the wheel of the VW Fisher had driven to the museum and instruct him to catch the earliest flight that evening down the air corridor from West Berlin to London. He rejected the idea that the SSD agent should accompany the two men to the check-point; it might arouse suspicion if anybody spotted him with Fisher and Blount; in any case, Blount would have to take care of the car and plane trips. When Blount had placed his valise in the car, Eberhardt led Fisher downstairs. At the door, he whispered in his ear, "Wake up, Laurence Hallam Fisher. Your friend is waiting for you in the car."

"Will he be all right?" Blount said.

"You can take him home," Eberhardt replied. "He won't give you any more trouble." Slamming the door shut, he and the albino watched the VW disappear down the driveway.

Twenty-one

When the bell pealed five minutes before closing-time, Maclean cursed and picked up his notebook and papers, motioning for Deirdre to do likewise. From his window seat he had observed Fisher drive through the main gate just after twenty minutes past four; they had lost his car when it circled the building and Maclean guessed that their man was testing his memory on the buildings and the area where they had indoctrinated him. Ten minutes later, the car had reappeared and now lay parked by the museum entrance. At closing time when they made their way downstairs,

Fisher had been inside the building for twenty-five minutes. As Maclean passed through the entrance hall, he noticed the door to the natural history museum was shut. Crossing the hall, he tried it and found that someone had locked it.

Deirdre and he did not walk directly to the flats where they had seen Hamlin park the Taunus half an hour before; they turned north and doubled back on their tracks to ensure no-one was following them. In the car, Hamlin briefed them about Fisher's movements since lunch-time and the detour he had made on the way to the museum. Maclean deliberated for several minutes. They could not afford to lose track of Fisher for a moment, so the museum had to be watched. He had an idea that Eberhardt or one of his successors would be waiting inside the museum to cope with Fisher and his defection. How he had no idea. It might be hours before anything happened.

He detailed his plan. Deirdre and Anne would walk to the small café opposite the main gate; they could drink coffee and keep an eye on the museum while watching for Hamlin's signals. Hamlin would wait in the car watching both girls and Maclean, who would be keeping a lookout from the fourth-floor landing of the flat to spot anything moving in the house or the park.

Within minutes they had taken up their positions. Maclean had a broadside view of the mansion; behind the main upstairs window on the eastern gable he thought he saw something budge; but the late afternoon sun was casting reflections and he could not identify anything definite. From the reconnaissance he had made earlier that day he knew that this part of the museum was kept locked and not even the caretaker had a key.

Gradually, the shadows began to thicken behind the trees fringing the park; upstairs on the far side of the museum, the caretaker's light gleamed. Soon they'd have to call off their vigil, move back through the Wall and hope to pick up Fisher the next day. Just when Maclean was beginning to cramp with his enforced stand at the small landing window, the mansion door opened and a figure that he did not recognize emerged carrying a suitcase. He got behind the wheel of the VW when he had placed his valise in the bonnet. In the café, both girls had risen showing that they, too, had spotted the man. Maclean signalled Hamlin to warm up the car and the SIS man raised his hand in acknowledgement.

Suddenly Fisher appeared, bracketed by an immensely tall man and a shorter one. They opened the passenger door and helped him inside. At that moment, Maclean started down the four flights of stairs and Hamlin revved the engine. However, they had ample time to pick up the girls, for they heard the VW stop at the main gate to wait for the porter to unlock it.

"Who's the little fat man?" Maclean asked when they dropped in behind the VW.

"Norman Blount," Anne said. "The man I told you about. My father's closest associate and friend."

Maclean and Hamlin looked meaningfully at one another, then peered ahead at the car they were tailing; in it they could clearly see the outlines of the two men, for Blount obviously had to feel his way down an unfamiliar road on the right-hand side at the wheel of a strange car; at the junction of Bucher and Hauptstrasse he drew in to ask the way, then headed south.

"Where do you think they're making for?" Hamlin said.

"Through the Wall."

"And then?"

"Templehof and down to Frankfurt or Hannover and back to London." As he spoke he was studying the shapes of the two men ahead; Blount's dumpy figure sat crouched over the wheel, but Fisher seemed asleep on the passenger seat. They had no doubt hypnotized him, but had they also drugged him? Hamlin kept muttering about Blount who was fumbling over busy crossroads and shaving the lights so that the SIS man had to take the Taunus through on the red. Down Berlinerstrasse, Schönhauserstrasse and into

Alexplatz they crawled with dusk, then darkness, fusing the sky and the tall buildings together.

Among the one-way streets the other side of Marx-Engelsplatz, Blount lost himself, finally stumbling by luck on Friedrichstrasse and the car queue waiting to cross the boundary between both Berlins. When the *Vopos* asked for passports, Fisher got out of the car as though making to return to East Berlin, but Blount said something and one of the policemen flipped the barrel of his machine-pistol at Fisher who got back into the car. Maclean noticed that he looked stiff and unnatural. Up swung the boom and the car crossed the dead area to West Berlin where they went through in seconds.

Hamlin had kept two cars behind. By taking risks and jinking in and out of the rush-hour traffic, he caught the VW before it turned left, following the signs for Tempelhof airport. A few minutes after they had eased into place behind the VW in Gneisenaustrasse, Maclean saw Fisher suddenly sit bolt upright as though he had woken up. He saw Fisher lean over to his left and grip the back of the driver's seat with his left hand. With his right hand he seemed to lunge or throw a punch at Blount. Only it wasn't a punch, more a push. Blount turned his head and began to wrench at the wheel. Maclean heard him shout something. After that, everything happened so quickly that Hamlin had shot past their car before he could brake to a halt.

Horrified, all four of them watched the VW skid to the left under the wheels of a huge lorry. During those seconds that he witnessed the accident, Maclean saw the lorry-driver try desperately but vainly to avoid the car. Then they heard the splinter and crunch of glass and metal. And as they flashed past the two vehicles, they observed the small saloon car being dragged under the lorry chassis and disappear beneath its wheels. Even in the uncertain light from the street lamps and headlamps, each nightmare fragment of the scene imprinted itself on their minds like a film reel stopped at each frame with the sound petrified. A long shriek echoed from the car, stifled by the bang and squeal of the lorry brakes; glass splintered and showered from the windscreen and windows of the car as the back axle of the lorry sheered its domed roof from the rest of the body. Sparks erupted from the tangle of moving metal; a wheel spun madly against their own car. Then silence. Broken at first by someone calling then someone crying, then the slamming of car doors.

Hamlin pulled their car on to the pavement. Before it had stopped, Maclean was leaping out, shouting to Deirdre to stay with Anne. With Hamlin on his heels, he sprinted back to the scene where a few people had already gathered. "*Ich bin Doktor*," he yelled, barging through to where the lorry-driver was crouching and aiming a torchbeam under the lorry. "Hamlin, listen – go and find a phone in one of the shops and ring the Free University Clinic. Get hold of Professor Ernst Linder and tell him to alert his casualty unit. Ask somebody to dial the police and ambulance while you're locating Linder. We're in Gneisenausstrasse by the Missionskirche."

"Wir brauchen Wolledecken (blankets) bitte," he said to the crowd and within a minute he had several coats and car rugs on the ground. Pushing these in front of him and with the driver beside him holding the torch, he crawled under the lorry. "He drove into me," the driver was muttering over and over again. "I saw the passenger pushing him into me."

"Shut up and hold the torch," Maclean snapped. "I saw it all, and it wasn't your fault."

Their torch and car headlights picked out the twisted wreck of the VW. However, its strong spine had kept it in one piece except for the roof; its main body had wedged against the Y members of the lorry chassis; both its doors and front wheels had gone with the roof. Maclean saw both Fisher and Blount sprawled across the front seat. Fisher's right hand lay across Blount's chest and they saw that it had a grip of the steering-wheel. "What did I say?" the German lorry-driver muttered.

"For God's sake hold your tongue," Maclean growled. Grabbing the man's torch, he examined the crushed car bonnet; both men were wedged between the dashboard and the front seats, but from what he could discern, Fisher's legs had not been trapped by the twisted bodywork. "Give me a hand," he ordered the driver. "When I release the seat lock, ease it back, but gently." His fingers probed under Fisher's legs, fumbled and found the lever locking the seat; he had to tug it free then swivel it. Between them he and the driver forced the seat back and the German held it while Maclean knelt, slid his hands under Fisher's back and thighs, then inched him free. He laid Fisher on a bundle of rugs and coats and covered him over. "Don't touch him," he instructed the driver. "And don't let him move."

One glance at Blount and he realized that he need waste no time on him. His skull had split open, presumably when the lorry had ripped away the VW roof. His chest had been pierced by the steering column. However, Maclean felt for his pulse, which was dead, and shone his torch into the lifeless eyes before coming back to Fisher.

Feeling under the rug, he found his wrist and a pulse that astonished him with its strong beat; he threw the torchlight on to the face to look at the pupillary reflexes and noticed that Fisher's eyes were open and he was blinking.

"*Ich bin kaputt.*" (I've had it) he said in a calm voice.

"No, you'll be all right," Maclean replied.

"*Wer sind Sie und warum sprechen Sie Englisch?*" (Who are you and why are you speaking English?)

"My name's Maclean. I'm the psychiatrist you stayed with in London. Speak English or the lorry-driver will understand us."

"What are you doing here?"

"Your daughter, Anne, asked me to help her find you when you disappeared."

"Anne! Is she here?"

"She's not far away. You'll see her when we get you out of here."

"Where's Blount?"

"He's dead."

"Poor bastard. And I'm alive ... But I'm kaputt ... I've no guts and no legs left."

Maclean slipped a hand under the rugs and pinched Fisher's thighs hard, then his more sensitive flesh. He did not even flinch. Somehow, when the VW embedded itself under the lorry, a blow or the whiplash effect had broken his back, probably fairly high up, and severed the spinal chord. But worse cases had survived. "Just lie quiet and we'll pull you out of it."

"It's no good, Maclean ... Know how I can tell I'm finished? ... I can remember everything, everything ... They've got no more hold over me."

"Who's they?"

"Never mind." He paused for a few seconds, breathed and sighed several times, then murmured, "I can remember everything, everything."

Maclean gazed at him, wondering if the shock had perhaps cured his amnesia. But no, it went deeper than that. Fisher was telling the truth; instinctively, intuitively he knew he was going to die. In so many ways, this man resembled a psychotic with his dual personality, his fugues, his schizoid and paranoid behaviour. And so often in his practice, Maclean had seen schizophrenics and paranoiacs suddenly turn sane and lucid at the final moment of truth; he had witnessed people immured in perpetual silence abruptly give tongue and lunatics speak words of wisdom in their final moments. Released from bondage, Fisher must have been experiencing that profound insight. All those barriers they had constructed in his mind and around his personality had crumpled before the approach of death. Even the hypnosis that they had used to inject so much pretence and falsehood into his brain had been exorcized by this fatal accident. In the distance he heard police and ambulance sirens; but they would probably have to come in from the north rather than through the blocked main street. "Why did you force Blount into that lorry?" he asked.

"I couldn't go on ... I didn't want to go back with Blount."

"But your family, your home? ..."

"I am home." Fisher's eyes flickered towards Maclean's face and he seemed to hesitate before saying, "I have to tell somebody ... you're a doctor, you won't say anything ... I can tell you." He put a hand out to grasp Maclean's hand. "I am not Laurence Hallam Fisher."

"Who are you then?"

"My name is Wilhelm Friedrich Müller and I was born in Schönebrücke in Brandenburg ... My parents were Walther Friedrich Müller and Ilse Müller, Becker by her own name. Will you remember these things? They are important to me."

To reassure him, Maclean recited the names he had mentioned.

"Don't ask me why I changed my nationality and took the name Fisher."

"I don't want to know," Maclean said.

"Ruth, my wife, and Anne must never learn my real name ... only you, Dr Maclean ... only you know why I couldn't go back."

"They'll never know," Maclean said. "What else do you remember?"

"There was only one thing I wanted to remember ... her, the girl I love ... Anna."

"Anna?"

"Anna Weber ... you remember I called her Jane sometimes ..." His voice, slow and slurred, punctuated and eclipsed now and again by the approaching sirens, was weakening. "Anna," he whispered. "I can see her as though she were here beside me ... her skin is honey and roses and her eyes are sapphires and diamonds ... her hair, her hair has the last fire of sunset in it." Again he paused, his eyes distant as though fixed on the image he had just described. He coughed, then said, "Dr Maclean ..."

"Yes."

"You'll remember her full name ... It is Anna Marie Paula Weber ... She lived in Landsberger Allee, number 143bis. You sure you can remember that?"

"I'll remember, I promise you."

"Don't try to find her."

"I won't."

Fisher smiled. "Nobody's dead as long as someone remembers them ... or even their name." His hand squeezed Maclean's, but now with ebbing strength. In the torchlight, Maclean noticed his eyes film over and thought for a moment Fisher was going before he realized he was weeping.

Just behind him he heard the crowd directing the police and ambulance men towards the lorry. Two men with a stretcher crawled alongside and Maclean explained that Fisher had probably broken his spine and crushed or severed his spinal chord; they must handle him carefully and take him to the Free University Clinic. Gently they eased him on to the stretcher, then hoisted him a few inches off the ground to transfer him to the two men waiting by the side of the lorry. Fisher proffered a limp hand which Maclean took and pressed. "Remember, doctor," he said, then, "Adieu!"

"*Und der andere?*" the ambulancemen asked, pointing to Blount.

"*Er ist tot,*" Maclean replied, adding that they'd probably have to cut the body out when they could move the lorry.

On the edge of the crowd Deirdre was waiting for him. Hamlin had alerted the hospital and Professor Linder had gone there from his home to wait for both men. Hamlin was with Anne in the car. He explained that Fisher had a broken spine. "Will he live?" she asked.

"No, I don't think so," he said. "And for his sake I hope he doesn't."

"Why? Because he'd be crippled?"

"That and all the rest."

"Anne might want to accompany her father in the ambulance," she said.

"I don't think she should."

"You mean, he might say something about the murders, or confess about himself."

"That's what I meant."

It took the police half an hour to get the traffic moving and Hamlin had to make two detours to double back into the Dahlem district before they sighted the ultra-modern clinic, its wards cantilevered over the main building like a giant seesaw. Linder was waiting by the reception desk and when Maclean had introduced him to the others, he broke the bad news. Fisher was dead. A massive internal haemorrhage had killed him just as they were transporting him into the casualty unit. They took the lift to the basement and Linder led them to a room near the surgical wing where they had placed Fisher on a bed.

Anne gazed at her father. Death appeared to have softened the stern contours of his face, conferring on it a calm that it did not have when alive. "It's sad, but I never once saw him as peaceful as he is now," she muttered, with a catch in her voice.

Maclean beckoned Deirdre and Hamlin out of the room to leave Anne alone with her father. "What are you going to do, Hamlin?" he asked.

"I'm not sure, except for one thing – this is my last job for my present firm," Hamlin muttered. "I suppose when I get back I'll have to look round for another job."

"You're something of a journalist, aren't you? So Anne could probably fix you up with some useful work." Maclean took him to one side and whispered, "Why don't you take Anne home and help her straighten things out? We'll square things here and bring both Fisher and Blount home."

"I'll see what she thinks about it," Hamlin said.

"She doesn't want to think about it and don't let her. Get her out of here before people and the press start asking questions none of us can answer truthfully."

Hamlin nodded. When Anne entered the small cubicle where they stood, Maclean easily persuaded her to fly home with Hamlin that night and break the news personally to her mother before the newspapers carried their perverted accounts of the accident and started badgering her mother about her husband's strange disappearance. He would give the newsagencies here his version of the story and Hamlin would help her deal with the press in Britain. As soon as the police gave them clearance, probably within a couple of days, Deirdre and he would fly home with her father's body and Blount's. They accompanied Anne and Hamlin to the car, then came back to discuss the formalities with Linder and the hospital staff; Maclean made a police statement exonerating the lorry-driver; while he did this, the ambulance team brought in the smashed remains of Blount.

When they had finished, both Maclean and Deirdre felt they needed air and walked from the clinic to the *S-bahn* station by the Botanic Gardens. Standing on the platform, waiting for a train, Maclean fell to wondering about the twists of fate and twitting himself for a superstitious Celt. Fisher might have said that, as in those Priestley plays he liked so much, time seemed to have kinked backwards a quarter of a century to the point where his strange narrative had begun, thus according him at least a second chance. It was surely ironic, Maclean reflected, that Fisher or Müller had stepped into the shoes of a man who had died after a car crash and then killed himself in the same way not many miles from the scene of the first accident. It almost seemed as if his masters had rehearsed that gesture of self-destruction as they had nearly every other move in the role they had given him to play as a spy. Yet Maclean preferred to believe that Fisher had finally broken their shackles, freed himself, then committed suicide as an ultimate act of self-will and defiance.

Deirdre cut across his musings. "What are you thinking about?" she asked.

"Oh, about a man who came back from the dead and did another twenty-five years, then decided he didn't want to live on somebody else's time and name any longer. So he tried to turn his personal clock back and restart it."

"And didn't succeed."

"He didn't do too badly."

She looked keenly at him. "What did Fisher confess?" she asked. "What happened under that lorry?"

Maclean smiled at her. As usual, she had hit the right word: Confess. He shrugged. So that it would not die with him, so that it would exist in somebody's mind, Fisher had entrusted him with his personal story, his personal secret. To Maclean, it seemed almost a sacred confidence, the names of Wilhelm Müller and Anna Weber and that part of their history that he alone knew. "Mavournin, one of these days I'll tell you, but not now. All I can say is that it's the saddest love story I've ever met."

"Love story!" she exclaimed. Was he having her on, as he often did? A glance at his face and that misty, faraway expression in his eyes assured her this time he meant what he said. That, and the way he grasped her hand and held it tightly as they waited for the train.

If you have enjoyed this book, you might wish to join the Walker British Mystery Society.

For information, please send a postcard or letter to:

Paperback Mystery Editor

**Walker & Company
720 Fifth Avenue
New York, NY 10019**